Cycle of Ages Saga:
Finders
Keepers

Cycle of Ages Saga:
Finders Keepers

by
Jeremy Hicks & Barry Hayes

Cycle of Ages Saga:
Finders Keepers

ISBN 13: 978-0998373607

First Edition published by Dark Oak Press & Media – 2013

Second Edition published by Dark Oak Press & Media – 2015

Third Edition published by Broke Guys Productions – 2016

Cover Art by Enggar Adirasa
Cover Design by Alan Lewis
Interior by Jeremy Hicks

This book is printed on acid free paper.

Printed in the United States of America

Dedication

As in the first and second editions, we'd like to thank our major inspirations for Faltyr and the Cycle of Ages Saga, namely Gary Gygax, Robert E. Howard, J.R.R. Tolkien, and Ronnie James Dio.

For this edition, our first independent printing of Finders Keepers, the authors would like to thank our family, friends, fans, and other supporters for their patience, love, and guidance along the road of life. You have our love and eternal gratitude. We would not keep writing without you.

FALTYR

Chapter 1

The gnomish captain of the *Nightsfall* perched in the crow's nest, unfazed by the imminent danger posed by the storm besieging the double mast caravel. Lightning flashed across the sky. Rain fell in sheets. Titanic waves and gale-force winds tossed about both ship and crew in a frenzied fashion.

Consumed by his desperate search for a long forgotten island, Captain Gneut stared through a luminous spyglass, ignoring the tempest raging around him. Thanks to the device, he peered through the torrential rain with ease, seeking but not finding what he sought: his coveted prize - the Hallowed Vessel.

The enchanted glass he now held, along with the magic compass pressed against his barrel chest, belonged aboard the elusive ship of legend. These priceless possessions, along with a set of detailed maps, were responsible for Gneut's final reckless adventure.

Spying a spire of a not-too-distant land, Gneut whooped and danced jubilantly as relief and joy welled up inside him. The diminutive daredevil celebrated even as the storm raged and roiled, oblivious to the peril surrounding him.

Turning to the situation below, he surveyed the scene like an overseeing god. Most of the two-score-or-so individuals aboard the *Nightsfall* gathered together to fight the elements threatening to send them to the bottom of the shallow sea. Concerned passengers worked in the rainstorm alongside his crew of surly barefoot sailors to take down the sails and secure the cargo and livestock.

He spotted Spensir, his conniving first mate, as the human struggled to keep the ship's wheel from spinning out of control. The captain whistled, signaling his subordinate to turn hard to port.

Struggling to stand upright against the winds, Spensir nodded to his superior and then barked orders to the others assisting him. Short and stout, the longhaired first mate lowered his center of gravity and heaved against the wheel with all of his might. The bulkier sailor at his side grunted with renewed effort as his feet slipped on the caravel's wet deck.

Although of slight build, Rayne aided the two hatchet-faced seadogs, the comely woman's muscles rippling under her pale skin and doused attire. Her fae features and slightly pointed ears betrayed her elven heritage, as did the slender sword of elven steel, one of many blades secured about her person.

An elderly bent sailor stopped amid the chaos and confusion created by the storm to watch in awe as a tattooed and pierced elf, one of the mercenaries he had hired, chanted and waved a long fingered hand over a nest of entangled ropes. In a flash, the hemp lines snaked their way into position, tying themselves into intricate and secure sailing knots. In the midst of the maelstrom, elf and human exchanged wide grins.

A giant of a man covered in scars and tattoos assisted Gneut's crew in securing the sails. Working without a partner, the dark skinned mercenary drew in the lines with ease. In contrast, the common sailors around him worked in pairs and still struggled to move their lines against the tension created by the raging winds.

The glowing stone set into the front of his wide wrestling style belt cast his shaved head and swarthy features in a severe light. The luminous stone resembled an unblinking Titan's eye. According to rumors, the girdle fastened around his waist supplied the source of his famed strength and endurance.

The *Nightsfall*'s second mate worked alongside a traveling knight to secure the panicky livestock on deck. As the nobleman from Oparre closed the gate, the mate blocked several animals from escaping the corral. Relief flooded both men's faces when the latch slid into place.

An ominous roar kept them from celebrating their fleeting victory. Holding onto the fence of the stockade, the knight-errant braced for the impact of another powerful wave. The rushing water battered the second mate, causing him to lose his balance.

The knight was a moment faster than the angry sea at claiming the second mate's life. He reached out a gloved hand and grabbed the off-balance sailor. Relief colored their faces.

As the mate staggered away to attend to the next task, his savior took the opportunity to run a loving hand along the snout of his fine white charger, its muscular flanks scarred from close encounters in countless battles. Gneut's omniscient survey noted how calm the knight's warhorse remained amidst the chaos as it nuzzled its master's cheek to reassure him.

Pushing his sword scabbard out of the way, the human withdrew a badly bruised apple from the folds of his tabard. The horse consumed the treat as its master whispered to it lovingly. However, the captain noted that the knight's gaze fixated on Rayne as she and the two sailors struggled to turn the wheel. As if feeling his eyes on her wet, taut body, Rayne's attention shifted from the wheel to the young noble. Blushing, she turned away, redoubling her efforts at the helm.

What history did they share? Gneut wondered, as a renewed gust forced him to tighten his grip to the crow's nest. Over the years, he had treated Rayne more like a daughter than an employee, but she'd never mentioned a dashing knight from her homeland, much less one that held her heart in his hand.

Lightning flashed anew, drawing the captain's eyes skyward. As the fury of the Nine Hells raged around him, Gneut wondered if he would survive to hear the couple's whole sordid tale...or if they would survive to tell it.

***

Down in the hold of the *Nightsfall*, Kaladimus Dor, a young man with thick unkempt hair, sat before a low desk in his private luxury accommodations. On the aged caravel, *private* amounted to a cramped closet. *Luxury* consisted of a soiled sea cot, a low desk, and an uneven stool.

Dor finished a notation in his mission journal. Satisfied with his latest entry, the Mage of Moor'Dru waved his hand dismissively toward the floating quill. The goose feather-writing instrument shot into the corner with enough force to embed its tip in the plank wall. Unalarmed by this turn of events, he shook his head in disgust.

A sharp crack of nearby thunder split the relative quiet of the cabin. Dor struggled to collect his writing material together despite his shaking hands. The subsequent flash of lightning outside the porthole caused the skittish wizard to flinch violently. He retrieved the quill but not without mangling the feather in the process.

He extracted a small metal chest from underneath the desk. He eyed the ominous item warily. A series of glyphs, symbols, and other ritual markings covered the box, some native to his homeland of Moor'Dru, others from far older cultures and races. Even the alloy itself appeared foreign to the young Protectorate Mage.

Taking a deep breath, Dor forced himself to relax. Try as he might, he could not shut out the sound of his pounding heart. He imagined he could hear another heartbeat from inside the chest. Of course, it had to be his imagination running wild again. Dor reminded himself that a Mage of Moor'Dru should be calmer, braver.

He raised the lid of the chest, stuffed the materials into its inky recesses, and snapped the lid shut. The lock clicked into place. Raising his fingers, he wove an enchantment designed to secure all manner of containers and portals from prying eyes.

Since recovering the box's contents from the ruins of a temple located in the war torn kingdom of Oparre, he'd dared open it on a few rare occasions while casting the same spell on the chest each time. Unfortunately, as a result of the young wizard's inherited affliction, there was no such thing as routine magic, especially magic cast in the midst of a thunderstorm.

Dor's fingers sparked, creating an arc between him and the container. The entire chest crackled with energy as it sucked in the static from the surrounding atmosphere. All of the shaggy hair on the shabby mage's head stood on end as lightning began to dance across the metal lid. He had enough experience with catastrophe to know that something had gone wrong, terribly wrong.

Sighing, Dor stammered, "Not…again!"

***

Lightning from all directions streaked through the low hanging thunderhead, coalescing above the beleaguered *Nightsfall*. Eyes wide, Captain Gneut watched as a ball of lightning blazed into existence, growing a thousand fold in the span of a heartbeat. Safety line in one hand and spyglass in the other, he leapt from the crow's nest as a single bolt snaked down from the glowing sphere of energy, splintering his perch and the mast below it.

Gneut kept from being blinded as lightning coursed through the main mast, illumining everything below him bright as midday. The freefalling captain stared in mute horror as the mast splintered and separated from the deck. The ruined beam of treated wood fell slower at the top than at the bottom due to the rigging on each side. As it kicked away from the base, the massive beam sent a shower of shrapnel outward that took several bystanders off their feet.

The falling mast slammed into an old sea salt, sending him into the turbulent sea. Plummeting toward the water, the tiny captain watched in a mix of awe and terror as the bulk of the main mast, sails, and rigging ended up following the elderly sailor into the swirling waters. The hull of the *Nightsfall* rolled in the same direction while the weight of the broken beam dragged the doomed ship toward the bottom of the shallow sea.

Defeat and despair filled the captain. As he rushed toward his fate, Gneut watched as people scrambled about with reckless abandon. Panic gripped most of those remaining on the swamped deck while a brave few remained sane despite the insanity surrounding them, including the battle-hardened mercenaries of Finders Keepers.

The stragglers who emerged from below decks appeared confused by the catastrophic events unfolding on the *Nightsfall*. Kaladimus Dor, the troublesome magician who'd come aboard in Kingsport, seemed more concerned with his precious baggage, the peculiar metal chest, than saving his own pathetic hide.

Before his body struck the unforgiving sea, Captain Gneut adopted a new caveat: Deals with wizards seldom ended well. And his deal with Dor had proven to be no exception. The bargain struck in mutual desperation had led the captain to believe he would find his coveted prize, the Hallowed Vessel. In the end, Gneut found his fate instead.

Chapter 2

Sir Caayl, noble son of the House of Regula, lifted himself out of the tideland and stared at the sea. The expanse of blue appeared gentle and inviting. Nothing remained of the tempest save scattered clouds on the horizon. The sun warmed him as the water dripped from his soaked garb.

Already unarmored, he examined his weapon belt to find his sword still in its scabbard. A piece of knotted cord tied around its cross-guard bound the long steel blade of the masterwork hand-and-a-half sword inside its sheath. He sighed with relief that the sword presented to him by the Order of Ishta'Kahl, Goddess of the Moon, had not joined his armor at the bottom of the sea.

Sir Caayl stumbled along the beach in search of survivors amidst the flotsam and jetsam. He traveled only a short distance before he spotted the body of his charger amongst the debris. Emotion welled up within him at the loss of his dear friend.

Caayl hurried over and fell to his knees in the sand beside the loyal steed. Mourning it like a fallen warrior, he gave noble Farsig the last rites of the Order.

As the knight murmured his prayer, Rayne placed her hand on his shoulder. Kneeling beside him in the sand, she situated herself so her array of blades did not dig into her side.

Though still a fair skinned beauty of slight build, Rayne had matured into a woman with qualities of silk as well as steel. From what Caayl had witnessed on the *Nightsfall*, her years abroad had hardened her body and tempered her demeanor. Despite these changes, Rayne wasn't that different from the girl he'd fallen in love with so long ago. He had discovered this during the voyage from Oparre.

"He's been with you since you joined the Order, hasn't he?" she inquired in a soothing voice. As he returned his gaze to the fallen warhorse, she placed her hands on top of his own.

Staring at his fallen comrade, Caayl replied, "Farsig was my oldest, most loyal friend."

Rayne asked, "And I?"

His emotion-filled eyes met her own. "I've always considered you to be more than a friend."

"Really," she replied. "Is that why I hadn't seen you in over a *decadus* until you came into that bar in Kingsport?"

"You know things had to be that way for the safety of your family," he explained, "as well as my own."

"Thanks. Always the perfect gentleman even as a lad."

"Sarcasm. Great. Some things never change," he responded with a grin, comforted by her familiar sense of humor. After all, she had always been able to make him smile.

His thoughts drifted back to an earlier time in his life, when he and the wild fae-like girl would meet near the stream on his family's estate. Rayne had resided to the north of his home, in the heart of the Everdew Forest. Before the horrors of the Blood Wars, her father's family would travel to the Regula estate and sell all manner of high quality elven goods. On market days, while the grown-ups conducted business, Rayne and Caayl would have the run of the forest adjoining the manor. He reminisced about the tree fort they had constructed deep in those woods.

They had shared their first kiss there a few years later, long before his father sent him away to serve at the behest of King Orson. Caayl had snuck a quick peck and then blushed crimson. Already chivalrous, he had apologized for soiling her honor. The buck wild young girl had responded by wrapping her arms around his neck and planting a wet open-mouthed kiss on the lips of the astonished man-boy. Due to circumstances beyond their control, they had kissed for the first and last time that unforgettable spring day.

Once news of King Orson's Purity Decrees had swept through their province, Rayne's father's people had become unwelcome anywhere within the boundaries of the Regula estate. Many turbulent years had passed before Caayl finally understood his father's decision to banish them. His father had managed to insulate her family--and by extension his own--from the predations of King Orson's oppressive, even genocidal policies against wizards, elves, fae, and other magic-users. Only Orson's own magi and priests of the Holy Trinitas and other state-approved faiths had received a reprieve from these bigoted decrees.

After a generation of warring with human kingdoms, King Orson had expanded his Blood War to include the elves of Silverbrook, a peaceful and honorable people that Caayl had learned to admire and respect during his childhood. Now, the guilt of his actions during the war left him with nightmares. The combination of grief and guilt made him want to stop and beg for forgiveness at the feet of any passing elf.

Serving under such a monstrous sovereign caused him to question his faith, his fealty, and even his sanity. His irrational, even rebellious thoughts and opinions became treasonous actions. Throwing in his lot with the few knights that had remained loyal to their Goddess instead of their murderous liege, he left Oparre to search for the true cause behind the King's affliction.

Although never a great ruler, Orson had been a good man before the Purity Decrees, before the Blood War. Now, the King of Oparre seemed more puppet than ruler, more devil than man. In support of Orson's doctrines, the Churches of the Holy Trinitas spewed a hateful, bigoted dogma of reformation, threatening to undo countless centuries of tolerant religious tradition.

Without having risked everything for the sake of a promise to a stranger, Caayl might never have seen his beloved again. Calm returned to the knight-errant at this realization. For a brief moment, the grief-stricken pair continued to peer into each other's eyes, causing something to stir deep inside him. His grief transitioned to a smoldering, almost desperate longing.

Blushing at the attention, Rayne looked away. Also embarrassed, he returned to his prayers. As the chaste knight tried to focus, the half-elven woman's hand caressed him with the reassuring familiarity of a lover and a friend. Her warmth filled him, pushing away some of his emptiness and filling him with hope that expressed itself in a prayer of a different kind than the one for his fallen mount. Instead, Sir Caayl prayed for a second chance at the life he'd wanted with Rayne all those years ago in Oparre.

***

Kaladimus Dor awoke on an alien shore, happy to be alive. Full of seawater, the nearly drowned magician rolled over onto his belly and vomited into the surf. Hacking and coughing, he tried to force his mind to focus on the events of the previous evening.

Raising himself enough to crawl, the pale-skinned young man clawed his way farther onto the beach. Moving like a newborn fawn, he rose to his feet and then tripped on the sodden robe as it tangled about him. After a brief fight, he won his freedom and his balance.

The blinding reflection of the morning sun on the white sand stabbed into his bloodshot eyes, forcing them closed. The sudden burst of light triggered a flashback of the shipwreck with vivid clarity. Guilt and then nausea overwhelmed him. Dor expelled the contents of his stomach onto the sand, dry heaving for several moments afterwards.

Wiping his mouth on the back of his sleeve, he felt his eyes grow both hot and wet. Blinking through the tears, he surveyed the beach, unsurprised but not unmoved by the scene of devastation. After all, Disastrous Dor, the calamitous mage of Myth, knew he was to blame for the misfortunes of those along the shoreline.

Most of Captain Gneut's caravel now lay at the bottom of the shallow sea, along with the bulk of its passengers and crew. In the distance, he watched as the survivors stirred, albeit slowly, and began to pick through the wrack of the *Nightsfall*. His green eyes continued to return to the forms on the beach that remained still despite the growing level of activity around them.

How many dead by my hand? Dor asked himself.

Sitting back in the sand, he grabbed his thick, unkempt hair and pulled at it in frustration. Rocking slightly, the wretched, weeping magician appeared the perfect picture of misery borne of a perfect storm. Nearly catatonic, he sat alone as the events of the previous evening flooded his mind again and again, threatening to drown him in a sea of guilt and self-pity.

Regaining his composure somewhat, he struggled to his feet. He scanned the beach for the chest. Though he could not see the accursed container, he figured the tide had carried it ashore. After all, one of the enchantments bound into the box ensured that it would float regardless of the weight of its contents.

As Dor searched for his missing chest, he surveyed the survivors moving amongst the wreckage. A few of them waded in the shoals to scrounge stray barrels, crates, and other potentially useful items.

In the distance, Spensir, the first mate, stood atop a parabolic dune and shouted orders. A stocky sailor and a black haired woman worked to carry them out while poking around the wreckage. He hoped none of them discovered the chest first, much less tried to open it. The very idea sent chills shivering down his spine.

Along the sandy seaboard, Dor observed that all four of the captain's sell swords had emerged unscathed from the storm. Breuxias, Yax'Kaqix, and the Cadogan twins strode down the beach in lockstep fashion. The members of Finders Keepers appeared to be in a stormy disposition.

Clenched in one meaty fist, Breuxias held a single boot of finer craftsmanship than the simple ones worn on his oversized feet. As the mercenaries proceeded along the beach, Dor wondered if the brute sought the other boot or its owner.

Breuxias's attire consisted of a plain shendyt, or cotton kilt, belted at the waist by his magical girdle and a pair of sturdy sandals. The brace of throwing daggers strapped across his muscular chest constituted his only visible weapons. However, the network of scars and intricate body art provided the brute with a textured, tortured appearance, leaving him as fierce-looking as the elf accompanying him.

Unlike the scruffy sailors, Yax'Kaqix dressed the part of a noble warrior. Tall and pale, the full-blood elf wore a long shirt of black scale-mail armor sandwiched between layers of eel skin. Yax's weapon belt featured pouches, potion holders, and a sword scabbard. The plain sheath contained an ancient elf blade named Demon Queller.

The elf carried an ornate jade wand known as Starkiller, thrust crossways into the front of his belt. Gold inlaid scrollwork covered the slightly curved wand from rounded end to tapered tip. The small pyramid inset into the tip of the wand looked to be forged from the same curious golden alloy. The device allowed Yax to channel Aethyr energies through the wand to disable or kill an enemy at a considerable distance. All elven Wand Bearers commanded this devastating ability.

Yax'Kaqix wore his hair in the fashion of the Unen'ek, the Elves of the South Isles - long hair in the back tied and limned into a wild design with the browline cut very high in an exaggerated widow's peak. Even dripping wet, his coif held the shape of a leafy jungle frond.

Very prominent, pointed ears also set apart Yax from his northern cousins, the Winaq'che, or the Elves of Ny, Faltyr's main continent. He decorated them with shiny silver rings and earplugs of pure gold as was the custom of his people. Dor noted that Yax's slender, long-fingered hands rarely drifted far from his powerful sword and curved jade wand.

Donal Cadogan was the taller of the fraternal twins. A long gingery mane and thick, drooping mustache provided the sword-for-hire characteristics that further distinguished him from his brother. The long-bladed fighting knife on his weapon belt marked him as one of the Gre people; fair-skinned, knife-wielding barbarians that conquered the Ireti and Baax empires in the wake of the Cataclysm. The rest of his arms and armor now rested with the *Nightsfall* at the bottom of the sea.

Shorter and stouter with the broad chest of an archer, Glynn Cadogan, the clean-shaven twin, carried an eel-skin quiver slung over his shoulder that contained his bow and remaining arrows. A dagger like Donal's hung at his side. Dor observed that the knives shared more similarities than the twin brothers carrying them.

Deciding to avoid the menacing mercenaries for now, he slinked past them, concealing himself amongst the ship's remains scattered along the beach. An expert eavesdropper, he hoped to overhear their conversation without being discovered.

"There's something about that guy I don't like," Breuxias said.

Dor assumed Breuxias meant him. But relief washed over the mage as the mercenary gestured toward Spensir. Dor empathized with the brute's sentiment; he too despised the greasy first mate.

"Nature's stormy disposition stranded us here, not that petty tyrant," Yax replied. "So focus. There are other survivors ahead. Gneut may be amongst them."

Behind the wreckage, Dor blanched at Yax'Kaqix's comment. Why would the elf deceive his comrades? After all, when he had fought his way up the flooding staircase and emerged onto the swamped deck of the *Nightsfall*, Yax had been the one to save him.

As the cumbersome chest threatened to pull Dor to the bottom with the ship, Yax had seized him by his robes, physically separating him from the anchor weight in his arms. Despite Dor's protests, the elf's viselike hold had wrenched him from his death grip on the lightning-scarred chest. Could Yax have missed the damage to its lid?

Perhaps he was being paranoid, Dor thought. Even if Yax had noticed anything amiss, why would the elf connect him to the sinking of the *Nightsfall*? The metal box could have become marred in any number of ways. That had to be it. Yax had not made the connection between the lightning strike and the scorched, smoking chest in Dor's arms.

The realization that there were no witnesses caused Dor to feel weak in the knees. Relief replaced his nagging paranoia, at least for the moment. Now all he had to do was live with his most recent magical mishap and its resulting loss of life. Dor wondered if that part would ever get any easier.

Farther down the beach, Breuxias stopped as he reached the body of a drowned man amidst the widely dispersed wrack. The boot in the mercenary's hand matched the one remaining on the shod foot of the sailor. Breuxias laid the boot onto the dead man's chest and then folded the corpse's arms over it.

"Damn it," Breuxias spat through gritted teeth.

"At least he's got both boots again. Makes for much easier walking in the afterlife I suppose," Donal Cadogan joked. Even his own brother failed to laugh at his gallows humor.

A survivor called out from the field of debris, "We found the captain. He's alive. Help us!"

Breuxias broke formation from his guildsmen, hurrying toward the origin of the voice. The Cadogan twins sprinted after their captain. Rather than leaving, Yax turned, his eyes settling on the patch of wreckage through which Dor observed them.

"I think you'll find the malignance you seek over there," Yax'Kaqix said, indicating an area not too far from where survivors gathered around the fallen captain. "Its foul presence stings my nostrils even from this distance. Be careful trafficking in dark magic. You will not find the others as accepting. Their ignorance and anger will destroy you before whatever you carry in that box does."

Emerging from behind the wreckage, Dor ventured a word of thanks to the concerned elf. Yax raced down the beach, sidestepping debris with the nimbleness of a stag. Slogging along after him, Dor considered the elf's words of wisdom but knew that he had no choice. The chest was his burden to carry alone. In Dor's mind, fate had led him to this island just as surely as it had saddled him with sole responsibility for the chest until time to destroy its contents.

Chapter 3

The group of survivors gathered around their trapped captain. A large splinter of the mast protruded through the right side of Gneut's chest. His eyes rolled back into his head as the group removed debris from atop him. His deteriorating condition forced them to ignore safety for speed.

Vaguely aware of events around him, Captain Gneut tried to focus as Breuxias lifted a large beam out of the way. The captain felt but could not see those who pulled his body free of the wreckage. Multiple sets of hands lifted him from the rising tide, laying him down on the hot, dry sand beyond the surf.

His sister, Asta, mumbled in his ear but her wailing words made no sense. Rayne pulled her away, allowing one of the passengers, a traveling priest, to kneel down beside him in the sand. Waving his left hand over Gneut's wound, Rafasi prayed aloud to his goddess.

"O Goddess, Lady of the Moon, hear my cry! I call to you not for my own sake but for the sake of another. By your grace and by your healing light, may he be restored? Hear his plight, O Goddess, so that he may be healed. I ask this in your name, Mighty Ishta'Kahl, for I am your humble servant. Fill me with your light!"

Gneut watched as Rafasi's tattooed hand began to radiate soft, warm light. The captain groaned as the wooden fragments extracted themselves from the wound and floated toward the priest's outstretched hand. Closing his hand around the bloody splinters, the priest blew once into his clenched fist. Opening his hand, he revealed an empty palm; even the luminous glow had vanished before Gneut's tired eyes.

"Thank you, Blessed Ishta'Kahl," Rafasi said, clasping his hands together reverently. "Though we are not worthy of your many blessings, your silver light continues to illuminate our path."

Then he removed a small leather pouch from the inside of his robe and pulled out a clump of dried herbs. Breaking off a small chunk, he dampened it with water from his flask. He rubbed the mixture into the oozing wound before placing an improvised bandage over it.

Rafasi spoke gravely, "I have done all that I can. It may not prove to be enough. You must pray. The Goddess may hear you and come to your aid before your spirit slips away."

Gneut raised his head, grimacing at the healer as he said, "If I only have a few moments, I'll spend 'em with my crew, not beseeching the gods for miracles I don't deserve."

Nodding, Rafasi turned and stepped past Sir Caayl. Gneut's keen ears heard the priest whisper, "Gnomes are a hardy lot, sailors doubly so. He's lost a lot of blood. It's in the hands of Ishta'Kahl now."

If his fate was in the hands of the gods and goddesses of Faltyr, the captain knew that he'd lived a questionable enough life that no deity would ride to his rescue during his final moments.

Spensir broke the group's silence by saying, "You heard the Cap'n, dogs. Assemble or disperse as you're ordered."

"I don't take orders from you," Breuxias reminded him.

The first mate's narrowed eyes shifted from the diminutive captain to the towering mercenary. Spensir took a step forward, but Gneut seized him by the tattered leg of his breeches. He glanced down into the disapproving eyes of his captain and halted his advance.

Gneut said hoarsely but forcefully, "It's my order! And my last request…to die surrounded by my crew, my family."

Breuxias's demeanor visibly softened. He nodded and then stalked away from the assembly toward the Cadogan brothers. Yax offered Gneut a wan smile before following his comrades down the beach.

The suddenness and severity of Spensir's order surprised Gneut, yet it pleased the dying captain to see him take charge of the situation. Perhaps he could trust his first mate after all.

Not that Gneut felt like he had a choice. To take the secret of the Hallowed Vessel to his grave would mean stranding the shipwrecked survivors on this long-forgotten island. In that case, his obsession with possessing the ship of legend would doom them all. He couldn't let that happen. Though he didn't merit divine intervention, he hoped to provide his crew with some measure of salvation and security.

Out of respect for the dying captain's wishes, everyone except the remaining crewmembers walked away. Noting the obvious disapproval from the members of Finders Keepers, Gneut realized he had made the right decision. Trusting mercenaries with his crew's sole means of escape from this forsaken island did not sound like a prudent idea, especially to the dying captain. Once he was dead, would Breuxias and the other sell swords even listen to Spensir?

Pale and gaunt from shock and blood loss, the captain summoned the energy to address his crew one last time.

"Come closer," Gneut managed. After several labored breaths, he continued, "What I have to tell you may save all of your lives."

Most of the assembly huddled closer to him, their faces filled with a mixture of astonishment and dread, mostly dread. All of them focused on the dying gnome's final words. He found some comfort in the fact that Spensir paid close attention as command of the remaining crew would fall to him. The passengers and the captain's hired mercenaries possessed contentious aims and came from different backgrounds; but Gneut hoped that their common goal, survival, would prevent any open bloodshed within the group.

"This island is our true destination, its secret our true purpose. The voyage to Myth was simply a means to an end. I brought you to Moor'Dru, to this island, for a prize; a ship of legend."

Captain Gneut coughed violently, unable to continue for several tense moments. As the fit passed, he spat up dark blood onto the white sand. Spotting Rafasi approaching the assembly, Gneut waved him away with renewed vigor. Collapsing back onto the ship's wheel, the captain fought to control his erratic breathing. He had more to tell them.

Rayne took his hand and smiled at him. "Captain, don't overdo it. Take it easy."

Chuckling, he replied, "I've overdone it for years. Now I'm done. Don't end up like me: shipwrecked and dying because of my own greed. My quest for this prize has doomed me. Don't let it doom you too. Find it. Master it. Use it to escape. The maps will guide you."

With great effort, Gneut managed to disentangle himself from a boiled eel-skin cylinder. Placing it in Spensir's care, the captain added, "As will the spyglass and compass."

Gneut handed Spensir the compass but floundered about searching for the spyglass. When the captain saw that his other hand held it in a virtual death grip, he realized he could no longer feel that arm at all. Nor could he move it. His life slipped from him as surely as the surf from the alien shore.

Taking his cue from Gneut, Spensir pulled the spyglass from the gnome's paralyzed hand. As the ancient Aethyr device came free, fresh sensation flooded back into Gneut's limb. It felt as though a thousand pins and needles stung at his exposed flesh. Crying out, Gneut seized the first mate with the spasmodic limb.

Badly shaken, Spensir shrank away from the gnome's intense gaze. Even as a dying man, the tiny captain managed to intimidate his first mate. Pain racked Gneut's body, causing him to seizure again. As he coughed uncontrollably, he clung to the other man even tighter.

The captain's vision dimmed even as he focused on remaining conscious. Every sentence that he could muster might save a life or two of his diminished crew. Staring into Spensir's fear-filled eyes, he uttered one final cryptic line.

"Know your prize by its true name…its true power you shall gain."

And then for Gneut, his story drew to a close. Even as it ended, he knew the others' tale had only just begun.

***

Thanks to the assistance of Yax'Kaqix, Kaladimus Dor relocated the metal chest in no time. The container remained secure despite its scorched lid. In fact, the extreme heat of the lightning melted the strongbox's heavy-duty lock mechanism.

Removing the chest from beneath the scattered wrack of the *Nightsfall* proved to be another matter entirely. Doing so while eavesdropping on the captain's final orders to his crew complicated matters further. Terrible at multitasking, his past attempts often ended in disaster, the fate of the *Nightsfall* being an extreme example.

Dor excavated the metal chest from underneath the pile of debris as quietly as possible. But, before he managed to reach it, he dislodged the material supporting the cluster of ruined cargo and splintered wood, causing it to topple down around him.

"So much for being subtle, stupid," he admonished himself.

Spensir and the ship's stocky quartermaster, Fergus, rushed around the wrack of the *Nightsfall*. They spotted Dor as he dragged the chest from the pile of debris.

"What did you hear, boy?" Spensir demanded.

Hoping to avoid a violent confrontation, Dor decided to feign ignorance of the captain's deathbed confession. The grubby magician chose to play the part of the self-absorbed fool. For him, that role came naturally, too naturally at times.

Stumbling in the surf, Dor glanced up at Spensir and Fergus. He asked, "Can you give me a hand with my luggage?"

"Not on your life." the first mate chuckled, lowering his weapon. "You're that infernal wizard with the funny name, right? The one from Kingsport."

"I'm the wizard but I'm not from Kingsport. Dor. That's my name, not where I'm from. I'm actually from--"

"I don't much give a damn, Mister Dor. We've lost our ship and our captain and I got no time for your yap. So stow it or start countin' your ivories." Spensir finished his threat by pointing to his own yellow teeth for emphasis.

"Wizard with the funny name." Fergus laughed. "I get it. Like a door."

"Yeah, clever one, aren't you?" Dor quipped, unable to fight these bullies in any other fashion under the present circumstances. And unwilling to tussle with them as long as they possessed those maps, especially the one that he had traded for passage on the *Nightsfall*.

"You mouthy sonuva--" Fergus spat, silenced by a loud slap across the mouth from Spensir. Rubbing his jaw, the cowed bully glared at both Spensir and Dor. Shock and shame colored his freckled face.

"And shut your yap too, Fergus," Spensir snapped, "Make yourself useful and haul Mister Dor's luggage outta the surf."

"Why me?" Fergus pleaded.

"Because I've gotta go lend my back to digging graves. Be happy yours isn't one of them."

"Aye," Fergus relented, stooping to retrieve the chest.

"I appreciate your help," Dor lied.

"Shut it, Dor," Fergus gibed. "Get it? Shut it? The door?"

"Never heard that one before. Quite original," the mage replied through gritted teeth, resisting the urge to slit the oaf's throat or set his balls aflame.

Behind Fergus, Dor's fingers sparked as the wizard rubbed them together in growing agitation. He fought to regain his composure as the sailor struggled with the chest. Dor managed to stretch a fool's grin across his scruffy face before Fergus freed the trapped object.

As Fergus turned back toward him, Dor sat in a pose that mirrored levitation. Gnarled black staff planted in the surf, he appeared to float a few feet above the lapping waves. The fear in Fergus's eyes spoke volumes for the effectiveness of the simple illusion. After last night, he dared not attempt true levitation; for now, parlor tricks seemed enough to enthrall and intimidate this superstitious lout.

Stepping down into the surf, he took a step toward Fergus.

Grunting from the exertion, the sailor asked, "If you can do that, why didn't you magic the chest out?"

Smiling, Dor replied, "I did. And presto. It's in your hand. And, upon my command, you'll return it to me. One way or the other."

"That's not magic."

"The most insidious magic is getting someone to do your dirty work for you."

Fergus paled at Dor's revealing remark. The mage saw that he had the sailor in his sway. *Now to cow the bully completely*, he thought.

"My chest. I'll have it at once." Snapping his fingers, Dor sent sparks flying, each one dying with a sinister sizzle in the surf below.

"Not like I want the damn thing anyway," Fergus chuckled nervously. "What am I gonna do with a melted chest that's far too light to contain treasure? What's in this thing anyway?"

The thuggish dimwit sounded as if he was trying to retain some semblance of bravado in a situation that had gone spooky on him. Dor hated to admit it to himself but he liked it when the bullies cowered. In the end, they always cowered before him, one way or the other.

Accepting the chest from the sailor, Dor cradled it to him as a heirless king would hold his bastard boy. He decided to be honest yet remain vague. That method helped him confuse overly curious parties.

"Dead things, mostly."

Fergus trembled at Dor's cryptic response. The wizard forced a sinister smile, holding it until Fergus slipped away down the beach.

The mage allowed the uncomfortable grin to slip. He trembled in the wake of the confrontation. Like most simpletons, Fergus feared the unknown, and as a result, subtle wizardry duped him easily. As a learned man, Dor feared the known, the calculable, and even the prophesized. For those reasons, he feared the instrument of undoing clutched in his trembling hands.

Chapter 4

Shortly before dawn, the exhausted survivors clustered around a dying fire. While the others slumbered, Yax'Kaqix lay watching the waning embers. Fire was not only his primary elemental affinity but also something he truly loved. Of its myriad forms, Yax considered the time he spent around a campfire his preferred form of communion.

Yax snaked his clawed fingers out of his voluminous cloak. Gesturing toward the glowing embers, he chanted in the language of his ancestors. The red-hot coals popped and hissed like an angry viper disturbed from its slumber. The rejuvenated flames danced brightly, illuminating the scarred, tattooed form of Breuxias who snored nearby.

Breuxias had been burned, branded, and scarred before he and Yax had met aboard the ferry to the island nation of Asterion. He also knew that Breuxias had earned several of his battle scars during his association with him. The very first of those had been on that island during the protracted goblin infestation of the capital city of Minotas and its neighboring city-states.

Yax and his only begotten son, Kan'Balam, had been drawn to the troubled island for the same reasons as Breuxias: gold, glory, and goblins. Initially, Yax did not take to the booming, bombastic giant but his son made friends with the human before they'd even reached the island. During the long months that followed, Breuxias and his mercenary company, the Gore Corps, had fought alongside Yax and his son against the horde of goblins nesting beneath Minotas. Before the bitter campaign ended, Breuxias had saved Yax's life on a few notable occasions, earning his respect and eventually his camaraderie.

In the end, however, Breuxias and Yax bonded over something of greater significance than gaining gold, seeking glory, or slaying goblins. The tragic loss of Kan cemented their friendship. Rarely a day passed that Yax did not replay those events in his mind's eye.

Commanding the mercenary forces at the personal behest of Aeogius Rex, Yax made the fateful decision to flood the labyrinth during the final desperate battle for the fate of Minotas and all Asterion. However, Aeogius wanted to sacrifice the mercenaries already inside the labyrinth to ensure that none of the goblins escaped their watery fate.

As Kan and Breuxias fought alongside the trapped forces, Yax chose to go against his wealthy benefactor, risk everything, and save his son and the other mercenaries. The sole means of draining the labyrinth involved eliminating the wall separating it from the city sewer system. Yax accomplished this explosive feat through a combination of alchemy and raw magical power. However, he failed to stop his son from being dragged out to sea with the goblin horde.

The betrayal by Aeogius Rex had upset him, but the death of his son had left Yax in a murderous mindset. Had it not been for Breuxias, he would have set fire to the entire city of Minotas. Instead, they exposed the king's nefarious plot against the mercenaries hired to protect the city, led an attack on the palace, and tore the tyrant from his throne. They took the remainder owed on their contract and anything else they could carry to the boats. Sailing north toward Fraustmauth, the new friends staked their fortunes with a new company of adventurers known as Finders Keepers.

His attention returned to his present situation as the ship's fleshy cook, Thrash, struggled to his feet with a soft groan. Yax drew his cloak around himself and pretended to be asleep. He heard rather than saw the human approach from the direction of the campfire. Thrash planted his hairy foot into Yax's side, cursing his own clumsiness under his breath as he stumbled over the elf.

Turning to face the awkward cook, he intended on spitting a few curses of his own, but the elf's excellent night vision afforded him a good view of Thrash's intended destination. Doubting the cook was going for a predawn swim, he took a guess on what Thrash intended.

Already annoyed at being awakened by the graceless human, he had no desire to watch a fat man fumble for his prick. Rolling over, he vowed to do his best impersonation of sleep until he transmuted it into the real thing. Unfortunately, his sensitive hearing could not block out the sound of the cook grunting and sighing by the shoreline.

Heightened senses could be a blessing and a curse, Yax reflected. Indispensable when one needs to hear a goblin slinking up in the night. A nightmare when one is trying to block out some guy pissing into the waters swirling around his bare feet.

A sudden, strong gust of wind blew across the beach encampment, stirring up sand and scattering sparks from the campfire. Yax heard something above the wind buffeting the humid night air with the beat of massive wings. While not large enough to be a dragon, he realized that the flying phantom sounded sizeable enough to pose a threat to the entire party. He had to warn everyone.

The elf's realization came too late, for the beast was already upon them. Yax closed his eyes to mere slits to avoid being blinded by sand and ash. He peered toward the shoreline through the sooty cloud in time to witness the cook's grizzly demise.

Thrash stared down at the long black scimitar-shaped appendage protruding from his ample gut. His contorted face conveyed a mixture of agonizing pain and complete surprise.

As the cook's strangled cries broke the relative stillness of the predawn, the other survivors scrambled about blindly, unsure as to the situation or the source of alarm. Most had not moved past assessing their own situations before blood began to rain from above. Thrash's panicked, gurgled screams moved up and away from the bustling, broken encampment before dying in the distance.

Yax's eyes glowed red in the dimness, sharpening his dark vision. He observed a huge winged predator clutching a squirming figure before the dense vegetation beyond the beach obscured his view. Definitely not a dragon, he reflected. Close enough kin for real concern though. Too many creatures could fit that description and behavior pattern for him to be sure of its identity at this juncture. To pinpoint it with any certainty, the Wand Bearer would need a much closer look.

Unfortunately, fate would provide him with just that chance.

Bearing torches, Breuxias and the Cadogan brothers hurried toward him. The trio stopped short of the shoreline as they reached the site of Thrash's gruesome abduction. Breuxias rubbed his stubble-covered head as he surveyed the grisly scene. The brute's jaw reminded Yax of chiseled stone.

After a moment of silence, the brute asked, "What did you see?"

Wiping specks of the stolen man's blood from his face, Yax answered, "An unexpected development."

***

In the gray light of the morning, the frazzled survivors of the *Nightsfall* finished gathering their remaining possessions. Spensir noticed that most of them kept a wary watch on the overcast sky for any sign of the creature that killed the hapless cook.

In the distance, makeshift tombstones marked the fresh graves of the bodies recovered on the beach. Sailors preferred to bury their dead at sea, but the lack of a ship made that difficult at the moment. The ship's wheel stood out as the most prominent piece scavenged from the wreckage. He supposed it served as an appropriate monument to the *Nightsfall*'s deceased captain.

Of the graves he'd bent his back digging since the shipwreck, he reckoned the most recent had by far been the easiest. The fat cook had become chow for some flying beastie, leaving no body to bury. The first mate judged the missing corpse a small kindness. It kept him from having to dig a grave thrice the size of the others.

Spensir waited beside his lover, Vorta, on the highest sand dune on the beach as Fergus approached. He had asked them to meet him away from the outsiders so that he could discuss the items he'd inherited from their late captain without being overheard.

The spyglass and compass fed the captain's guarded obsession with this island and its mysteries. Both possessed powerful enchantments, including one that linked them to the Hallowed Vessel.

He witnessed Gneut using the spyglass on numerous occasions, including the night of the shipwreck. No fog bank or blinding rain ever stymied the wondrous powers of the device.

The compass, on the other hand, seemed to be broken or fixated. Neither genius nor magician, Spensir still knew enough about navigation to know that no compass should keep a fixed point other than magnetic north. Regardless of how he tilted the instrument, its needle pointed in a non-northerly direction.

The maps were another matter entirely. The largest map featured the most detail, including the home island of Moor'Dru as well as its hundreds of outlying islands. This map had provided Gneut with the exact location of this island. By all indications, this particular map would not be of any further use until they located the ship of legend.

The pigskin map of the island itself was crude but clear. It indicated a solitary settlement on the far side of a nearby bay. If the scale was accurate, the body of water cut deep inland, diminishing in size until it was not much wider than the river system that emptied into the bay. Looking down the shoreline, he noted that the shortest overland route was impassable due to a reedy wetland.

As he stared across the bay, Spensir realized that the compass's fixation appeared to be the lone occupied area indicated on the map. The walled fortification sat atop a rocky ridge spur. From this perspective, he could discern neither a seaward approach to the keep nor any safe portage along the waterline at the bottom of the sheer cliff face.

With the aid of the spyglass, he observed that the walls of the ridge top fortification consisted of stacked coquina blocks, a common building material used along the southern coasts of Faltyr. Turrets built of the same type of shell concrete protruded from either end of the wall. These smaller, flat-topped towers were perfect for coastal defense since they were capable of supporting siege engines.

A taller, broken tower composed of a darker, glassier stone stood beyond the coquina wall, probably within the grounds of the fortress itself. His eyes narrowed to mere slits as he spied the jagged, broken terminus of this otherwise impressive structure. Although the composition of this ruinous building escaped him, the stone reminded him of a waxier version of obsidian or onyx.

Tearing his attention from the foreboding place, his inky eyes met Vorta's own abyssal ones. She wore her raven-colored hair cropped short and dressed as a common sailor with few female accentuations. A false corset highlighting her pert bosom and her thigh-high boots served as notable exceptions. Spensir had insisted on both of them despite her protests. Her agitated expression ruined the alluring effect created the wardrobe choices he'd made on her behalf.

Wondering what had tilted her kilt, he asked, "What's wrong?"

"We've got company," Vorta whispered as several of the other survivors drew near their gathering atop the dune.

Rayne led the contingent of the survivors up the broad windblown dune. Sir Caayl walked hand in hand with her like lovers. Spensir's suspicions grew as he observed the level of fraternization between the outsider and someone Gneut had considered one of his most trusted associates.

Putting the spyglass away, Spensir glared at the half-elven woman and her human lover. Jealousy tugged at his heart and twisted his mind against her. Vorta had damaged their friendship and ruined any chance of developing something friendlier; but he still didn't like seeing Rayne with anyone else, especially some pious pretty boy from Oparre.

Two of the surviving members of the mercenary company hired by the captain for this particular voyage accompanied the interlopers. According to their substantial reputation, these sellswords from Finders Keepers were dangerous men. Spensir did not relish the idea of tangling with either the elven war-mage or his muscle-bound companion.

However, he could not afford to have his newfound command compromised by dissent and disloyalty. For better or worse, Gneut had seen fit to leave him in charge. Casting his gaze downward, Spensir realized he needed to draw a line in the sand. Better now than later.

Drawing himself up to his full height, he placed one hand on the clamshell-shaped pommel of his scimitar. Spensir stood almost a head and a half shorter than Breuxias, but he was almost as broad as the towering mercenary.

Although no warrior-for-hire, the first mate rarely shrank from a challenge or a fight. Despite Spensir's many faults, the captain trusted him to preserve his interests and protect his crew for this very reason. Commanding a crew of scoundrels such as these took someone hard as a coffin nail, someone like him.

Taking the initiative, he addressed the gathering crowd, "There's one marked settlement on the island. And that's yon keep..." Gesturing to the map, Spensir continued in his clipped manner, "...Frolov Keep according to the maps. Gonna be a coupla days before we get there. Gonna have to cut inland and try to find a way to approach from the landward side. Flyin' devil or no flyin' devil."

Fergus, the ship's stocky, bull-faced quartermaster, nodded his assent. "Seems simple and sensible enough," he commented, seconding his friend's plan. "After seeing Thrash thrashed, I got no desire to remain in the open any longer than necessary."

As Vorta was not a sailor by trade, Spensir knew she typically stuck close to his opinion on matters of ship's business. However, when she had spoken out against him in the past, she normally made sound suggestions. When he had followed her advice, the results had been satisfactory if sanguine. In fact, though he wouldn't admit it, Spensir owed his meteoric rise to her influence.

Sir Caayl posed a question, pulling the first mate's attention back to the business at hand.

"What'll we do about tonight? With something on the prowl for our flesh, I don't recommend sleeping outdoors."

Breuxias crossed his bulging arms and commented, "I'll second that sentiment. Not sure about this keep idea, especially if the natives do prove to be hostile. Too many of you are unarmed to risk a straight-up fight."

Countering with his own proposal, Fergus said, "We make a shelter out of the wreckage and some of the taller palms. Leave the weak 'n wounded here with that healer and this knight. Once we make it to the keep, we'll send back help for the rest."

"Speak for yourself, friend," Breuxias interjected. "I'm not leaving anyone here to be carried off by that thing. No telling what else is lurking in the bush either. We stay together. There's safety in numbers."

"I'm not your friend, *friend*," Fergus responded. "I'll speak whenever about whatever I please. 'Specially ship's business." Gesturing between Spensir and Breuxias, he added, "You tell him."

"Ship's business!" Breuxias laughed. "Isn't that like an empty-headed seadog? You have no ship! The business at hand is survival."

Before Spensir could call either man down, Fergus barked, "Empty-headed seadog! I'll…"

Red-faced, Fergus took a step toward Breuxias while reaching for the leaf-shaped blade hanging on his hip. Unfazed by the threat of imminent violence, the mercenary stared at Fergus with murderous intent. In Spensir's mind, he had to intervene to avoid bloodshed.

However, before Spensir could take action, the elf at Breuxias's side drew his own sword in a blur of motion. The tip of Yax's silvery blade pressed against the thick neck of the hotheaded quartermaster.

Realizing his friend's mortal peril at the hands of a paid killer like Yax'Kaqix, Spensir reigned in the belligerent sailor. Cutting across Fergus's rant, he shouted, "Stow that yap, dog! We got no time for that now."

Faced with a showdown against an arcane, inhuman blade master, Spensir watched as his companion's fear mastered his hotheaded nature. As his friend's hand moved away from the hilt of his weapon, Spensir sighed with relief. They'd avoided killing each other, for now.

Continuing with his reluctant peacemaking efforts, Spensir rhymed, "Everyone here who wishes'll have their say. But mark my words. In the end, the keep'll be the only way."

For him, almost any course of action beat waiting on the beach for their mysterious attacker to return. And, in light of a better suggestion, he knew that his plan to reach Frolov Keep seemed like a reasonable place to start. Despite their differences, Spensir wagered that the sell swords employed by Finders Keepers felt the same.

Chapter 5

The string of survivors sidled along the narrow trail cut through the jungle vegetation. As Dor stumbled after the others, the overcast sky became darker, giving way to a steady drizzle. His insatiable, even unhealthy curiosity shut out the foul weather, causing him to focus on the wide variety of flora rather than the precarious path.

As a result, he failed to notice the sharp stobs left over from the group's trailblazing efforts. Catching his robe on it, the clumsy mage tripped and fell hard in the mud. Tumbling downhill a short distance, he came to a stop in a puddle of cold rainwater.

"Sonuva…" he began but failed to finish as thunder boomed.

Glancing toward the warring heavens, the calamitous mage of Myth struggled to his feet. He searched about for the metal chest but spied a nearby stand of valerian nestled in the undergrowth. He set about gathering the valuable roots and became distracted once again.

Playing in the mud and gathering herbs took Dor back to a happier, simpler time. His master didn't enjoy leisurely pursuits, much less encourage them, yet Braigen's love of gardening had been a notable exception, a passion he had cultivated in his apprentice from childhood onward. Even as an adult, Dor possessed greater confidence in his skills as a gardener and herbalist than in his ability to weave spells and combat the forces of darkness.

"This'll be the perfect thing after a long hard day on the trail," he murmured, stuffing the prized herbs into his expansive belt pouch. "A pipe full of the good stuff and a cuppa this'll do us fine."

Regaining his feet, Dor recovered the accursed chest. After slogging back up the embankment, he emerged onto the trail. As he did so, the rain increased from a drizzle to a downpour, obscuring his vision further. There was no one to be seen.

He had been talking to himself…again.

Thoroughly saturated, he trudged along in the pouring rain, alone while struggling to carry his cumbersome chest. Vicious snake lightning flashed overhead followed by rolling thunder. Flinching, he looked skyward. His breathing became shallower as he stood transfixed for a long moment by the phantasmagoric display.

For the first time since the accident had happened, Dor let his mind drift back to the shipwreck. The guilt of his fateful actions on the *Nightsfall* and his inability to confess them to the others threatened to overwhelm the young Protectorate Mage.

Standing there in the midst of the storm, his tears mixed freely with the rain. Sometimes his burden and its unpredictable, often destructive consequences were almost too much to bear.

Would these survivors understand, like the Council of Three, and see him as a powerful yet cursed individual to be feared as well as pitied? Or would they react like the people of his late parents' village and want the wild mage lynched regardless of his affliction? Knowing something about human nature, the sniffling young man bet on the latter. That realization brought Dor little comfort.

Continuing along the trail, Dor struggled with the chest as much as his composure. The rain left the metallic box slick, making it difficult for him to carry. He felt the muscles in his slender arms start to burn but dared not attempt another spell under these hazardous conditions. And he didn't dare stop to rest, realizing he'd be left even farther behind.

At some point, the group's trek through the godsforsaken jungle had to end. Then Dor would be able to rest, maybe even sleep for a few hours without something or someone trying to kill him. Long past the point of exhaustion, he wondered if death would be preferable to the torture of carrying his burden another league through this downpour.

"Keep up, numb nuts, or you're gonna get someone killed," a voice boomed above the din produced by the rain, wind, and thunder.

Focused on avoiding a repeat of his earlier clumsiness, Dor started at the unexpected belligerence. He looked wide-eyed from his mud-caked shoes to the familiar faces of two of the mercenaries.

The bombastic voice belonged to Donal, the heavily mustachioed Cadogan twin. He returned along the trail, accompanied by Breuxias. Donal carried a makeshift spear composed from his long-bladed knife, a section of bamboo, and a length of supple vine. Breuxias held an improvised weapon as well: a staff hewn from a slender, springy tree.

Striding past Donal, the other mercenary asked, "Need a hand?"

Dor became acquainted with the mercenaries after they came aboard the *Nightsfall* during a stopover on the island of Corr Deyraire. As a result, he considered the most conversant one, Breuxias, to be the closest thing to a friend that he had on this island. The mage figured that if Yax'Kaqix, a centuries-old elf from the South Isles, trusted the likeable brute, then he figured him for an honorable man.

"Thanks," Dor replied. He smiled despite his sodden state. "Be careful with it. It's fragile."

Taking the lightning-scorched chest, Breuxias hoisted it onto one muscular shoulder with ease. He tossed the sturdy walking staff he'd fashioned earlier in the day to the magician.

"Catch!"

And Dor did. Deftly even.

Looking surprised, the brute said with a grin, "Impressive. And don't worry. I'm no porter, but I know my way around a box. Just make sure that you don't fall and impale yourself with that length of wood there. Catching it is one thing. Using it's another matter."

"I'm a fully registered Magus of Moor'Dru. I may not be accustomed to trailblazing, but I know my way around a staff."

Donal quipped, "I'm sure you do, mage. I'm sure you do."

Leaning on the walking stick, Dor followed the other men in silence for a moment before he finally got the jest.

"Hey! That's not funny."

***

Using his heavy curved blade, Spensir hacked a rough trail through the soaked subtropical undergrowth. Sweat stood out on his brow and caused his long hair to hang wet and loose. Despite the thorns and vines, he had chosen to remove his shirt and belt it around his waist. Scars from numerous skirmishes and lashings crisscrossed his tanned, chiseled exterior.

Pausing for a moment, Spensir checked and rechecked the compass entrusted to them by Gneut. No matter which way he turned the device, the needle remained buried in the direction of the keep perched on the high bluff across the distant bay. Salty perspiration stung his eyes as he failed to discern more details of the structure. The stretch of fauna between them and the shoreline blocked most of the compound.

Squashing another mosquito feasting on his vital fluids, Fergus asked, "Any luck?"

"It's still pointing straight at the keep."

"To the keep then. Sure as Hells don't want to be caught out here after the sun goes down."

Slicing a long runner of liana out of the way served as Spensir's response. He continued cutting at a pace that kept them well ahead of the others.

"What about Rayne?" Fergus asked. "Can we trust her?"

Taking a break from trailblazing, Spensir turned back toward Rayne and Sir Caayl. As the pair of lovebirds paused on the trail, Caayl offered her his canteen. Rayne took a long pull on the container before handing it back to him. As she did so, the first mate noticed that she drew intimately close, letting her pert breasts press against Caayl. The knight blushed as Rayne kissed him on the cheek. His eyes narrowed and his blood burned as he watched the lovers' display.

Spensir felt the jealousy roiling inside him. He and Rayne had been coworkers and casual friends on the *Nightsfall*, yet that hadn't stopped him from satisfying himself countless times to fantasies about her full lips stretched over his cock or her lean, flexible form contorted into a variety of positions. Despite his lusty intentions toward Rayne, he didn't consider his feelings to be entirely sexual in nature. He feared losing one of his few remaining friends to the likes of that blasted do-gooder.

Though Spensir had never been particularly loyal to anyone save himself, he wondered if her association with Sir Caayl would affect her loyalties to the crew and their pursuit for the ship of legend. They'd already suffered a shipwreck and the loss of the captain and most of the ship's hands. Now a winged demon stalked them as they hunted for a magic ship that may or may not exist while he attempted to keep this contentious, diverse group of survivors from tearing each other apart. Spensir needed fewer complications in his life, not more.

Answering Fergus, he said, "Don't trust anyone personally."

His rust-tinged scimitar emphasized the point as it cut clean through a nest of vines entangling a stand of trees growing along the low hillside.

Behind him, Fergus grunted in agreement.

Hours later of hacking away at the undergrowth, they emerged from the wild, tangled jungle onto a section of unpaved, rut-filled roadway. Though mostly reclaimed by the island's invasive flora, this overgrown wagon trail appeared to parallel a raging river. Spensir could not see it but he heard it above the sound of the steady downpour.

The high-banked waterway lay beyond the shallow road cut. Stepping up onto the steep bank of the river, the first mate looked down at the torrent below. He sighed dejectedly. Even if they could descend the treacherous banks on this side, it would be impossible to ford its storm-swollen depths.

He glanced at the compass in his hand. The shimmering needle never wavered during their trek as it continued to point in the direction of Frolov Keep. Judging by the azimuth, he determined the settlement to be downriver from their position.

The first mate figured that any wagons in use on the island would have required a securer crossing than a simple ford site. Since their most likely cargo would have been timber cut from the dense stands of vegetation in this region, he deduced that the keep's residents would have constructed a sturdy bridge to support their logging expeditions.

The other survivors emerged onto the roadway as Spensir weighed their limited options. Sir Caayl, Rayne, and Rafasi exited the foliage behind the remaining crewmembers. Dor and the four sell swords from Finders Keepers brought up the rear.

The first mate eyed the mercenaries with suspicion. Though he had no particular disagreement with any of them, he considered their contract null and void when Gneut had passed beyond this world. He felt like he owed them nothing. He planned to offer them safe passage off the island if they helped him acquire the ship.

Though he wouldn't maroon anyone without a good reason, Spensir considered the safety of the passengers secondary to that of his crew. If any of the wayfarers proved hostile to his band of sailors or stood in the way of their pursuit for the ship of legend, he would have to leave them behind. Abandoning the guilty parties would be a damn sight easier than resorting to unnecessary bloodshed, especially if that meant an entanglement with battle-hardened mercenaries.

Rolling up the pigskin map, he cleared his throat before addressing the other survivors. Speaking loud enough to be heard over the river and the rain, he declared, "We're gonna follow the road a piece. I think it'll be easier going until we find a place to cross."

Crossing both massive arms over his chiseled chest, Breuxias replied sardonically, "You think? I feel safer already."

Spensir glared at Breuxias but remained unable to bear the brute's withering gaze for long. He glanced over at Fergus who shook his head slightly. His friend was right.

Now was not the time for this, he surmised, yet the time would come. Before they sailed away from this place, he hoped to find a discrete way to silence that mouthy sonuvabitch permanently.

Obviously flummoxed, Spensir muttered through clenched teeth, "Make sure you keep up. We'd hate to have anymore…casualties."

Chapter 6

The rain slowed to a drizzle as the group approached the confluence of the river with a wider, slower-moving waterway. The faster-moving oxbow terminated in a dramatic fashion at the confluence. A tall, scenic waterfall cascaded over the steep limestone bank a few yards beyond a sharp bend in the abandoned roadway.

Yax'Kaqix considered the scenery impressive, even by his standards; he'd roamed the main continent and the outlying islands of Faltyr going on seven centuries. Wanderlust and a curiosity for the unknown afflicted him the same way that gambling, drinking, and carousing took hold of others with addictive personalities.

In the dimness of the waning day, Yax spotted an old stone bridge less than a league beyond the river fork. The high arch of the uncovered structure indicated that the designers intended for it to facilitate boat traffic along the waterway. Despite its age, the bridge looked to be in serviceable condition.

The aged structure served as additional evidence of a sizeable, lengthy occupation on this part of the island. He wondered when the group would make contact with someone from the keep; surely its troops patrolled the fiefdom and its shores. Would the survivors be perceived as the unfortunate victims of a shipwreck or trespassers with malicious intent? Either way, those encountering them would be correct.

Beyond the bridge, the road progressed along the gentlest part of the landform before disappearing into the dense foliage on the opposite bank. Yax'Kaqix could see Frolov Keep situated on the highest elevation in the area at the end of a prominent ridge spur.

He strolled past the others, ignoring the Cadogan brothers' ribald discussion about how they'd like to relieve Spensir of his sultry, willowy prize. Yax grinned as Glynn made an obscene remark about Spensir preferring his quartermaster to the tattooed woman.

Indeed, the pair seemed unusually close, but the elf viewed their relationship in a different light than the twins. He saw Spensir and Fergus as co-conspirators adhering to Captain Gneut's final orders.

Finders Keepers had been hired to perform an acquisition job for Gneut, but the gnome had passed before briefing them on the details. Apparently, Spensir felt the same as Breuxias and considered the contract between the adventuring company and the late captain null and void. As a result, he had cut the mercenaries out of the loop.

From past experience, Yax knew that keeping secrets in this kind of situation could get them all killed. Regardless of the dangers present on the island, internal dissension and hidden intrigues would eventually tear their group apart. Hopefully, they would find passage off this speck of rock and sand without further bloodshed. He, however, doubted it. The brewing storm concerned him far greater than any raging in the skies above the ragged band of survivors.

Yax took Breuxias to reconnoiter the area around the confluence; they investigated what they hoped to be a relatively safe, dry campsite suitable for their sizeable party. While the others went to check out the integrity of the bridge and search for suitable candidates for firewood, they decided to check out a sizeable cave opening partially obscured by the waterfall.

The pair of adventurers worked their way along an overgrown trail that wound down to the river's edge. Though the path became steep and slippery, Yax considered himself as sure-footed as any creature on the face of Faltyr. Breuxias maneuvered along behind him with caution while using his staff for support.

Following another rocky path along the sheer rock face, the pair of adventurers sidled to the opening beneath the falls. The cascade of water echoing around them sounded like an ominous roar issuing from the yawning mouth of the cave. Curious to a fault, the elf loved ominous. It drew him like a dwarf to a vein of gold.

Gesturing toward the rough arch with his staff, Breuxias asked, "Does that remind you of the goblin caves of Chi'kakal?"

Grimacing, Yax replied, "You bring that up every time we go near a hole in the ground. How many times am I going to have to apologize?"

"I wasn't talking about that bit." Breuxias rubbed the stub of his right pinkie. "But you do owe me a finger."

Holding his palm up in a gesture of peace, the elf commented, "I told you not to take that ring."

"You could've mentioned the damn curse before I put it on my finger."

Shrugging, Yax proceeded to the mouth of the cave without further comment. He knew that logic was of little use when it came to arguing with Breuxias. A stubborn streak ran through him as wide as the river.

Yax peered into the cave's stygian depths. He scanned the interior with all six of his senses as a cursory inspection.

"Opens up into an amorphous gallery after a few yards. I can make out another passage on the far end." Sniffing at the ground, he added, "Doesn't smell like it's inhabited. No tracks either."

"Only one way to know for sure," Breuxias replied. "Let's investigate."

Their brief examination of the cavern complex revealed not one but two roomy chambers. Of the passages radiating outward, all but one of those dead-ended after a few paces. A single route at the rear of the cave wound back to the main chamber behind the waterfall.

The sound of rushing water reverberated through the walls of the subterranean grotto. Drainage from the tributary above trickled through the porous limestone to form shallow pools in the dome pits scattered across the floor of both chambers. Although the water could be mistaken for potable, Yax, a veteran spelunker and explorer of Faltyr's Underworld, knew it to be full of calcium and other minerals. A thimbleful would lead to a night of intestinal tortures.

They detected no signs of current occupation but definitive evidence of previous humanoid inhabitation. Charcoal stains on the cavern's domed ceiling indicated that countless fires had burned within the confines of these chambers. Graffiti composed of pictograms, sigils, and initials from a half dozen alphabets defaced the lower half of a column formed eons ago by the union of stalagmite with stalactite.

Beyond the main gallery, a smaller grotto with a lower ceiling formed a rough horseshoe before rejoining the larger chamber through a portal in the far wall. Although not as spacious as the first room, Yax found this chamber to be much drier and a bit quieter.

"I think this will do fine," Yax said as they emerged from beneath the waterfall.

"Let's hope so," Breuxias replied. "If that thing can get to us in there, no place on this island may be safe."

***

Later that evening, the group of survivors huddled around a small fire in the roomiest chamber of the cavern. Kaladimus Dor sat staring at the chest, watching as the light from the flames danced across its scarred surface. Though scarcely a score of cycles old, he felt he'd aged far beyond his years since that burden had come into his life. He'd barely had time to mature to manhood before becoming worn as a pebble lost in a raging river. The Council had seen to that.

Pursuing this disastrous mission on behalf of Braigen and the Council of Three had started his transformation. Narrowly escaping the Temple of Ra'Tallah with the chest's odious contents and then losing his party in the Sands of Sorrow had escalated it, but the sinking of the *Nightsfall* shortly before completing his mission had assured it. Dor saw himself as an old man trapped in a boyish body.

Looking across the cavern, he wondered how Yax'Kaqix managed it; living for untold centuries and dealing with all of the pain, all of the regret. No lines, no crow's-feet, no wrinkles marred the elf's unblemished face. Was that the secret of elven longevity? No regrets?

Judging by the haunted look in Yax's inhuman eyes, Dor doubted it. The idea of finding himself reincarnated as one of the seemingly ageless Children of the Stars one day both appealed and frightened him.

What would he do with all that time? If it involved worrying as much as he did now, Dor considered it to be a curse that he wouldn't wish on anyone. His short miserable life seemed torturous enough; a life that stretched on for countless centuries would have to be a living hell.

Breuxias sat between Dor and Yax and fed the fire with wood collected earlier in the day by some of the others. The wet branches smoked before catching fire, due in large part to the flames projected from Yax'Kaqix's bare palms. Dor wondered what other powers the mysterious elf had at his command. As one of the infamous Wand Bearers of the Unen'ek, the mage knew that they had to be considerable.

Reaching into his belt pouch, he pulled out two large loaves of bread and a whole wheel of cheese. Breaking them into portions, he handed out the food without further explanation.

His feat of conjuration failed to do more than raise a few eyebrows. All but the most provincial of Faltyr's peoples had heard of the Magi of Moor'Dru. The young Protectorate Mage carried their seal, the Iron Circle, emblazoned on much of his gear.

Some of the group slumbered near the fire and were too exhausted to be lured by the bread and cheese. Stripped of most of his soaked rags, Gilly, the ship's carpenter, snored in a corner of the chamber. Curled up against Spensir, Vorta dozed in a similar state of undress. Dor averted his eyes from the tanned bosoms of the sleeping woman. If Spensir noticed his lingering gaze, there'd be hell to pay.

Dor's cheeks flushed with embarrassment. If outrageous fortune made him an old man before his time, then he vowed to be a dirty old man. For as much as his harrowing experiences had aged him internally, Dor's desire for the carnal pursuits of the flesh rose after each one.

Was this the real reason why so many men on Faltyr enjoyed the rush of adrenaline that came from pursuing a life of adventure? For the magician, gold and glory seemed insufficient reasons to risk life and limb, yet Dor considered golden-skinned beauties with glorious curves another matter entirely.

Turning his attention back to those with whom he had literally broken bread, he watched as the conscious survivors wolfed down the simple but filling meal of bread and cheese. Some of them made wordless gestures of thanks. After washing down their dry repast with river water, a few of them went so far as to remark on his benevolent gesture.

Cupping the food reverently, Rafasi first thanked his Goddess, Ishta'Kahl, and then his benefactor.

"Bless you, my friend. May the Goddess smile upon thee."

Typical, Dor carped. *Thank the gods and goddesses for the feats of men.* After all, he didn't beg, plead, and cajole the Aethyr, the unseen forces of the universe, to respond to his wishes; he ordered them to obey his command. Despite a few notable—even disastrous—exceptions, the Aethyr energies tended to obey.

The Book of Five Elements defined this as the nature of the distinction between priest and wizard, between supplicant and sorcerer. Before she brought about the Cataclysm, Artemis bridged these concepts in her *Book of Golden Moons.* Dor loathed asking anyone for anything, including power, so he didn't put much stock in her Aethyr theories.

"Agreed, Father," Sir Caayl seconded. "Thank you, Dor."

Dor smiled weakly. "It's no trouble at all. Glad to help."

"Thanks a lot, Dor," Rayne commented, tearing her gaze from the handsome knight at her side. "You've been quite helpful. How'd you come to be with us again?"

Dor blushed at the attractive half-elven woman's compliment. He grinned and averted his eyes, handing a piece of the loaf to Asta, the gnomish woman nestled beside Rayne.

"Thank you, dearie," Asta added in a tired, detached fashion.

Gneut's sister still appeared to be in shock from the loss of her brother. Try as he might, he could not meet the gnomish woman's gaze, though not wholly out of remorse. Sometimes his maleness amazed him.

After all, how could he ignore the half-elven beauty sitting beside Asta and the wet, diaphanous top clinging to Rayne's pert nipples? Dor believed himself to be a virtual encyclopedia on a number of subjects, though clearly not the study of women or human sexuality. So Dor did what he always did; he stared and admired her from afar.

Dor knew more about summoning elements from the Aethyr, solving complex polynomials, and creating alchemical remedies than he wagered he would ever know about the fairer sex. Or even sex for that matter, he thought. If he lived long enough to ever have it again.

Summoning an answer to Rayne's question, he said, "I required passage back to Myth. Captain Gneut told me that there'd be two stops before home. Didn't mean for this to be our final one."

Sitting across from him, Fergus studied the scorched lid of the chest. Noticing the sailor staring across at him, the magician looked around nervously. Dor realized it would be better to think before he spoke in the future, if he had a future. He repositioned the battered box in his lap, casually covering it by folding his arms over its lid.

"Nor did Gneut, love," Asta responded. "Accidents happen."

"Yes, accidents happen," Dor answered, truly sorry for her loss.

Chapter 7

The fire burned through the growing night. Half asleep, Rafasi watched Sir Caayl poke at the bed of embers with the smoldering end of a stick. The knight became agitated as he finished telling them why he'd broken an oath to his king and fled his home. Living in a similar state of self-imposed exile, Rafasi empathized with Caayl's tale.

"And that's why I left. King Orson is mad, blaming elves, fae-folk, and magicians for the woes of all. War came. The rivers ran red with blood. There's something wholly evil at work in Oparre and it's spreading."

Jabbing the fire with renewed vigor, Caayl added, "I've got to find the source and stop it. I figured the Council of Three would be of help."

Drawing his bisht tighter around him, Rafasi reflected on his own reasons for leaving home. Though similar to the knight's motivations, the priest admitted his intentions had not been as lofty. They involved a desire to avoid all things political and military. He had chosen the priesthood to be a man of peace. The only war he had any interest in fighting involved the fate of the souls of humankind. However, his countrymen and fellow clergymen had other ideas.

Rafasi's homeland of Panglov was a stretch of desert intermixed with lush oases that formed the hubs of trade and community for its nomadic tribesmen. After their sheikhs had entered into trade agreements with Oparre, each caravan returning from the rapidly expanding kingdom brought wilder tales of horror and bloodshed than the last. By all indications, the Blood War was spreading like wildfire, engulfing central Ny. How long before the winds of fate blew the fire east to the desert nation of Panglov?

Several prominent clergymen spoke out against the alliance, afraid their people would be tainted by associating with such an evil land. Although Rafasi agreed with their position in theory, he did not join them. Disavowing any political associations, he tried to remain neutral in the polarizing atmosphere sweeping through the church.

As a healer and holy man, he did not feel that it was his role to get involved in politics. What had once been a place of serenity and security now reminded him of an ancient Ireti proverb: the Lords of the Underworld reserved the hottest level of the Nine Hells for those who would remain neutral at a time of moral conflict.

Both factions pressured him and his few associates who opposed intervention by the church in political affairs to pick a side. Instead he cast aside a prominent position in the church hierarchy and chose the life of a poor pilgrim, a wandering cleric tied to no one church in particular. Unwilling to play a part in either a religious or political schism, he sailed away, leaving it all behind him.

Taking his few possessions, Rafasi ventured to the nearest port, secured passage, and stumbled upon this adventure. He did not believe an event such as booking passage on a ship ferrying a questing Knight of Ishta'Kahl to be a coincidence. In his eyes, the Goddess of the Moon had provided him a new opportunity to serve.

"You speak truth, sir knight. A dark cloud hangs over Oparre," Rafasi shivered as he glanced back at the entrance to their impromptu refuge. "Much like the one over this island. Unseen forces are at work both here and there. Your pious soul is drawn to these currents of malignant energy in the same manner that a sailor seeks the next horizon. It is the way for all Seekers and all True Believers."

"Dark clouds abound in this world, priest," Dor responded, disdain evident in the mage's voice. Clutching the metal chest on his lap to him, Dor continued, "One hangs over my master even now. If I don't get this container home to Myth, he'll die under it, just like…"

Dor trailed off rather than finishing his statement. The priest wondered what the magician had left unsaid, what weighed so heavily on the young man's conscience. He had taken too many confessions from men haunted by their past not to see it on Dor's face.

Rafasi watched as Fergus whispered into the ear of the slumbering first mate. Spensir opened his coal black eyes, locking them on the guilt-ridden magician. The priest's pulse pounded in his ears as Spensir reached for his sword. Rafasi's voice caught in his throat.

"I'm sorry to hear about your master, Dor," Rayne responded, gently squeezing his narrow shoulder. "We'll make it home. All of us. You'll see."

Yax's menacing laugh echoed in the confines of the cave. Its inhuman sound drew Rafasi's attention away from Spensir. He feared the wild Unen'ek war wizard more than the hotheaded first mate.

Sitting up from his position away from the firelight, Yax'Kaqix quipped, "All of us. That's a bit optimistic given the circumstances. In case you haven't noticed, we're being hunted. I'd be less worried about nebulous forces and foreign wars and more concerned with the here and now. Not sure about you lot, but I can take care of myself."

"I can attest to that." Breuxias laughed. "In over a decade of travels and travails with Yax here, I've never seen anyone best him. Except for that old beholder below Agranak."

Grinning at the gibe, Yax replied, "Tell me about it. Some mornings I still wake up feeling stoned."

Snorting loudly, Glynn Cadogan asked, "Did you?"

"Did I what?" Yax responded.

"Never mind, Glynn." Breuxias grinned. "You know he doesn't have a sense of humor. Traded it for martial prowess."

"Shut up. Elves do have a sense of humor," Yax countered.

"Yeah, just not you," Breuxias jested.

Spensir rose to his feet, upsetting the half clothed sleeping woman by his side. He slid his scimitar from its battered sheath. The sound of ringing steel interrupted the mercenaries' moment of levity. Spensir leveled the rust-tinged blade in the mage's direction.

Though Fergus backed his superior's sudden, violent play, Rafasi noted that the quartermaster drew no steel. A sword fight in the cramped confines of the cavern would cause unexpected casualties, and the priest did not desire to be one of them. Thankfully, at least one of Spensir's crew seemed to have the same reservations about close quarters combat against seasoned mercenaries.

Breuxias bellowed, "What in the Nine Hells is going on here?!"

"Stow that yap, mister," Spensir spat at the muscle-bound mercenary. "I've gotta point o' ship's business to conduct with this 'ere whelp."

Breuxias stared through Spensir as though the sun-addled seadog had lost his damn mind. As he cut his eyes over at the elf, Yax drew a clawed finger across his slender throat. Breuxias shook his head. Rafasi prayed cooler heads than Yax's would prevail.

The elf settled into a crouch, looking like a cobra ready to strike. Two fingers lightly tapped on the handle of the jade wand stuck into his belt. Yax eyed Spensir like a tiger eyeing its prey. Rafasi surveyed them both warily. He prayed to the Goddess for a peaceful ending to their showdown.

Gesturing toward Dor with his blade, Spensir roared, "How'd that scorch mark get on that chest there, boy?"

When he didn't get an answer, Spensir stepped toward the rattled young mage. Sir Caayl placed himself in a defensive position between Dor and the irrational sailor. Although he gripped the handle of his sword menacingly, Caayl stopped short of drawing down on Spensir.

Rafasi moved to back whatever play the knight made. If he had to choose a side, he would stick with the questing knight, one of the Moon Goddess's True Believers.

Shaking with rage now, Spensir erupted, "Stay outta this, do-gooder! I wanna know! We all wanna know! We have a right to know! Ship destroyed by lightning! More'n half our number dead and a devil huntin' us in the night! I'm gonna ask you one last time. Where'd that scorch mark come from?!"

Rafasi focused his attention on the container in Dor's pale hands. His eyes settled on the black mark scorched into the lid. Clearly, the chest had been exposed to extreme heat, even the lock itself appeared to be melted.

What in Ishta'Kahl's name happened to it? the priest wondered.

The cornered magician looked fearfully, guiltily at Spensir and the others. Dor's voice appeared to be caught in this throat. His mouth worked like a fish floundering on dry land.

Stammering, Dor managed to say, "It...it was an accident."

Roaring madly, Spensir charged forward. Sir Caayl drew his Order sword, moving directly between the sailor and the unarmed man.

Rafasi backed away from the fray as Caayl raised his sword to guard Dor from Spensir's impending blow.

As Fergus fumbled to unsheathe his blade, Breuxias clubbed the stocky quartermaster to the ground with a powerful overhand right. Rafasi had expected Fergus to put up more of a fight. By the look of surprise on the tall man's face, so had he.

Drawing his wand with practiced ease, Yax'Kaqix uttered a phrase in his native tongue. A bolt of golden energy lanced out from the wand and split the air like lightning. The missile hit Spensir in the chest, putting him on his backside. The wand's blast dissipated on contact but not before burning a hole through his tunic. It left Spensir scorched and blistered but alive. The elf had shown him mercy.

"That'll be enough of that. No one's killing anybody..." Rafasi boomed. Everyone paused, interrupting a skirmish that could have turned deadly in the confines of the cavern.

Turning toward Dor, Breuxias added, "...yet. Not before I get some answers. So you better start talking."

With his prayers answered, Rafasi breathed a sigh of relief. Sometimes it took a thousand small victories to win a war, especially the war for hearts and minds. Maybe Ishta'Kahl guided him here to prevent bloodshed amongst the survivors of the wreck of the *Nightsfall*.

The priest viewed the others as lost sheep being hunted by a wolf in the night. With tensions running high, someone could get hurt or even killed over a simple misunderstanding or miscommunication.

Fortunately Rafasi was a shepherd, albeit a reluctant one. He had fled from one conflict to end up stranded in the middle of another. The Goddess worked in mysterious ways indeed.

***

After accidentally sinking the *Nightsfall* and killing half of the people onboard, Dor figured that he owed the survivors something, if only an explanation. As he couldn't be completely honest with his victims, he figured that a half-truth would have to suffice.

He started his tale honestly enough. He told them that he had been heralded into this world by a tempest, one that had baptized him by lightning and left him an orphan all in one fell stroke.

Dor's mother went into labor on the night of the storm, her contractions increasing with its intensity. Flash floods stranded the local midwife across a sea of inundated fields and pastures. Unable to wait any longer, his father delivered the baby.

The birth was difficult, even painful, for both mother and child. Mercifully, most babes did not enter the world so aware, so capable of thought and feeling. Kaladimus Dor was not one of them. He remembered everything. He felt not only his pain but also his mother's.

He cried for her, even as they placed him in his crib by the window. He remembered her face twisted in agony and the blood. There was so much blood. Turning away, he squealed with fresh lungs, his infant eyes wide as lightning snaked by the chamber window.

As booming thunder rattled the windowpane, Dor called out to the elements. The wailing child begged them for one thing, to end his mother's pain, to ensure she never suffered again. And they did.

In a flash, the warring heavens answered his cries. A single bolt fell from the stormy sky, striking the infant's crib, setting the tapestries behind it aflame.

Strong, familiar hands plucked the screaming infant from his flaming crib. His father handed him to his uncle and then went back for his beloved wife, but a burning beam collapsed, trapping the lovers together in their bedchamber.

When the rescuers discovered their remains in the ruins, they realized the heat had fused the bodies together. Forever inseparable, Dor's parents had been buried together in a single grave marked by a heart-shaped arch. He never visited it, but he dreamed of it often.

Though lightning would never harm one such as Kaladimus Dor, the burns he'd suffered that night left wounds both physical and emotional in nature. After using his sleeves to mop the tears from his eyes, he pulled the hem of his robe up to his knees. He showed them the network of scars still visible on his lower extremities.

The lingering scars served as not only a testament to his burden, his curse, but to his raw magical power. As a babe, he had commanded elements that some wizards failed to manifest in their entire lifetime. And as a young man, he hesitated to tap into the Aethyr too deeply for fear of creating another Cataclysm. He was an engine of destruction.

"My very presence seems to make magic twist and bend around me. It just happens sometimes, but storms seem to trigger it with frightening regularity. It's like I'm a living lightning rod. It's always been that way. This affliction, curse, or whatever in the Nine it is, can make spell casting pretty risky. That's what happened on the *Nightsfall*. An accident. A terrible accident. I swear."

He could see sympathy, even empathy on the faces of some of the survivors huddled around the campfire, including Rayne, Caayl, and Rafasi. But others, hardened by the trials and tribulations of the world or blinded by hate, were unmoved by his tale.

Yax'Kaqix stared at him with intensity unrivalled by any save Spensir and maybe Fergus. However, Dor detected neither hatred nor malice in the elf's gaze whereas the two sailors exuded those emotions. Unlike them, Yax seemed to have the stoic detachment of an inquisitor or even a monk. Looking at the expensively adorned elven war-mage, Dor suppressed a laugh at the mental image of Yax as a simple ascetic.

"*Maelanfaidh*," Yax said, almost under his breath.

"Bless you," Rafasi called from across the campfire.

"I didn't sneeze," Yax clarified. "I said: *Maelanfaidh*."

"But that's a fairy tale," Rayne exclaimed.

"To some people so are we," Yax reminded her.

Sir Caayl inquired, "What does that even mean?"

To which Spensir interjected, "It means he's the cause of all our bloody sufferin'! And he's the reason we're stuck on this damn island!"

"Here, here!" Vorta seconded. "I say we feed him to the thing that's hunting us."

"Serve him right," Fergus said, spitting at Dor's feet.

So much for the sympathy vote, Dor thought.

"No one is killing or feeding anyone to anything on my watch! I'm sick of all this fighting! Got it?" Rafasi boomed. The priest's authoritative tone silenced the intersecting lines of debate.

"Agreed," Breuxias assented. Turning to Yax, he said, "So what's a *Maelanfaidh* anyway? Enlighten us, old friend. Your dramatic pauses grow as long as your ears."

If Yax knew something about his condition beyond what the Council of Three had told him, then Dor wanted to hear what else the elf had to say on the subject.

After waiting for everyone to grow quiet again, Yax said, "There's no direct translation for it in your tongue. It's an old word with Draconic origins, but we know people like this wizard.

"You see, there is a difference between using magic and being magic. Elves and fae-folk are magic. Typically humans merely wield it. Our new associate here blurs the line with some unintended, sometimes unfortunate side effects. But with time, discipline, and careful tutelage, Dor may yet master the forces inside him before they destroy him or anyone else."

The vagueness of the elf's explanation confirmed that Dor wasn't the only one telling half-truths here. Yax knew more than he was telling; Dor was sure of it. He had to find out what had been left unsaid, especially if it related to his curious affliction.

Chapter 8

In the end, the majority of the group voted to let the wizard live. Their decision incensed Spensir anew, but Vorta's quiet, sensual ministrations convinced him that discretion was the better part of valor. He didn't relish the idea of a showdown in the confines of the cave anyway. Easier opportunities to get rid of the mage and his allies would present themselves in the near future.

Spensir waited the better part of a decade for the opportunity to become first mate on the *Nightsfall*. Vorta's presence provided that opportunity after meeting her in a portside tavern while he was recruiting for Gneut's ship. Despite both being suspicious by nature, they clung to each other immediately, as if drawn by some inexplicable force. On the next tide, Vorta followed him out to sea to learn her new lover's trade. In return, she taught him to be bloody, bold, and resolute.

And now Ole Obadiah, the former first mate, slumbered in the deep, dark abyss of the Ireti Sea. Weak, simpering, and eager to please, Obie would have voted against stringing up the wild mage. He wouldn't have wanted to rock the boat or risk a confrontation with the do-gooders. The murdered mate's drowned face emerged from the swirling chaotic seas of Spensir's unconscious mind.

As he slept on the floor of the cavern, he dreamed of a raging river. He floated in a pilotless ferry perilously close to the edge of the falls. He fought his panic by relying on his training as a sailor. Spensir checked the thick hemp tether that formed his lifeline to the shore. Seeing the stout rope and secure knot set him at ease.

The boat glided across the river, seemingly under its own power. As it moved toward the center of the waterway, faces from Spensir's past swam up from its depths to greet the backstabbing bastard responsible for sending them to the watery depths of the Underworld.

The bloated, rotting carcasses of corsairs, sailors, merchantmen, and prostitutes reached up from the churning water. As Spensir flailed about in the boat, the corpses of his victims clawed at him, beckoning him to join them in the Underworld. He felt panic rise in his chest as Obadiah's bluish, bloated face rose from the watery depths of the river. Knife in hand, the phantom of the former first mate sawed at the rope tether. As the boat swayed on the frayed rope, Spensir lunged for Obadiah.

The tether snapped as his weight shifted in the boat. As the ferry rushed toward the horizon of the falls, he watched Obadiah sink back into the white water. Spensir could have sworn that the blue-lipped bastard was smiling.

A few frantic heartbeats later, he plunged over the falls. As he plummeted toward the churning water at bottom, he found he could not scream, or he couldn't hear himself yelling over the roaring sound of the waterfall.

Jarred into consciousness, Spensir awoke before he impacted the frothing waters at the base of the falls. Feeling hands grasping at him, he swung blindly and connected. Blinking away the dream, he saw Vorta sprawled on the floor of the dimly lit cavern, spattered in blood.

Spensir was as confused about the situation as he was concerned about her welfare. Her freshly swollen lip looked to be Vorta's only visible wound, but a copious amount of blood covered her face, blouse, and beyond.

Regaining full possession of his faculties, he listened for any signs of imminent danger while he scanned the cavern for evidence to corroborate her tale. He discovered the pool of blood near the opening of the cavern moments later.

One of the mercenary twins, Donal Cadogan, had been assigned to guard the entrance. Now he had disappeared from his post. What in the Nine Hells had Vorta been up to while Spensir slept?

Grabbing her by the shoulders, Spensir hissed, "What've you done, woman? Are you insane?"

Vorta seemed more hurt by his accusation than his haymaker. Tears streaked her blood-spattered face. What had scared her so badly?

"It...it killed him," she sputtered. "Not me."

"That thing?! Here? How?" Spensir whispered.

"Donal got too close to the waterfall. Then he was gone."

She clung to Spensir, burying her face in his broad chest. Her entire body shook as she cried hysterically. If she was acting, her performance warranted the royal stage of a king's theater.

"We have to go," she implored, "before it comes back. We're not safe here. If that demon doesn't kill us, those mercenaries in the next room sure as Hells will."

Would the mercenaries blame the beast or them? Spensir feared he or Fergus would be blamed for Donal Cadogan's death in the wake of his disappearance. No clear evidence of his fate existed.

For that matter, all that remained of the Cadogan twin was the blood and gore covering the floor, signs of a violent end. The heated disagreement the night before had almost ended in bloodshed. Now blood had been shed.

With an unexplained death in the mercenary company, he expected deadly reprisals. He wagered the men of Finders Keepers would beat his crew in a straight-up fight. Even if he could fight dirtier than the elf, he doubted he could fight meaner.

So what option did they have left but to run, far and fast? Beat them to the ship of legend and sail away, leaving them and this cursed island on the fading horizon. With the maps and enchanted items, Spensir had the advantage. All he had to do now was keep it.

As the sun rose toward midday, Spensir stood on the far side of the steep-banked river. He peered across the dilapidated stone-and-plank bridge. Flames covered the end adjoining the opposite bank. Thick white smoke mixed with ash spiraled up from the burning bridge. The sticky resin-like material coating the ancient planks popped and sizzled loudly enough to be heard over the rushing river.

The efforts of Spensir, Vorta, and Fergus spread the flames swiftly. Hacking with his leaf-bladed sword, Fergus chopped down stands of bamboo growing around a waist high stone stele and then cut them into impromptu cups. Although they noted their presence, neither he nor Fergus paid the least bit of attention to the arcane glyphs on the standing stone.

Gilly filled the bamboo cups with the flammable resin of a bulbous tree. The milky white fluid bled from a deep gash hacked into its trunk.

"This ought to slow 'em down," Spensir called back toward the carpenter. "Great idea, Gilly! No way in the Nine Hells am I takin' it in the arse over this deal."

"Aye, Captain," Gilly responded. *Captain*, Spensir thought. He had never considered it before, but he *was* their new captain. With a smug grin, Spensir turned back to the matter at hand.

Vorta carried the cups across the bridge where she flung them onto the burning planks with obvious glee. The flames leapt higher, dancing for a few moments before resuming an even burn. In the light cast by the fire, the grin on her face looked sinister to Spensir. He reflected that she might enjoy arson a bit too much.

Sometimes the wild woman worried Spensir. His mind returned to the night before and the sanguine events in the cavern. Fleeing while the others slept, he had tried to push away his doubts yet something kept nagging at him.

Had the Cadogan brother been killed by the winged devil as she'd claimed or had the mercenary died by her hands?

After all, Vorta was no innocent. It wouldn't have been the first person that his lover had killed nor would it likely be the last. In the end, Spensir had erred on the side of caution and slipped away with her, Gilly, and Fergus. He didn't want anyone questioning her about Donal's disappearance.

Vorta pulled Spensir out of his reverie and back to the present. He flinched at her touch. She looked hurt as if he'd struck her a physical blow rather than an emotional one. Spensir forced himself to smile, trying to reassure her.

"Ya startled me, woman! Don't sneak up on me like that."

She stood right in front of him, resin-filled cups in hand. Confusion and concern colored her countenance.

"Don't worry, baby," she purred. She gave him a quick kiss and then added, "We have two pieces of the prize and the maps. The ship of legend is all but in our grasp."

Grabbing her by the wrist, Spensir hissed, "Hush! You'll jinx us with that kind of talk."

"Baby, don't be silly. Sailors are supposed to be superstitious by nature but that's ridiculous."

An arrow stuck into a plank beside his foot. Spensir swore Vorta had to be an albatross and her bad luck contagious. He grabbed the troublesome woman, nearly snatching her off her feet, as he rushed back toward Gilly and Fergus. Held in his viselike grip, she fled close on his heels as arrows rained down around them.

"Run for yer lives, ya dogs!" Spensir called to the others.

An arrow zipped past Fergus's ear and shattered against the stone stele. Sword in hand, he sprinted ahead of Spensir toward the wooded ridgeline.

Gilly hesitated long enough to collect the last of the resin-filled cups. In doing so, he caught a metal-tipped shaft of wood in the back. Crying out, he dove into the undergrowth in a desperate move to escape another volley of arrows.

Dragging Vorta by the hand, Spensir plunged into the wood line. Regardless of his doubts about her veracity, he cared enough about Vorta to ensure her safety as they fled for their lives for the second time that day. Once the arrows had started flying, he no longer cared whether or not she had killed Donal. Circumstances beyond his control had dealt him this sorry hand. Not the type to fold under pressure, Spensir intended on playing to win until his dying breath.

Cresting the rise, his group observed the remains of a village bordering the dilapidated walls of Frolov Keep. His first glance told him that the settlement had been abandoned long ago. The deathly stillness hanging in the air confirmed his suspicions.

Following the compass bearing, Spensir led the others through the village and onto the grounds of the keep. As he did so, he imagined the eyes of a thousand specters upon them, spirits of the former residents unaccustomed to regular visitors from beyond the sea. He wasn't a superstitious man; he understood the haunted landscape of faraway Faltyr, a land where myth and legend walked hand in hand.

The ancient temple of Damarra loomed over the courtyard of the deserted keep. The building served as a testament to the skill of the engineers who had built the structure untold centuries ago. Whistling, Spensir appraised the imposing architecture of the cathedral.

The ravaged domed construction showed signs of deterioration and decay yet remained intact. Thick creepers and vines covered the walls, stretching toward the dome itself. Perched atop the main entryway, a large carved statue of a half-eagle, half-tiger creature perched, guarding the temple.

The statue's stony eyes stared down on those who dared enter. He tended to steer clear of temples, shrines, and any other sacred structure, but the pigskin map placed the Hallowed Vessel beneath this structure. Returning the stone guardian's empty stare, Spensir ventured into the temple, hoping like the Nine it wasn't a golem. The terrible constructs of the ancient ones terrified him far more than the restless spirits of the dead though he accepted both as a reality.

Inside the dim interior of the chapel, Spensir examined the tapestries that hung along the wall. The original images had depicted scenes from Damarra's most famous scriptures, myths about the Sun Goddess so common that even an old salt like Spensir knew them by heart. But the tapestries had been desecrated in the most profane ways imaginable. Spensir could tell that none of the damage was recent. A thick layer of dust covered everything inside the structure.

Shards from urns shattered long ago littered the area around the altar. A larger, darker tapestry now hung over the desecrated one that bore the Sun Goddess's holy symbol. The tapestry featured an outstretched skeletal hand. Its background faded from crimson to black, giving the bone-white appendage the appearance of having a bloody aura.

Sounds of destruction filled the defiled place of worship as Fergus and Vorta searched for the hidden entryway to the crypt below the temple. In the process, they desecrated the temple in fresh new ways.

Away from the ruckus of their searching and ransacking, Spensir examined Gilly's injury. Fresh blood oozed from the gaping puncture wound as he removed the broken projectile from the old carpenter's shoulder.

"Damnable Hells, I wouldn't have guessed you'd have had that much blood left in you."

"If I weren't tough to kill," Gilly replied, "I'd not have survived so many seasons with our late Cap'n."

Spensir cleaned the wound with water collected earlier at the river. After packing the hole with cloth from an old priest's vestment, he cinched it semi-tight with an altar sash.

Satisfied that the grizzled carpenter would not bleed to death, he said, "Keep an eye out for the others. They'll be here soon enough. With any luck though, we'll be long gone."

Gilly replied, "We'll be needin' luck, by gods, because I doubt Damarra'll be helpin' us."

"I reckon not." Spensir smiled as Fergus toppled a decorative pedestal, cracking the floor. Frankly, the first mate feared the threat of live steel and hired killers to the wrath of foreign gods.

***

Scouting the road to the bridge, Sir Caayl chanced upon some time to talk to Rafasi without Rayne around. While she and the other survivors in their group searched for Donal's body, the knight and Rafasi followed the road back to the bridge. They hoped to catch up to Glynn and stop him from confronting Spensir and his cohorts alone.

Confident in his ability to handle a few ruffians, he used scouting ahead as an excuse to speak with Rafasi in confidence. He sought to unburden himself to the Priest of Ishta'Kahl, the first one the knight-errant had encountered since leaving Oparre. For Caayl, confession washed away his nagging sense of guilt and growing inventory of regrets, at least for a little while.

During his flight from Castle Grymsburg, he had committed a multitude of sins. In fact, he would be committing another if he got as close to his childhood love as he intended.

Under the current laws of Oparre, coupling with elves was illegal, punishable by death. Regardless, the modern tenets of his Order forbade any interracial relationship, punishable by loss of station and excommunication. Much like his homeland, the Churches of the Trinitas (Kahl, Damarra, and Ishta'Kahl) had not changed for the better over the centuries. Hatefulness and bigotry had wormed their way into clergy and dogma alike, signs of troubling times for Faltyr.

In his heart, Caayl knew what was right; however, he still found it difficult to betray king, country, and his knightly oaths without guilt eating away at him. But before Caayl could unburden himself, Rafasi broke the silence between them.

"Smoke is generally regarded as a bad omen, right?"

Rafasi pointed toward the horizon. Lost in his thoughts, Caayl had missed the ashy plume rising from the direction of the bridge.

Sighing, he replied, "Think positive, Father. Could be a barbecue."

Stroking his beard sagaciously, Rafasi responded, "That's what I'm afraid of. Should we wait for the others before proceeding?"

"I'd prefer going boldly forward. But perhaps we should err on the side of caution. Survey the scene then report back."

"As I leave heavenly matters to the powers above, I shall leave military matters to the soldiery. Lead on, good sir."

A short time thereafter, they stood at the bend in the road, watching the bridge burn. The smoldering fire started by Spensir's group had grown into a full-blown conflagration.

Smoke filled the river valley obscuring their view beyond. Even at this distance, the acrid cloud hung so thick that it stung Caayl's eyes, causing them to water. Beside him, Rafasi covered his face using the front of his hooded robe. Though it gave the priest some relief, like Caayl, he too appeared to be weeping at the sight of the bridge's destruction.

A burst of sudden movement in the undergrowth alongside the road drew the knight's attention. Reaching for his sword, he noted that whatever lurked in the bushes was moving in their direction.

He raised his weapon to attack as something large burst forth from the smoke-laced foliage. Recognizing the figure to be Glynn Cadogan, his surprise and alarm dissipated as quickly as it had arisen. Caayl lowered the blade but did not sheath it. Either someone had been pursuing Glynn or, in his grief, the man had become unhinged.

Tears streamed from the mercenary's smoke-stung eyes despite an improvised mask of fabric covering his nose and mouth. The poor man looked exhausted and out of breath as he leaned on his small but stout bow for support. Caayl noted that a handful of arrows remained in the archer's quiver. The mercenary had been shooting at someone.

"Are you okay? Did you find them?" Rafasi inquired before Caayl had the chance to speak.

"Got there too late for the bridge," Glynn responded with some effort. Wheezing, he continued, "Wounded one of the bastards though. Wished I'd killed him!"

Regardless of Donal's fate, blood had been shed between the contentious groups of survivors. Caayl realized that there would be no peace, no compromise now; only open warfare until one of the groups managed to escape from the island or killed the other in the process.

"No killing--no matter how justified--is justified, my son," Rafasi cautioned Glynn.

To Caayl, Glynn looked as confused as he felt by Rafasi's logic.

"You know what I mean," Rafasi continued. "Let's get out of this smoke and wait for the others. I can't think much less proselytize."

As Damarra passed midday, Her light shined down upon their reassembled party on the steep bank of the river. In the heat of the day, Sir Caayl watched as fragments of flaming planks rained down into the river below. This close to the burning bridge, he felt as if he stood before one of the gates of the Nine Hells.

At this point, the bridge looked as if it would be better suited as a route to the Underworld rather than across the river. And, if his group couldn't get across this waterway, then Spensir and his allies might escape the sell swords' wrath. Perhaps there would be no war after all, he hoped.

"They burnt the damn bridge," Glynn shouted, drawing the knight's attention away from the river.

"We can see that," Breuxias responded.

"Sorry, not thinking too clearly."

Scowling, Breuxias clasped a meaty hand on the remaining Cadogan brother's shoulder then he said to Glynn, "We can see that too. We're all sorry about your brother but nothing you do today or any day is going to bring him back. It hurts. It's gonna hurt. But, if you don't start thinking clearly, you'll end up joining him."

"He's right," Caayl interjected. "Honor your brother and seek justice, not revenge."

Rising from his seat in the road, Dor cut between him and Rayne. Heading toward the bridge, the mage mumbled under his breath.

"What do you think you're doing?" Caayl inquired. Although he had defended the magician's life, after last night, the knight could no longer be sure if he'd made the right choice. Dor's confession had polarized the group and had possibly led to Donal's murder at the hands of Spensir's faction.

"I'm tired of sitting here so I'm helping," the mage replied.

Dor marched down to the edge of the bridge, pulling up the sleeves of his grubby robes. As the Protectorate Mage made a series of complicated gestures, he spoke in an arcane tongue. He punctuated the spell by clapping his hands together loudly.

Caayl watched in awe as a cone of forceful, freezing winds projected outward from the unkempt wizard's outstretched hands. The winds blew fast and cold, chilling the air around them and leaving icicles on the undergrowth.

Dor's spell extinguished the remaining flames and left the superstructure of the bridge coated in frost. The icy winds passed beyond the opposite bank of the river. The unnatural cold left irregular formations of icicles clinging to the arches of the bridge.

Caayl shivered despite the heat of the day. Exhaling a visible puff of air, he marveled at the frost coating his hands and whiskers.

"Impressive," he chattered, "but how does that help us cross a burnt bridge or ford a raging river?"

"It doesn't," Yax'Kaqix interjected, "but it does facilitate the process. Remember, patience is a virtue."

The knight watched as Yax withdrew a tiny leather pouch from underneath his scale-mail cuirass. Opening the bag, the elf poured a fuzzy round object onto his outstretched palm.

"Not that thing again," Breuxias lamented, rubbing the stump of his missing pinkie finger.

"You're lucky that I keep things like this around for sticky situations."

"Did you make a joke?" Breuxias inquired.

"Me?" the elf grinned, exposing his filed teeth. "Never."

As Yax uttered a phrase in an elven dialect unfamiliar to Caayl, the object in the elf's hand uncoiled, revealing itself to be a fat black spider. As Caayl watched in a mix of awe and horror, the spider crawled across the back of Yax's left hand and onto his ring finger.

With the bottom of its abdomen positioned toward the elf's pointed fingernail, the spider proceeded to latch on with its mandibles while securing its legs against Yax's flesh. As the animated creature settled into place, it took on the appearance of a shiny black ring.

No one uttered a word as the elf stepped up to the remains of the bridge and flung his arm outward. At the end of his extended arm, the ring spewed thick streams of spider silk. The sticky, seemingly endless webbing covered the area between the bridge's stone arches, anchoring themselves to every surface. With the flick of his wrist, the webs ceased. Yax wavered like a sapling in a strong breeze, visibly drained by his efforts.

To Caayl, the webbed structure looked like a trap rather than safe passage. Stepping onto the silk-covered bridge, Yax illustrated that if they moved slowly and carefully, the webs would support their weight. Caayl was amazed, if a bit repulsed, by the entire concept of a blood-sucking spider ring.

"Coming?" Yax prodded them, another grin touching his lips.

"Wow!" Dor exclaimed, following Yax onto the bridge. "Where do I get one of those?"

"Pray you never have to find out," the elf replied. "Some treasures cost more than they will ever be worth."

As he turned away from Dor, the expression on Yax'Kaqix's face darkened. Though no mind reader, Caayl figured the venerable elf had learned that lesson in a most painful way. Looking back at Rayne, the knight hoped that wouldn't be the case when it came to her.

Chapter 9

Kaladimus Dor followed Breuxias and Yax as they led the small band through the remains of the long abandoned village bordering the dilapidated northernmost wall of Frolov Keep.

Situated on a broad, flat ridge top that extended out into the sea, the village bordered the keep to the south and east by terraces leading down to steep rocky sea cliffs.

To the west, the river emptied into a wide bay. The land got progressively steeper and rockier until it transitioned to a sheer drop off. The keep complex lay beyond the village at the far end of the landform.

As Dor walked through the village, he could see inside the shops and homes that lined the unpaved road. Windows had been shattered long ago. Doors had either been bashed in or torn away from their hinges.

Breuxias moved ahead of the group, checking for signs of traps or an ambush. Behind him, Yax'Kaqix's keen eyes darted back and forth from building to building.

Dor followed them but at a discrete distance. In case something attacked, the master-of-disaster wanted to be sure to have enough room to cause some damage.

Various noises could be heard in the village, but as the group walked through, the noises would either stop entirely or suddenly change position. Dor shuddered as he imagined possible sources for the cacophonous cries. Each hypothetical scenario he envisioned grew grimmer and grislier than the last.

Breuxias paused on the road ahead. He took a long drink from his canteen as he waited for the rest of the group to catch up to him. Dor lingered a bit, so he remained near the back of the party.

Breuxias said, "It's not much farther. If we can maintain the pace we have now, we should be in the keep before nightfall."

"Agreed," Sir Caayl seconded.

Dor and the others nodded their silent assent.

Walking in silence, the group started their trek toward the keep once again. The path that they followed led out of the town and passed a large graveyard on the southeastern side.

The necropolis filled much of the flat area between the structures of the absent citizenry and the walls of their long dead lord. Shrines to the Father, the Mother, and the First Daughter—Kahl, Damarra, and Ishta'Kahl—dotted the landscape of the peasant cemetery.

Dor recognized a low stone pillar set apart from the burial plots. Approaching it, he brushed back a stand of tall oats for a better look at the glyphs and pictograms covering the stele.

After reading the warning, Dor stood lost in thought, oblivious to his surroundings. Fear threatened to overwhelm him. Dor grew weak in the knees, swaying in the wind like the tall grass in the cemetery.

"Someone you knew?" Rayne asked.

Dor jumped as if having a seizure, startled by the silent approach of the half-elven woman. The chest slipped from his grip, striking the stele with a metallic clank.

The sudden impact jarred it open, causing Dor's look of shock to turn to one of abject terror. The damn box was open again! Bending over, Dor snatched the container from the ground. Rayne shifted her body as if to look inside it. Dor snapped the lid shut.

Dor hoped for her sake that she had not glimpsed its sinister contents. His nightmares hadn't stopped since he first laid eyes on the item in the Sands of Sorrow even though his background fortified him for close encounters of the supernatural kind. To his knowledge, Rayne had no such training in defending herself against the dark arts.

"Thanks, um, been trying to get that open," he said.

That was a lie. Somehow that infernal thing inside always descried a way to get the lid open even with the lock melted. Though Dor blamed himself for sinking the *Nightsfall*, he knew his decision to open the chest had been influenced by another insidious intellect.

Honestly, having the chest sealed had been a blessing for Dor. In his mind, it protected the contents from convincing him to open the lid. The last time that had happened he'd foolishly tried storing his mission journal and writing materials inside and, as a result, he'd sunk the *Nightsfall* less than a league from landfall.

"All it takes is a professional's touch. You never answered me," Rayne awaited Dor's answer.

Holding the chest to him, Dor replied, "Uh, it's no tombstone."

Sir Caayl inquired from behind him, "What is it then?"

Dor jumped again, though not quite as high this time. "Stop sneaking up on me," Dor snapped as he turned toward the knight. "It's dangerous! For both of us."

Dor's ire dissipated swifter than his level of agitation. His outburst had gained him everyone's undivided attention, whether he desired it or not.

Dor wanted to be honest with his fellow survivors but he couldn't discuss certain types of privileged information with anyone other than a registered magus from his homeland. And the dire warning on the stele was one of them. Oaths existed for a reason, even if they proved inconvenient at times. So he told them what he could for now.

"It marks a boundary. Protectorate Magi employed by the High Council use them to mark a protective enclave. Or sometimes..." he trailed off, muttering the last bit, one of his more annoying traits.

"Or what, Dor?" Yax asked.

"A warning to trespassers," Dor stated.

"Trespassers," Breuxias parroted. He did not look pleased.

"Yeah. Before the Great Scourge started," Dor explained, "Protectorate Magi used magic to protect whole villages or castles, safeguarding them from supernatural or magical threats. That's what markers like this one usually depict. It could mean a free floating specter or a full blown infestation of nocturnal Underworld beasties."

Dor gestured to a line of steles disappearing in both directions into the tangled undergrowth between the village and Frolov Keep.

"These are supposed to mark a boundary. In this case, an exterior perimeter," Dor continued, "that we shouldn't cross."

"I'm not one to interfere in the affairs of wizards," Rafasi interjected, "but I agree, young mage. There is something terribly wrong here. A powerful evil is at work. A dreadful darkness casts long shadows over these lands."

"I feel it too," Sir Caayl volunteered. "The Father is right. The wind here blows cold and stagnant despite the sun and the sea. A cold that chills to the bone is in the air."

Yax nodded in agreement. His eyes focused on Dor as if peering into his very soul. The human withered under the elf's unrelenting gaze. He knew whatever the mage kept in that box was more malevolent than anything lurking in the keep. He sensed it despite the dampening effect the enchanted chest had on his extrasensory abilities.

Breuxias settled the debate when he said, "You're welcome to wait out here, wizard. As for me, I'm braving the unknown. There might even be someone alive inside who can get us off this damn island. If not, I'm killing Spensir, taking those maps, and sailing us to Moor'Dru on the back of his bloated corpse."

Eyes forward, Breuxias strode toward Frolov Keep. The others took the hint and left Dor standing alone at the edge of the cemetery.

"Who's the real fool," Dor muttered, "the one full of bravado running headlong into danger or the idiot who follows him?"

Sighing, he drifted toward the ruinous keep. At this distance, he saw that Frolov Keep was no longer the pristine mirage it had seemed to them from across the bay. He spotted several holes in the keep's massive stonewalls. In many places, entire sections needed repair. Curiously enough, the front gate itself was missing, most likely ripped or blasted from its hinges by mages from Moor'Dru.

Dor noted it looked less like a place of refuge and more like a place of deep foreboding. The complex of structures seemed as devoid of life as the village itself. To him, Frolov Keep might as well be renamed the Keep on Haunted Hill. After all, he could feel the vague presence of the restless dead even from this distance.

Dor passed through the gaping entrance to Frolov Keep. His watchful eyes scanned the expansive courtyard. After the warning on the markers in the cemetery, he understood that there could be grave consequences for all those who dared trespass. However, he knew their means of escape lay somewhere beneath the keep.

Long shadows cast by the setting sun obfuscated a great deal of the keep's bailey. As Dor walked through one such pocket of darkness, created by the rotten remains of the gatehouse, he heard murmuring in the wind. He couldn't make out the voice, but it was no hallucination. Phantasm perhaps, but the spectral sound had been no daydream or trick of light and shadow.

The rest of the party took no notice of it, but Rafasi and Yax looked uneasy about treading on these haunted grounds. Both proceeded as if they trod upon quicksand. Like Dor, they knew that the dead on Faltyr often roamed in the land of the living to avoid the Nine Hells.

Continuing across the courtyard, he found his view dominated not by the keep itself but a far older structure within its crumbling walls. Despite its obvious state of disrepair, the broken tower had impressed him from a distance. Up close, the abbreviated structure was a wonder to behold.

Fat at the base and tapered like the trunk of a great oak, the tower had been sheared off about two-thirds of the way up. Dor based his calculations for its probable natural terminus on the assumption that the structure had been engineered using conventional means. Engineering was another discipline at which the mage felt proficient. However, his education focused on siege warfare and other combat applications rather than civilian ones. He might not be able to design a city's sewer system, but he could defend it or even sabotage it.

Unfortunately, Dor's mastery of geology left something to be desired. The black stone composing the tower did not appear native to the island, but the exact nature of the material eluded him. Judging by its glassy appearance, he figured it was a byproduct of volcanism.

Pausing at the base of the black tower, Dor searched its exterior for an entrance. To his surprise, there seemed to be no visible way into the structure. Shifting his eyes subtly, Dor failed to discern a magically concealed portal either.

"No door," Dor mused aloud.

"Damn peculiar isn't it?" Yax'Kaqix commented, his eyes flashing red in the dimness.

"Wonder if the entrance was at the top of the tower?"

"Possible. If so, it dates the tower to the time before the Cataclysm. That's pretty old, even by elf standards."

"I doubt it," Dor scoffed, shuddering at the implications. "What's the likelihood of a dragon tower surviving this long?"

"Next to zero. Either way, the entrance is most likely underground. No telling how far down it goes into the island, possibly into the world below."

"The world below." Dor laughed. "Surely you jest. How would this tower connect to goblin tunnels and ghoul nests?"

"You forget one of the basic metaphysical tenets, wizard," Yax scolded. "As above, so below. Depending on whom you choose to believe, there is as much going on inside this world as there is on its surface. I've seen enough to believe. If you live long enough, you may too."

"Why a tower then? What would a dwarf, a goblin, or some other dweller in the dark want with a tower *above* ground?" Dor cautioned.

"It could have been a stellarium or a lighthouse."

"A stellarium?" Dor scoffed. "That doesn't make any sense. Why would denizens of the Underworld build an observatory?"

"Why else? To observe the machinations of the heavens and unravel the mysteries of time and space itself," the elf added. "Even the faceless masses of the Underworld contemplate the infinite and seek answers amongst the stars."

Yax's inhuman eyes bore into Dor's own. He could not hold the elf's unsettling gaze for long. Left pondering the possibilities, Dor wandered away from the broken tower toward the manor house.

***

The whelp had much to learn, Yax surmised as Dor retreated from their debate. The elf had learned much about Faltyr's expansive Underworld during countless decades of exploration and subterranean warfare. His time studying with the monks at the High Holy Temple of Kümatz on the sacred island of Ch'ab had enlightened him to many of its ancient mysteries as well.

One of the primary charges of the Unen'ek was to police the world below, culling the demons that lurked in the darkness beneath the feet of the Star Children. The Elves of the South Isles still fought the Eternal War, a millennia-old war of attrition against the denizens of the Underworld. However, few reliable allies remained after the Schism split the Unen'ek and created the Winaq'che, most notably Free Dwarves and Deep Gnomes.

Unable to rule above, lesser noble sons such as Yax'Kaqix considered the Eternal War below their sacred duty, one he'd fought off and on for most of his current incarnation. His adventures had earned him wealth, glory, and as much fame as infamy. However, they had also brought him loss, grief, and too many encounters with horrors that would literally turn one to stone. The Eternal War took its toll, even on the infamous Blue Macaw who, after six centuries of globetrotting internecine warfare, considered himself unbeatable.

Cursing to himself, he spat at the base of the shattered tower and stalked off toward the keep's manor. Regardless of its previous function, he considered the structure an ill omen. In his mind, it now served as a stovepipe to the Nine Hells, a chute allowing any creatures from the Underworld to come screaming to the surface.

Many who knew him for any length of time considered him paranoid. While fighting alongside him during the protracted goblin invasion of Asterion, Breuxias became one of them. *Ironic*, Yax thought, *since Breuxias himself had grown paranoid after losing his pinkie finger to the spider ring*. Technically, he had severed Breuxias's finger with Demon Queller; the alternative had been to allow the ring to drain the human dry and then pluck it from his lifeless body. Being much older and wiser, he understood that sometimes the lesser evil was the only alternative.

The keep's domed cathedral became visible as he rounded the base of the tower. The temple stood beyond an overgrown garden, its tangled flora dominated by medicinal herbs and wild roses. *A human church consecrated to Damarra*, Yax concluded. Better the Sun Goddess than one of the darker, destructive deities of Faltyr's human pantheon.

As he crossed the bailey, Demon Queller's blade burned into his hip through its wood and skin scabbard. In his experience, the sword's reaction was the polar opposite of a good sign. In fact, he referred to this type of situation as an OSM, an Oh Shit Moment. Dread replaced the sense of relief that had washed over him moments before.

Drawing Starkiller from his belt, Yax approached the three-story manor house. The crumbling building loomed over the far end of the bailey, intruding into the main walls that overlooked the precipitous drop into the sea below. The support columns on the porch had cracked at some point, allowing the balcony above to slump slightly.

A sole window loomed above the broken balcony. A corroded vent covered the circular portal. The rust stains running down the stone below the window gave it the appearance of an eye weeping blood. Yax noticed that it shared a curious commonality with every window visible from this side of the manor: the windows were either shuttered or barred with cold iron. To him, the building looked like a prison, not the former residence of a noble family.

A soft glow emanated from the structure, faint but visible to his inhuman eyes. Judging by the subtle luminescence, a variety of Aethyr-fueled protection spells warded the entire manor house. The obvious hotspot was the main entrance, a large set of cast bronze doors.

A massive beam of cold iron barred the tall double doors. The seams around the doors had been sealed with molten silver. Unlike the doors themselves, neither the iron bar nor the shining seams showed visible signs of age or corrosion.

An ornate insignia inset into the doors featured a coat of arms, presumably that of the Frolov family. Its circular design incorporated symbols of status, wealth, and power into a maritime theme. He recognized these as common heraldic devices used by noble clans associated with coastal fiefdoms. And the presence of the Iron Circle indicated that this bloodline hailed from the island of Moor'Dru.

One look at the Frolov family crest caused Dor to flinch. The dopey mage wandered off toward the temple garden muttering too low for even an elf to hear. Yax wondered what he had missed in the design that the whelp had observed. Should he be preoccupied with Dor or the doors? Breuxias made Yax's decision for him.

"Glynn, keep an eye on Dor," Breuxias ordered. "Yax and I'll handle the door situation."

Bow in hand, Glynn headed off toward the overgrown garden.

"Let us check out the chapel, brother," Rafasi encouraged Caayl.

"There?" the knight inquired, gesturing toward the looming church with obvious reluctance. "That's a Temple of Damarra."

Rafasi explained, "I'd like to make sure that holy ground has not been desecrated." The priest added, "Fear not, brother. Did you not see the look on the mage's face? This is our path. The Goddess has steered us to the accursed place for mysterious, wondrous reasons."

Sir Caayl relented. "Regardless, we should be careful poking around in there."

Yax shook his head and turned his attention back to the doors. The eternal warrior scoffed at the idea of being led into following someone purely out of some fanatical religious obligation. Unlike Spensir, he understood his ironic even hypocritical position. An elf of vast complexity and longevity, he had made peace with his inner hypocrite long ago.

Forcing himself to relax, Yax focused his inner flame through Starkiller. As a *Choj'Ajaw*, or Wand Bearer, for the Unen'ek, he used the device to amplify his natural magical abilities. He channeled energy from the Aethyr through his body and into the wand. The Golden Wedge situated at its tip began to glow. Once this metallic pyramidal array burned white hot, it emitted a tight beam of directed energy.

Using the wand like a dwarven cutting torch, Yax ran Starkiller along the door seam. The soft metal yielded to the intense heat produced by the wand's beam. Soon, silvery streams ran down the face of the massive bronze doors. Greedy by nature, he stifled the impulse to produce a cup and collect the molten metal flowing onto the porch.

"Hurry up," Breuxias hissed in his ear. "I don't like being out in the open after dark. I feel exposed."

"How many times do I have to tell you? Put on a shirt," he gibed at the bare-chested mercenary.

Breuxias snorted with laughter at a familiar jest. "Seriously, what's taking so long?"

"I'm preoccupied," Yax said, grimacing in pain. "Don't take this the wrong way, but I think my sword is trying to burn a hole in my ass."

"You gotta be kidding me! "Why didn't you say Demon Queller was warning you?"

Breuxias trusted the instincts of the magical blade to unerringly detect evil, malicious intent. Having worn Demon Queller on his hip for going on three centuries, Yax knew better. In the past, the sword had been wrong on occasion, sometimes with deadly consequences. He didn't want to raise a false alarm, not with poor Asta in the throes of shock and grief.

"You think I'm paranoid," Yax quipped, "but that daft blade does the same thing around barking dogs and crowing cocks."

"Now you're trying not to frighten the womenfolk," Breuxias exclaimed. "Cut faster!"

"Whatever," Yax chuckled, continuing his deliberate pace. In his experience, melting the bronze doors into the frame would ruin his most recent attempt at breaking-and-entering.

Behind him, he could hear Glynn yelling at someone, probably Dor. With his senses focused on the task at hand, he failed to grasp the content of the Cadogan brother's warning. Yax reckoned Dor had wandered too far astray. Now Glynn had to shepherd the dopey wizard back this way.

"Cut faster!" Breuxias repeated, tapping Yax on the shoulder for emphasis. "Seriously!"

"Now who's being paranoid?"

Louder, indistinct shouting from behind him interrupted his concentration. The beam from the wand fizzled to nothing as morbid curiosity gnawed at him. Turning on his haunches, he looked around in time to see the winged nightmare take flight.

As the giant beast soared from the top of the broken tower, Yax realized that he'd been right about the ominous structure. Apparently, the creature had used the tower as a nest or a channel to the surface, allowing it to take them by surprise.

From his position by the manor doors, he could see the animal in exquisite detail. As it glided toward them, he could not help but be impressed by nature's infinite variation. The monster measured over forty feet from tip to tail. At a cursory glance, it resembled a miniature dragon, but its hide appeared chitinous rather than scaly. With its scimitar-sized stinger, the flying beast could have been a species of rock wyvern. However, its long head tapered like a crocodile snout to a set of wicked tri-hinged mandibles.

Though Yax had never heard of an eyeless variant of wyverns, this particular creature had no discernible eyes or ears. Instead, three hornlike structures protruded from around its toothy maw. He wagered that these served a remote sensing function for the beast. Numerous species on Faltyr used echolocation, sonar, telepathy, or similar remote-sensing adaptations in place of conventional senses. Regardless of its specific taxonomy, he knew of few large, winged predators as aggressive as the blind wyvern diving toward Dor, Glynn, and the others in the courtyard. Its appetite seemed insatiable.

"Move," Breuxias barked, "I'll take it from here."

"Gladly," Yax replied, stepping to the edge of the porch.

Across the courtyard, Dor, Caayl, and Rafasi rushed back toward the manor house. Utilizing a weave to hasten his speed, Dor streaked across the bailey. He passed Glynn and overtook Caayl and Rafasi despite carrying the cumbersome chest.

The Cadogan brother stood his ground using his few remaining arrows to buy the others time to escape. Yax saw it as not only a strategic move but also a sacrificial one on the part of the grief-stricken twin. Unfortunately, Yax knew of no means magical or mundane to save the suicidal.

Glynn's arrows punched holes in the right wing of the wyvern, causing it to overshoot its intended prey. Screeching, the wounded yet quite aerobatic creature banked slowly, maneuvering for another pass.

Gripping the wand as a fencer would his foil, Yax waited for the wyvern to come into range. Though he had other spells in his arsenal, none of them would be able to target the creature without causing collateral damage. With the other survivors rushing toward the doors, Yax didn't want to risk incinerating them along with the eyeless beast.

Glancing back, Yax watched as Breuxias forced the doors. With the gem in his belt glowing in the twilight, Breuxias grabbed one end of the heavy beams barring their access to the manor. He heaved once, snatching the iron bar free of its moorings. It slid with the ease of a thrown bolt and landed with enough force to crack the porch.

"Rayne! Asta! Inside! We'll hold the door," Breuxias called.

Dor avoided colliding with Yax as he raced past him on the stairs. The panicked expression on the mage's face indicated that he had little to no control over his rate of acceleration. As Dor vanished into the unlit manor, Yax wagered the mage would stop one way or another. A loud crash echoed from inside the unlit manor. A groan followed a moment later, satisfying his curiosity about Dor's fate.

Turning back to the courtyard, Yax'Kaqix surveyed the chaotic scene before him. The wyvern finished its midair turn over the dome of the chapel. Caayl and Rafasi mounted the steps of the manor as the beast dove toward the lone archer in the courtyard.

Drawing a bead with his last arrow, Glynn let it fly. The steel tipped missile imbedded itself deep into the wyvern's chest but did not dissuade the beast. As it roared by the mercenary, its prehensile tail whipped around, slicing across him.

The razor-sharp stinger cut through Glynn's torso at an obscene angle. In a gruesome display, the mercenary's top half slid free from the rest of his body. Trailing the twin's bloody entrails, the savaged torso fell to the ground with a wet plop. Mouth agape, Yax watched as the dead man's lower body took its final spastic steps before slipping in a puddle of its own gore.

Brave but foolish, Yax thought bitterly. Forcing himself to focus, he fired one bolt of energy after another from Starkiller. The golden beams lanced out but dissipated before they reached the wyvern.

"Damn," he cursed. "Still too far away."

Breuxias clapped him on the shoulder and urged, "Inside, brother. This isn't over."

Yax retreated to the relative safety of the manor, but his eyes never left the enemy. The last thing he saw as Breuxias reached for the doors was the open maw of the wyvern as it swooped in for the kill.

Chapter 10

Breuxias barred the doors behind them. Stepping back, he stood protectively in front of the other survivors. His reflection faced him in the polished interior door panel. The brute looked fierce bathed in the menacing red light of the shining gem in his belt.

The creature smashed against the barricaded entrance yet the sturdy portal held. The beast roared and redoubled its efforts. The doors rang like a church bell as the monster crashed into them again, this time hard enough to crack the stone around the doorframe. The wooden beam barring the entrance bowed inward, splintering under the stress. A less energetic thump against the door and a half-hearted shriek signaled that either the creature's strength or its patience had reached its limits.

Breuxias bet on a short attention span rather than a shortage of raw power. An eerie silence engulfed them after the ravenous beast retreated from the barricaded doors. No one seemed to breathe for a long moment. He knew he didn't. Finally, he inhaled deeply, trying to stem the tide of adrenaline threatening to consume him.

He resisted the urge to rip the doors from their hinges and set upon the winged demon that had killed Glynn. As he exhaled, he let go of the rage and the anger. He knew that there would be a better time to even the score with the monster outside. Soon enough the hunter would become the hunted.

"This isn't over," Breuxias seethed. "Not by a damn sight."

He forced his rapid heartbeat to return to its normal rate with his controlled breathing. As his rage dissipated, so did the baleful light of the eye-shaped gem. Crisis averted.

Even those who knew him misunderstood the purpose of his magical belt. Though he wore the device every day, he had not known its true purpose for many years. For a good deal of his life, he'd labored under the delusion that the belt enhanced his strength and endurance so that he could survive in the harsh environment of the Broken Lands.

Tosk'Kiante, the ogre shaman who'd raised him as an adopted son, had bestowed the Belt of Titan Strength upon him as a child. After Breuxias's capture by a rival tribe, he had realized that no one could remove the belt without his permission.

As a mischievous human child with the power to rival any ogre, he had caused his captors no end of trouble. The beleaguered tribe had sold him into the service of a wealthy Baax merchant family so they could have some measure of peace and quiet.

Unable to remember his childhood before Tosk'Kiante's canyon pueblo, Breuxias had learned these details while recuperating from a harrowing quest in the home of the infamous Metron Illbringer. The odious sage had tasked him with the quest in exchange for translating a letter penned by his birth father.

Returning to the Broken Lands as a young man, he had located the piece of fire-damaged correspondence amongst a cache of items within the ruins of Tosk'Kiante's abandoned pueblo. In addition to his father's letter, he had found the protective bracers that shielded him from most forms of magical attack.

Unfortunately, the damage from the fire had erased the identity of Breuxias's birth father from the document. However, the smudged heraldic device present on the parchment had enabled him to trace his family's lineage to the island nation of Moor'Dru.

As a result, their extended layover in the port of Myth provided his motivation for volunteering for this assignment. After finishing their job for Gneut, he planned to conduct research on his origins. The family crest gave him a place to start.

Yax agreed to accompany him on this assignment because of how much finding his father meant to Breuxias. Now, his friend was in danger and the Cadogan twins were dead, all because of his obsession with a father that didn't want to be hunted down.

No, Breuxias shouted at his nagging subconscious. *I'm not taking the blame for this bloodbath*, he told himself. *This is that damned gnome's fault. If Gneut had lived, I'd kill him myself*, he brooded, fresh rage welling up inside him.

Deciding to channel his anger into productive action, he addressed the other survivors. "We should stay close. No splitting up." Pointing an accusatory finger at Dor, he added, "Especially you. Pull another stunt like that and I'm putting you on a leash."

Bathed in the light produced by the spell glowing in his trembling palm, Dor looked more pathetic than apologetic. Without a doubt, the young magician possessed incredible power but he lacked confidence, discipline, and self-control. *All of the traits desired in a wizard*, Breuxias lamented. If Dor qualified as a Protectorate Mage in Moor'Dru, he was the most inept, bumbling one of the lot, or else he had been playing them all for fools.

Unwilling to trust anyone who'd lied to him already, Breuxias bet on the latter. He suspected that Dor had more information about Frolov Keep than he had told the others; was the mage unwilling or unable to share the details? Either way, he tired of Dor's mistakes having fatal consequences.

The mage needed to start pulling his weight and maybe he'd learn something about personal responsibility in the process. Breuxias decided to force Dor into using his privileged information to keep them alive. He decided to employ the same tactic against the secretive mage that he used with backstabbers, pickpockets, and suspected traitors.

"Since you read that marker in the village and recognized the seal of the doors outside, why don't you take point?"

"Me?" Dor asked Breuxias.

"Yeah, you got the magic hand there so lead on."

"I'll do it," Sir Caayl interjected. "Could be dangerous."

"No, Dor's gonna do it." Breuxias prodded, "Aren't you?"

Unable to bear Breuxias's stony gaze, Dor cast his eyes down at the mage-light radiating from his open palm. Relenting, he answered with a slight nod. Long accustomed to disciplining his own errant children, Breuxias figured shame would be a powerful tool for dealing with the chaotic behavior of the calamitous young wizard.

***

Perhaps Breuxias had a right to be angry with me, Dor pondered as he wandered down the entrance hallway of Frolov Keep. What had he done other than bring death and destruction to everyone aboard the *Nightsfall*? Even now his oaths of allegiance to the Council of Three prevented him from being open with them about the situation on this godsforsaken island. Dor knew that his inability to be forthcoming about the implications of the markers outside of Frolov Keep could lead to additional deaths before this night was over.

As he looked around, the signs of danger lurked all about him. Thick cobwebs filled the hallway and the adjoining rooms but he had yet to see a single spider. In the jungle beyond the keep, spider webs stretched between every gap in the foliage. In addition, Dor noted neither rat droppings nor any other visible signs of vermin. Even his magically augmented senses failed to perceive a single, solitary sign of life in the entire manor, save for their ragtag band of survivors.

Only able to provide them with vague warnings about Frolov Keep, he hoped that it would be enough. Seasoned campaigners Yax'Kaqix and Breuxias stayed vigilant despite their surroundings. Rafasi discussed his feelings about the unholy emanations coming from this place with Sir Caayl. *What about dear, sweet Rayne and poor, grieving Asta*, Dor wondered.

Though Rayne stayed close to Sir Caayl, Asta became her primary concern for the moment. Badly rattled by recent events, the teary-eyed gnomish woman looked exhausted and semi-catatonic. No longer able to bear the sorrowful sight of her guiding Asta's listless form along the corridor, Dor turned toward the gallery at the end of the hall.

The main hallway ended facing a broad hearth situated between two winding staircases leading up to the next floor. A large dusty painting hung above the fireplace's thick ironwood mantelpiece. Under the layers of dust and grime, Dor could see the rendition of a magnificent ship emerging from the mouth of a river onto stormy seas.

The vessel had three masts but no flag flew from any of them. Nor did the ship feature its name inscribed alongside its sleek hull. The hull closely resembled the anthropomorphic longboats used by ancient Gre raiders or similarly styled ones still in use by the fierce barbarian tribes of the Broken Lands.

However, its sails resembled those of the Chi'Zhan junks that'd made the four-thousand-league voyage from the Empire of Chi'kakal to Myth. The amidship's deck cabin was also consistent with Chi'Zhan maritime designs. He remembered spending countless afternoons during trade season waiting for one of the junks to sail into the busy harbor.

Examining the wide wood frame, he spotted a tarnished gold nameplate affixed to it yet the engraving looked nonsensical. Not magical but mundane, the script defied decryption upon cursory inspection. After setting the chest on the mantel, he fished the mission journal out of his pouch. After the mishap on the *Nightsfall*, he would never store it in that damnable box again.

After opening the volume to a fresh page, Dor ran his glowing hand along the nameplate. As he did so, a perfect copy of the unknown script appeared on the page. Satisfied with the results, he returned the book to his seemingly bottomless bag. As he did so, he took his eyes off of the mantelpiece.

The gallery became cold as ice. Exhaling, he noticed that his breath was visible, almost tangible. Gooseflesh stood out on his pale skin, causing him to shiver from the base of his spine to the top of his shaggy head.

Looking up from his pouch, Dor jerked backward as a shadowy figure crossed his field of vision. In the time that it took him to blink, the shadow had flitted to the top of the stairs. A panicked heartbeat later, the retreating phantom had disappeared into the stygian interior of the upper floor.

Behind him, Yax drew his wand, its red-hot tip adding another source of illumination to the keep's forbidding interior. Weapons at the ready, Breuxias and Sir Caayl stood on either side of the elf.

"What in the Nine Hells was that?!" Dor shouted.

"Whatever it was, it's gone now," Yax replied, lowering his wand. "Relax. Either we'll be fine or we won't."

"That's reassuring," Dor answered, hoping sarcasm worked to mask the fear in his voice. Bravado in the face of certain death; yet another lesson learned during his brief associations with Finders Keepers. *Not likely to be the last lesson either*, Dor reflected.

Turning back to retrieve the chest, he discovered a leather-bound folio lying beside it.

"And where in the Nine did you come from?" he inquired, hoping like Hells he didn't get an answer from the phantom tome.

Dor lifted the book from the mantelpiece. He sighed, relieved that it didn't strike him dead or steal his soul like another tome had tried with him on more than one occasion. According to the stelae outside, similar fates had befallen the previous residents of Frolov Keep. However, the mechanism of their demise eluded him.

He lingered so long with his find that Yax passed him by, ascending the staircase to the second floor. Breuxias glowered at the mage as he followed Yax up the stairs. Dor allowed the mercenaries to lead the way.

Who was he to corner the market on imminent danger and unseen peril? After all, as adventurers, Breuxias and Yax thrived in tense, threatening situations. In his opinion, a combination of fate and bad luck landed him in these types of scenarios. If pressed, he managed to sort things out, though rarely without collateral damage.

Dor stashed the folio in his pouch and then hurried after the rest of the party. He didn't have time to read the book's contents now, but his instincts led him to believe that the unseen hand of fate had saddled him with another burden. Why did fate always have to feel like the swift, stiff hand of a jilted lover across his stubbly cheeks?

The majority of the second floor of the keep consisted of a series of apartments. These elaborate bedchambers contained a suite of rooms with a single door leading out into the hallway. One doorway in particular drew the attention of Yax and Breuxias.

Dor came to a stop behind the others in the corridor. From his perspective, the door looked as if someone had mistaken it for a tree in the forest, someone with a sharp ax and a murderous hatred of trees. At least he hoped it was an ax. He shuddered at the implication of any creature that could do that much damage with their bare hands. He wondered if Breuxias could perform such a feat, another damn good reason for not butting heads with the grizzled sellsword.

As the mercenaries led the group toward a set of doors at the end of the hall, Dor paused before the open portal of the bedchamber. Trampled toys littered the floor. Their presence filled him with dread. *A child's bedroom*, he thought. *Nothing creepy about that in a haunted house.*

He spotted a small figure seated upon the bed and froze in his tracks. The shadowy form faced away from him, its attention fixated on a ship's trunk situated beneath a shuttered window. Though he could not positively identify it through the rotten fabric of the canopy, he hoped by all the gods and goddesses that it was a doll.

Anything but the body of a child, he despaired, fear flooding him anew. Raising his glowing hand, the mage-light cast a pale pall over the end of the long room. Its luminescence revealed alabaster skin, curly blonde locks, and a dress long out of fashion in Moor'Dru.

Sharp, pointed claws dug into his skin through the fabric of his robe as something grabbed him by the shoulder. Dor screamed like a girl and tore away from his unseen assailant.

"Oh gods! She's got me! She's got—"

The mage flayed about using the chest as an improvised weapon.

"Hey! Calm down, it's me," Yax chuckled.

Dor's panic receded once he realized his phantom menace was the elf. Several moments passed before he regained enough composure to speak. *Some Protectorate Mage I make*, he lamented to himself.

"What in Hells' names are you trying to do?" Dor asked. "Find out if I'd bring the roof down on us or if I'd just pee my robes?"

"I'd prefer the latter to the former."

"Same here. But we may not get a choice if you do that again."

"It'd be preferable to letting you walk into that room."

"That room?" Dor asked. "Why that room?"

"Spooky house sealed up by wizards. Spirits roaming the halls. Creepy doll on a bed. Bad combination if you ask me," Yax responded.

"You're telling me. I thought it was a ghost, ghoul, or maybe something worse."

"If this week keeps its current trend, it'll be worse," the elf said. "So don't go inviting any unwarranted danger. Asta's barely hanging in there now, and everyone else's ass is dragging. Follow me and we'll get some rest. There's a library at the end of the hall."

"Sounds good to me," Dor said. And it did. The muscles in his thin arms burned past the point of aching from carrying the chest so far and for so long.

As he turned to follow Yax toward the library, he felt someone watching them. If the elf noticed, he didn't communicate it to Dor. Hazarding one last look back at the room with the ruined door, the mage spied the doll seated on the bed. Only this time, its glassy eyes fixed on him.

Rushing past the elf, Dor burst into the anteroom of the two-story vaulted chamber that had served as Lord Frolov's library. The stacks of dusty, mildewed tomes lining the walls of the room would have made any sage salivate. His eyes widened with the realization that Lord Frolov had been one of the first mage-lords of Moor'Dru. The Iron Circle built into the tile floor confirmed it.

Though now a strict mageocracy, meaning that the ruling caste consisted solely of magic-users, the island nation's past included several different forms of aristocratic arrangements before settling into its current governmental model some three centuries ago.

Dor knew from the warning inscribed on the stele in the village that magi of Moor'Dru dispatched to this island had besieged the keep. For that to happen, the Lord had either lost control of his fiefdom or betrayed his noble contract. Either way, the former master of this island had been deposed violently. However, had Lord Frolov been deposed before the magi had arrived or had they performed a political coup as part of their assignment? Neither crushing a peasant uprising nor launching a coup d'état would not be out of the scope of their duties as Protectorate Magi.

The question remained: had Lord Frolov been a victim of whatever fate befell the keep and its inhabitants, or a willing participant in the nefarious events perpetrated here centuries ago? If the Lord and his confederates proved to be the true villains, Dor reasoned that this might serve as their jail instead of their tomb. Something evil had been imprisoned within the walls of Frolov Keep.

His mind raced, generating more questions than answers. Who or what warranted such extensive magical safeguards? And why would the Protectorate Magi sent here confine these forces of darkness instead of eradicating them? Could protecting the Hallowed Vessel have warranted preserving a lesser evil? If so, did that make the ship of legend the greater evil? Or did the greater evil refer to anyone who would trespass on these unholy grounds to seek the prize?

"Got something over here," Yax called, pulling Dor's attention to a hidden recess between two bookcases. "Rayne, can you take a look at this?"

Rayne and Breuxias joined Yax near the concealed cubby.

"It's a lockbox," Breuxias exclaimed. "Time to get paid!"

"Can you open it safely?" Yax asked Rayne.

"Is it trapped?"

"Definitely," the elf responded. "And the few ways I know to open it might damage the contents."

"I'll see what I can do," Rayne replied, kneeling down to examine the chest secreted within the cubbyhole.

Despite his natural curiosity, Dor wandered away from the trio huddled over the strongbox. In his mind, his objectives remained loftier than looting the keep. Though he loathed the idea of opening his mind to the potential horrors contained within its pages, Dor hoped that the folio from the mantelpiece would shed some light on the dark fate of Frolov Keep.

Chapter 11

Dor sat at one of the tables in the Lord's library with the found folio splayed open before him. Smoke from the smoldering incense hung heavy around the young magician. Lowering his head, he closed his eyes to shut out the distractions created by the others around him.

Chanting in the old tongue of Moor'Dru, he performed the spell required to read the impressions left behind by the journal's owner. The weave enabled him to look between the lines to read the writer's state of mind during each journal entry. He considered psychometry to be an excellent tool in any sort of investigation, but he hated the mental and emotional toll that came from reliving the personal experiences of others.

Finishing the incantation, Dor opened his eyes. As he passed his hand over the journal, his eyes changed from their normal blue hue to a swirling, stormy gray. The vista that materialized before his eyes proved painfully familiar. It was Myth. It was home.

Lady Natalya Frolov appreciated the simple joys of fresh sea air and the gentle breeze on her face, especially after weeks of stale air while quartered in the lower decks. Her tired eyes looked out over the rails of a ship sailing into the port of Myth.

Two young girls, obviously identical twins, flanked the dowdy noblewoman. Love and joy welled up inside Lady Natalya as she saw the curious and excited looks on her daughters' faces. Golden haired Sanya and Natasha wore their best finery for their father, not having seen him in several Lunares.

The Lady Natalya wondered at what point she'd lost her enthusiasm for seeing her husband. Probably around the same time she'd lost respect for him and their union.

"We have arrived at our first destination, children. This is the port of Myth. The old capital of Moor'Dru sits in the shadow of the Tyrus Mountains. Don't get too attached though. Before you know it, we'll set sail for our new home on the far side of the main island."

The twins looked up at their mother and then back across the large bay toward the historic city. Almost nine hundred years ago, the seat of the government had been moved to the larger city of Lore, deep inland on the island. However, ancient Myth remained a major port and a wondrous sight to behold, sprawling far and wide along the coast. Its marble structures towered over the myriad tiny ships docked along the shoreline. Mount Belgulla, the tallest peak of the Tyrus Mountains, dominated the horizon beyond the walls of the city.

Behind her, a chilling voice called, one that caused gooseflesh to race down her slender arms. "We'll put into port for a short time. The other vessels will meet us here in a few days and then we will be on our way to the island."

Turning, her eyes met those of her husband's closest advisor and friend, Father Harbin. She considered Harbin to be a self-proclaimed holy man, the ringleader of a dangerous cult. She considered her husband's association with this man as his reason for accepting the appointment to the remote island fiefdom.

Dor noted the symbol hanging around Harbin's neck, a sinister icon representing Darconius, God of the Underworld and Awakener of the Dead. It was unusual for a priest from Moor'Dru to wear such a symbol, especially in modern times. Most of his followers had been destroyed in the century-long Cleansing War, one of the bloodiest wars in the history of the Great Isle and a dark time for all of Faltyr.

Dor felt her gnawing fear of the priest and her concerns about his future role in her husband's affairs and intrigues. Turning the page, he peered through the mind's eye of Lady Frolov once again.

Lady Natalya stared at the fine clothes and intricately carved figurines displayed on countless tables at the largest bazaar she had ever seen. A fine white dress caught her eye and she had to possess it. Compared to it, her homespun garment appeared downright dowdy. Her own mother would be ashamed to see her dishonor her noble lineage by dressing in such modest, inexpensive fashions.

A rough, deep voice spoke from her side. "I must get back to the ship and take care of some matters. Don't be frivolous. Where we are going, there will be no occasion to wear such indulgent foolishness."

Her eyes fell upon the speaker's broad, bearded face. Unable to bear her husband's stern, scornful gaze any longer, she turned her attention back to her children. Natalya fancied that she could still feel his cold eyes boring into her.

Continuing to scan the entries, Dor skipped ahead in the journal to a scene similar to the first vision he had witnessed.

Back on the crowded transport, Lady Natalya headed for her final destination. She found the exotic flora of the island intriguing but the location too isolated and sparsely populated for her cosmopolitan tastes. The sole sign of civilization was perched high above the sea at the top of a sheer cliff face. From the bow of the ship, she beheld a pristine version of Frolov Keep.

She stared up at the imposing walls of the keep. From this distance, the dressed blocks of stone so closely resembled the local stone that the walls seemed to extend upward from the cliff itself. Only the presence of the sundered tower broke the illusion that the hilltop fortification could have been a natural phenomenon.

Their transport ship bore them across the bay toward the cliff. Alarm turned to panic inside her, but her husband, Lord Cranthus Frolov, settled a heavy hand on her shoulder. His grip held a painful reminder instead of needed reassurance, a reminder that he was in complete control of their lives, their destinies.

He whispered a single word to her, "Watch."

But she could not. The illusory wall was too real for her conscious mind to bear. She fainted.

Lady Natalya regained consciousness upon the deck of the ship, staring up at roughhewn rock. With the assistance of the oarsmen, the transport maneuvered through a watery tunnel toward a wooden dock. It took some time for her to ascertain their location, a secret cove far below Frolov Keep.

Braziers full of burning oil lined the walls of the narrow channel leading to the pier. The oil lamps illuminating the landing and its adjacent structures broadcast the vastness of the cavern complex. The entire area bustled with life as people milled about performing a variety of tasks. Many of the laborers involved offloading passengers and cargo from another transport.

A third vessel floated in the inky waters of the cove, cloaked in shadow. This curious ship appeared to be missing its figurehead.

Dor could not see the other watercraft from the Lady Frolov's perspective, yet in his gut, he knew this to be the ship of legend: the Hallowed Vessel. Probing further into the impressions left behind with this particular entry, he confirmed his suspicions. In her opinion, her husband considered the ship to be a greater treasure than his entire fortune, more valuable than his wife or children.

After their ship docked beside a smaller transport, Lady Natalya herded the twins onto the dock. She kept the girls close to keep them out of mischief. No telling what lurked in those shadows, she fretted, casting her eyes about the gloomy, crowded subterranean cove.

Her eyes settled on a pale young woman walking down the gangplank of the other transport. The raven-haired beauty looked statuesque, like a goddess cast in marble, but lithe and ageless as if the blood of elves flowed in her veins.

"Sierris will be helping with the children," her husband explained, his tone that of a politician. Lady Natalya knew it well, though he rarely used it with her. "I wanted you to be able to pursue your painting and gardening undisturbed."

She didn't consider herself to be a jealous woman, but something about this attractive au pair gnawed at her. Was it the way Cranthus watched Sierris with his wolfish eyes? She recognized that lusty look, even if her husband had not cast it upon her for longer than she cared to recall. So much for a fresh start for their marriage, for their family, she lamented.

Dor learned that he shared the concerns of the Lady Frolov. The longer the spell continued the greater the level of empathy and the greater the toll on the caster. As Natalya's thoughts became paranoid and then distraught, so did his own.

Flying through the journal entries now, Dor skimmed the surface impressions of each to get the her story without experiencing every tedious, agonizing detail. He stopped when he came to one set several months later. The strong psychic impression left upon it drew his complete attention.

One afternoon, Lady Natalya sat in her sun-drenched studio high above the sea trying to exorcise her darker thoughts. Like many artists, she took her fears and frustrations out on the canvas. Even her current piece, a picture of her husband's prized ship, featured a threatening storm and rough seas.

Sanya and Natasha came to her in tears. The twins told her about climbing to the forbidden upper level of the manor during a game of hide-n-go-seek. There they had entered a curious circular chamber filled with bottles, jars, and other strange ritualistic paraphernalia. The twins described arcane symbols and pictograms covering the room's floor, walls, and ceiling.

The girls called it the Witch's Lab, "Witch" being Natalya's nickname for the twins' nanny. The girls told her that Sierris had discovered them there and flew into a rage. After dragging them from the room, the nanny warned the girls that curiosity could kill a kitten as well as a cat.

Lady Natalya comforted her children and cautioned them to go to their room and bar the door should trouble arise. She saw something insidious in Sierris's motives and knew that no good would come of having the interloper in her household. If her husband would not see reason, she would appeal to another authority, a higher authority.

Strong impressions left behind by Lady Frolov highlighted her growing fear of Sierris, a fear that grew faster than the twins. Natalya wrote about a letter sent to her mother asking for advice. In a tragic turn of events, her correspondence returned to her unread along with news of her mother's recent passing. Dor empathized with the Lady's unfortunate luck. Without bad luck, he wouldn't have any luck at all.

The loss of Natalya's mother served to spur her creativity. Once again in her studio, she sat before a family portrait in progress. Despite her reservations, she asked Sierris to be her model during sittings for the portrait. Like her husband, the Lady Frolov used the wicked woman for her body.

When she'd finished with Sierris, Natalya painted in her own face with the aid of a mirror. She had never felt as isolated as when she saw her own aging reflection within the mirror. Her fears and frustrations about her waning beauty had influenced her expression in the Frolov family portrait. Her pain showed through her art.

The sadness and sense of hopelessness emanating from the pages of her journal threatened to become too much for Dor to endure. Cheeks wet with tears, he turned the page and discovered fresh pain, fresh misery.

Coming across another passage with a strong impression, Dor absorbed every detail, stitching it into his memory. She wrote about how Sierris and Cranthus would spend countless hours in his private chambers late at night. Natalya feared being replaced by a younger woman. Her fears turned out to be half right. At the time, she did not know that Sierris was older, far older.

Lady Natalya opened the heavy door to one of the manor's many bedchambers. Lord Frolov and Sierris lay naked on a large ornate bed. Their bodies entangled, writhing in a passionate embrace. The lovers fornicated furiously even as she stood frozen in the doorway.

Sierris looked up from suckling Cranthus's neck and smiled wickedly at her. Lord Frolov rolled over to see his wife staring at him and shouted a stream of obscenities. She backed out of the room, slamming the door behind her.

As the noises of their raucous lovemaking started anew, Natalya fled back to her studio. The haunting sounds echoed in her head, placing an even heavier burden on her broken heart.

Dor empathized with the Natalya's sentiment. The island seemed cursed. Her concerns about the attacks on the villagers and her husband's affair with Sierris competed with her growing concern about the safety of her daughters. A woman of deep compassion, the Lady Frolov had come to care for the people of her husband's fiefdom. After all, one of the nobles here had to take responsibility for the welfare of their people. If her husband wouldn't, that noble duty fell to her.

Villagers, some of them children, went missing at an alarming rate. The Lord's Watch claimed that these people had fallen victim to some nocturnal predator lurking in the jungle. However, she connected the attacks on the villagers with the insidious threat much closer to home.

She left behind a small note in the margins of a journal page mentioning the name of an old wizard whom she met through her family in Moor'Dru. Flipping forward in the journal, Dor discovered she had sent a letter to this wizard in the hope that he would be able to further investigate the sinister matters on the island.

The Lady Frolov had included details about how Sierris seemed to avoid the sun, noting her deathly pallor and total absence of appetite. Those few dreaded details caused Dor's blood to run cold, likely as cold as Sierris's alabaster skin.

Proceeding with his psychometric study of Natalya's journal, Dor flipped to another entry embedded with a strong psychic impression. This particular entry drew Dor's attention as surely as he'd drawn lightning to the *Nightsfall*. She wanted him to read this one.

Shouting incomprehensibly, Lord Frolov stormed into his Lady's bedchambers and confronted her with one of the letters his spies had intercepted. Tossing it at her in a fury, he headed for her father's war ax hanging on the wall. Lifting the antique weapon, he turned toward her, a look of murderous intent fixed on his pale face.

Frantic, she ran through the hallway, yelling for her daughters. Passing the intact family portrait hanging on the wall, she scooped up Sanya and dashed into the twins' bedroom locking the door behind them.

Lady Natalya embraced her terrified child. Looking around the twins' doll-filled bedchambers, she realized her other daughter was nowhere to be found. She had to find Natasha. But what would she do with Sanya in the meantime?

Hide-n-go-seek leapt to her distraught mind. Spying a large trunk beneath a narrow shuttered window, she rushed over to it. Overcome with grief, she began to weep. She kissed her daughter on the forehead and forced a smile.

"We're going to play a game, baby. Get inside the chest."

Sanya stared fearfully at her mother as she crawled into the trunk. Crying, she begged her mother, "What's wrong with Papa? Why is he mad at us?"

"Shush, baby," Natalya whispered to her daughter. "You've got to be quiet now. No matter what you hear, don't come out until I come back for you. I'll be back with Natasha soon."

Startled by a loud splintering sound, the Lady Frolov spun toward the door. In her excitement, she bumped the lid of the trunk, causing it to fall shut behind her. The lock clicked into place as it engaged, the sound all but lost as the ax smashed through the chamber door.

Tears streamed from Dor's weave-clouded eyes as the spell reeled out the final few minutes of Lady Frolov's life. As one dire implication became clear, his pulse pounded in his ears.

How could she write of her own demise?

Lady Natalya's eyes fixed on the chamber door as the head of the large ax penetrated it. The door shuddered as the heavy blade slammed into it once more, dislodging one of the hinges from the frame.

Lord Frolov charged through the ruined door, swinging the weapon wildly. Screaming obscenities at his panicked wife, he swung again, this time striking her in the back. Pain wracking her small frame, she crashed to the floor with the taste of blood on her lips.

Grabbing his wife by her hair, Lord Frolov lifted her face to his own. Smiling menacingly, he flashed a set of prominent, pointed canines. She screamed until he bit into her neck, ripping out the chunk of flesh that had once been her windpipe.

Her vision grew dimmer as blood flowed in a river from her twitching, semiconscious form. As she hoped to breathe her last, Sierris entered her field of vision.

"Death is too good for you, haughty bitch," the witch taunted. "So you won't be allowed to go free. Instead you'll serve me forever...as will your husband, his retainers, and even your children."

Peering deep into Lady Natalya's eyes, Sierris chanted an incantation designed to cheat the noblewoman of death's final release. Her life fled, only to be replaced by gnawing hunger.

Much to Dor's chagrin, her journal contained one final, fateful entry. Scribbled in haste, the chaotic passage seemed to be written in blood. Judging from the mournful yet murderous intent of the undead entity composing the entry, he bet it was human blood.

Catching its reflection in a polished mirror, the wraith stopped scribbling in the journal. A shadowy translucent mass—the undead remnant of the Lady Frolov—hovered a couple feet from the floor. Luminous gases seemed to flow through her veins. Her eyes blazed like burning coals.

Through her phantom self, the undead Lady Frolov caught sight of the discarded corpse of a chambermaid. The servant's body lay crumpled against the wall. Blood pooled on the rug underneath the corpse's savaged neck. Drained of its vital essence, it looked sunken, dry, and withered. She had not wanted to kill the poor woman, but the wraith was always hungry...so damned hungry.

Lord Frolov entered the room, his countenance as pale as death. The undead Lady clutched the folio to her torso in an attempt to conceal it. Bullying her past the point of death, Cranthus stalked toward her restless spirit. With a blood-curdling howl, his widow's shadowy revenant fled into the hallway, escaping with her journal.

An inhuman scream echoed down the hall, causing Dor's weave to waiver then fail. The spell's abrupt end startled him so that he fell backward in the chair and crashed to the floor.

Regaining his composure, he stood using the table for support. His haunted, tired eyes fell on Rayne standing before the open lockbox. The half-elven beauty held a journal similar to Lady Frolov's in her slender hands.

"What's going on? Where in the Nine is everyone?"

"No time for a proper explanation," she barked. "Asta wandered off and it sounds like she's in trouble."

"You have no idea of the possible troubles." Dor shuddered.

"We need to catch up to Caayl and the others." She replied, thrusting the book into his hands. "Hold onto this for safekeeping."

"What's this?" he inquired.

"It was locked in that trapped chest we found. Now let's go!"

Books in lockboxes boded badly for the young mage. He'd dealt with too many of them since leaving home. And, if his luck held, he'd be stuck with the newest acquisition as well. Dor pushed aside his fear, pocketed both journals, and then followed Rayne into the hallway.

Chapter 12

Sir Caayl watched Rayne work at one of tables in the spacious library. Using a set of fine metal tools concealed in her utility pouch, she probed the lock on the strongbox recovered from the hidden cubby. She disarmed the poison gas ampoule and extracted it, but the corroded lock mechanism resisted her best efforts.

As he stared, Caayl appraised far more than her skills as a locksmith. The chaste knight enjoyed any opportunity to appreciate the beautiful woman into which his childhood love had flowered. Love and lust mingled in his mind, forming an intense longing to have and to hold Rayne now and for the rest of his days. He would not let her slip away from him again, oaths and allegiances to foreign powers be damned.

"Making any progress?" he asked. Uncomfortable with his own increasingly erotic thoughts, he sought distraction with small talk.

"This is one tight bitch, but the lube is helping already," Rayne commented, trying once again to leverage the lock's tumbler.

"I hear the proper amount of lubrication is key."

Turning from her work, she smiled up at him and gibed, "And what would one of the Goddess's champions of purity and goodness know about proper lubrication?"

Called out on the incongruity of his innuendo with his Order's tenets, the knight could not help but blush. What else could he say? He loved her. He wanted her.

"Not a bloody thing," Caayl replied. With a meaningful smile, he added, "But that could change."

"Could it?"

He kissed her. And she responded. He drank in her warmth and passion. He felt her kiss restore him in ways that duty to king, country, and even his Goddess could not.

When their lips parted, both of them were smiling. Caayl felt like a kid again. Childhood had been such a simpler, easier time, before he had allowed oaths and duty to separate them. However, he had to admit that he relished the titillating possibilities of this new adult dimension to their relationship.

When he'd encountered her in Kingsport, he knew he'd been led to her for a reason. He needed quick passage out of the country, and Rayne happened to be working for the captain of a ship departing that very afternoon. Ishta'Kahl had brought her into his life again but for what reason? This question had gnawed at him daily since they'd left Kingsport.

Caayl did not believe Rayne represented temptation to be avoided. It made no sense to him that the Goddess would put her in his path to test him. Instead, he had come to see Rayne as a reward, confirmation that he'd been right about fighting against the modern dogma of the corrupted church, subverting the illegal decrees of his mad king, and sacrificing everything to help save the life of a woman and her unborn child. Every child deserved a chance at life, even the bastard half-breed offspring of the late Crown Prince of Oparre.

Rayne turned back to her work on the stubborn lock, but the kiss had affected her concentration. She fumbled with both lock and pick. Caayl liked that he'd had that kind of effect of her. After all, he felt that she'd affected him to his very core, shaking the foundations of his beliefs as much as Orson's genocidal reign of terror.

He cringed at the sudden sound of a chair scraping across the stone floor of the library. She lost what little concentration remained and snapped the delicate pick in half. Leaving part of the tool stuck in the lock, she buried her head in his shoulder. Her muffled curses sounded cute rather than obscene.

Hugging her to him, Caayl looked around the library. Dor sat ensnared in some kind of trance, his glowing hand hovering over an open book. Yax kept a wary eye on the magician from afar as Breuxias and Rafasi moved toward the library's open doorway.

Voicing his growing concern, Caayl asked, "Where's Asta?"

"She got up and walked out," Breuxias said. "I didn't want to grab her in case she was sleepwalking. But we should follow her."

"Good thinking," the knight replied. "Never wise to wake a sleepwalker."

"That's an old midwives' tale," Rayne commented. "You should have stopped her. She's in shock."

"No, he's right, child," Rafasi responded. "A century ago, an old dervish traveled the trade road between Imputnim and Jerishiya. He would spend all day healing the poor in the slums and then wander back to the other city by night, making the hundred-league journey in his sleep. One night on the new moon, a band of brigands beset him on his way to Jerishiya. One of the men tried to awaken the wandering dervish. But he was struck dead, transformed into a pillar of salt. Even today it stands alongside the road as a warning to anyone who would wake a sleepwalker."

"That's a good story, priest," Yax chided, "but I am quite familiar with that road. That mineral formation is much older."

"And how would you know that?"

"Because I first laid eyes on it about two centuries ago."

Rayne released Caayl and turned toward the others. Her concern for Asta turned to anger over their failure to act. She possessed the protective instinct of a mother bugbear, only twice as vicious.

"If you're all going to stand around and swap stories, I'm going after her," Rayne interrupted, tossing down her broken lock pick.

"No, I'm on it," Caayl volunteered. It provided him with the perfect opportunity to take his mind off her for a while. "You work on the lock. I'll look for Asta."

"But you can't go by yourself," she protested.

"I'll go with him," Rafasi said. "I'm curious to see what drew her attention."

"Wait here," Caayl said, caressing Rayne's cheek. Her warmth reassured him despite the bitter cold of the keep. "We'll be right back. I promise."

Breuxias yawned again. "Sure you don't want us to go with you?"

"I think Rayne could use some help with that chest you found," Caayl replied. "With her broken pick buried in the lock, it's liable to take brute strength to get into it now."

"If she disarmed the trap, it shouldn't be a problem."

"I know what I'm doing," she interjected, sounding offended. "I was distracted...that's all."

"Hmp," Breuxias grunted. "I guess we'll find out."

Sir Caayl and Rafasi left them to deal with the lockbox and followed the corridor leading from the library back toward the private bedchambers. They advanced cautiously, a scavenged lantern providing their only source of illumination. The sputtering flame cast irregular shadows that danced along with them as they neared the next turn.

Rounding the corner, they passed another painting set in an expensive frame. The knight did not recall seeing it earlier but it had to have been hanging here all along. He must have been too preoccupied with Rayne to notice.

He gasped as the lantern revealed the disturbing nature of the painting. The Frolov family portrait had been defaced. The faces of the twin girls had been left untouched, but the faces of their parents had been ripped to shreds.

As he stared at the portrait, Caayl fancied that he heard a low murmuring. Listening, he could identify a child's voice mingled with that of the gnomish woman, but was it an echo or phantasm?

Rafasi asked, "Do you hear that?"

An echo then, Caayl surmised. He nodded.

Raising the lantern higher, Rafasi took a few steps down the hallway. As he peered into the shadows, he caught a glimpse of Asta as she turned the corner.

"Asta! Wait up," he called out, hurrying down the hall.

They turned the corner seconds behind Asta, but they didn't see her in the hallway. The gnomish woman had to have gone into one of the adjoining bedchambers.

Shining the lantern through the doorways on either side of them, Rafasi asked, "Where did she go? Why would she run away?"

"Who knows? Grief does funny things to people," Caayl commented. "After King Orson's father died, he became a terrible, hateful person."

"True. And very insightful," the priest replied. "Maybe Asta's regressing to a simpler time. Playing a childish game to avoid dealing with a very adult loss."

"Let's hope so. "I don't like the alternatives."

Shivering, Rafasi withdrew his holy symbol from within his robes. The two men came from different nations and even ethnicities, but the priest's silver medallion, the physical embodiment of Ishta'Kahl's protection, appeared nearly identical to the knight's own.

"Neither do I," the priest responded. "There's a most unholy presence here. Can you feel it?"

"Vaguely. Like a gnawing in my gut."

Before they could check the next set of bedchambers, a frantic cry issued forth from a doorway to the left. Maneuvering around the ruined door hanging by its hinges, the brash knight rushed into the room before he was cognizant of the danger that awaited him there. Steeling himself, Sir Caayl faced the terrors inside.

Rafasi followed on the knight's spurred heels. The glowing symbol in his hand cast more light on the situation than the aged lantern. His prayers caught in his throat as he drew even with Caayl.

Asta hung before them, suspended in midair by a shifting, shadowy mass of ectoplasm. The shade drained the life force from Asta as she writhed in its grasp. The gnomish woman aged rapidly, withering before their eyes.

"We have to do something," Caayl said, drawing his sword.

"Exactly," Rafasi added, touching the Moon Goddess's silvery symbol to the knight's exposed blade. "We shall banish the darkness with Ishta'Kahl's light, my son."

He watched as the priest blessed his Order sword, bestowing the cleansing power of the Goddess on the weapon. Fueled by Her Aethyreal fire, the knight's shining blade illuminated the bedchamber. The foul creature holding Asta howled madly.

"Release her, foul spirit," Sir Caayl cried. "By the Goddess, I command it!"

He slashed across the tendrils of pulsing ectoplasm between the shadowy mass and Asta. Feeling emboldened by the energy surging through the sword, the knight surged forward, forcing it backward.

Maneuvering with the ease and rapidity of smoke, the shade flanked him, moving between him and the others.

"I fear you not, evil one!"

Raising the shining sword high, Sir Caayl prepared to defend himself. If he could keep its attention long enough, perhaps Rafasi could get Asta to safety.

The undead thing wailed, "You should!"

As it rushed at him, the knight saw a twisted face manifest within the ectoplasmic mass. Its dead eyes were dominated by sadness and regret, yet tinged with a mad, insatiable hunger. The spectral visage became sunken, drawn, and aged. Though Caayl did not comprehend it at the time, he gazed upon his own twisted reflection.

***

Entering the room on the heels of Yax and Breuxias, Rayne beheld her love's ghastly predicament. The writhing shade held Caayl in its transparent grasp. Rayne screamed as the creature drained her trapped lover of his essence. Though not dead yet, he aged at an accelerated rate. The human wouldn't last long, judging by the condition of the gnomish woman's desiccated corpse.

Someone had to do something, Rayne thought, her mind racing.

Drawing her sword, she charged between Breuxias and Yax.

"Stop her!" Dor cried, digging around in his magic pouch. "We can't let that wraith touch anyone. It feeds on life."

Breuxias seized her before she made it into the fray, lifting the sprite-like woman aloft. She struggled against the brute. She kicked at him over and over again, but he held her tightly.

Caught in his iron grip, Rayne watched the scene unfold before her. Agonizing over her lover, she realized that they were once again caught up in events that conspired to separate them when they needed each other most. If Caayl died this night, she would never forgive herself...or Breuxias for that matter. Even if she couldn't save him, she wanted the brute restraining her to at least respect her right to die defending a man whom she loved with all her heart.

As the lovers continued to struggle against those restraining them, Yax advanced on the shade. The elven adventurer held the red-hot sword in his hand loosely, almost leisurely. Licking his blue-tinged lips, the elf grimaced as the blade became whiter, hotter as he closed on the wraith.

Beside Yax, Rafasi stood unmoved by the horrors. If anything, the priest seemed at ease confronting a creature from the Underworld.

"Demon of the Nine Hells, be gone from this accursed place," Rafasi shouted, flinging a fluid Rayne presumed to be holy water from an ornate flask. The wraith wailed as if hot coals were burning it.

"Stop throwing that stuff at it," Yax cautioned. "You're just making it angry."

Rayne watched as Rafasi took his cue from Yax, retrieving the knight's glowing sword from the toy-strewn floor of the chamber. Both the priest and the elf advanced on the wraith as she squirmed against Breuxias's broad chest.

Rayne felt hot tears on her cheeks. Accustomed to fighting for what she wanted, it hurt her to watch her tortured lover and not be able to do something to ease his suffering.

As the wraith recoiled from the blessed blade wielded by Rafasi, Yax took the opportunity to attack. In a flashing display of swordsmanship, the elf made two shallow cuts across the amorphous body of the retreating shade.

The inky form shifted, howling again. The rage-filled face of a woman became visible for a moment in the swirling, phosphorescent mass of the creature.

"Holy Hells!" Dor shouted from behind Rayne and Breuxias. "It's her! It's really her!"

"And who in the Nine would that be?" Breuxias bellowed.

"The Lady Frolov!" Dor added, "This is her journal. If we don't stop her, the knight's a dead man."

Dor dropped the chest and the journal to the floor. The wizard then reached into the bag on his belt and extracted a blackened staff.

Seizing her opportunity, Rayne elbowed Breuxias in the mouth. Bellowing again, the tall man staggered backward. Rolling as she hit the ground, Rayne stood, took two steps, and flung the silvered dagger at the wraith. It flew between Yax and Rafasi and hit the specter. The dagger sunk deep into its shifting ectoplasmic form.

Smoke rising from its many wounds, the wraith retreated toward the room's single shuttered window. In its hasty retreat, the shade released its suffocating hold on Caayl and dropped him to the floor.

Ignoring the danger posed by the wounded creature, Rayne scrambled toward Caayl on her hands and knees. Yax and Rafasi kept the wraith at bay as she extracted the injured knight. The monster hissed and howled, stymied by their enchanted blades.

Grabbing him by his collar, she dragged the knight out of harm's way. She examined him, relieved to find him alive, unconscious but alive. As she brushed his salt-and-pepper hair, fresh tears flowed down her fair cheeks. Pulling him to her bosom, she vowed to never let go of her beloved again.

In the midst of the chaos, Rayne heard Dor's call over the wailing wraith. Cutting her tear-filled eyes in the mage's direction, she saw him holding the black staff at hip level. Snakes of lava swam down the length of its shaft. A visible shock wave erupted from the staff as the rivulets of fire reached its gnarled tip, sending the wraith hurtling across the room. She watched as the inky entity crashed to the floor in front of the trunk below the window.

Praying in his own tongue, Rafasi began what Rayne perceived as an aggressive exorcism. The undead thing flailed about on the floor, trying to regain its physical form. The wailing spirit managed to briefly manifest the anguished face of the Lady Frolov. Not giving it a moment to recover, the priest planted the blessed sword in the formless, smoking puddle of ectoplasm.

The wraith's disembodied voice echoed off the walls of the bedroom as it howled, "No! Not without my children. They're not safe with him! Not safe!"

As Rafasi ended his exorcism, Yax performed a fiery coup de grace on the undead thing. Liquid flame spewed forth from the elf's free hand, filling the bedchamber with welcomed warmth. The remains of the wraith turned into a gray, bubbling fluid before sinking into the seams in the stone floor.

Rayne cradled Caayl to her in an attempt to warm her aged love's shivering form. While he had survived his ordeal, she wondered how much of a toll it had taken on his mind, body, and soul.

As she kissed his forehead, Rayne became aware of someone crying, someone else rather. The tearful lament of a child filled the bedroom, echoing off the walls. Several moments later, the phantasmal sobbing died away, leaving her with the sound of her own bittersweet tears.

Chapter 13

Sir Caayl sat atop a large table in the anteroom of the Lord's library. He stared into Rayne's eyes, trying to focus on his ravenous hunger for her rather than on the throbbing pain racking his entire body. Wincing as she caressed one of the fresh gray streaks in his hair, he realized that even his hair ached.

The wraith's attack had taken quite the toll on the knight-errant, physically, mentally, and, as he would soon learn, spiritually. Caayl gasped as he attempted to take off his tunic. His muscles burned as if he'd fought an entire army in the span of a night. Seeing the knight's plight, Rayne aided him in removing his bloody garment.

Three rows of lacerations along the left side of his chiseled torso marked where the wraith had made contact. The exposed wounds, although not very deep, appeared blackened and bright red along the edges. To him, they looked as much a burn as a cut. Though no healer, the knight could see obvious evidence of infection. Even worse, he could smell his own rotting flesh.

Sniffing the air, Breuxias asked, "What's that odor?"

Pointing to the green pus oozing from the cuts in Sir Caayl's side, Rafasi responded, "Essence of evil. That foul shade's attack left something in its wake - its unholy taint."

"Hmm, by the looks of him, that thing took more than it left," Breuxias commented, staring into Caayl's bloodshot eyes.

Rayne took his larger hand into her own. Her fingers traced the lines of newly formed wrinkles. Her faelike hands, unblemished by age, stood in stark contrast to his old man's hands. And what of his old man's face? Would she want someone so wrinkled and worn?

Looking once more into her bright, teary eyes, Sir Caayl dismissed his insecurities, for her love for him shined there still. Using his free hand, he brushed a tear from her porcelain cheek. Sniffling, Rayne returned his smile with a tired one.

"Rafasi is going to fix you up," she reassured him. "You have nothing to worry about."

"I have no doubt about that," he lied. He had been full of doubt for longer than he cared to admit, yet he had no doubts about his growing hunger for her. He added somberly, "The Goddess's blessing is upon me. My injury is a small price to pay to release these poor trapped souls. May they rest in peace."

But was that a lie too? He admitted to himself that he was no longer convinced that Ishta'Kahl's blessing alone could sustain him. Once his love of Goddess and country had been enough for him, but now the knight-errant hungered for a different kind of love.

"We do not hate the sinner, just the sin," Rafasi replied, his black eyes boring into the knight's own.

Can the priest sense my doubts, Sir Caayl wondered.

As if reading his mind, Rafasi added, "Like all those purified of sin, they will have peace."

Breuxias said, "I hope there aren't other souls trapped here."

Sir Caayl didn't relish the idea of dealing with any more trapped spirits either. One had almost been enough to kill him.

"I'm sure there aren't," Dor muttered. "Not souls anyway."

Breuxias seethed, "You seem to know an awful lot about this place to have never been here before. What are you hiding?!"

Caayl watched as the mercenary's nostrils flared. The knight had restrained his own impulse to throttle the secretive magician. He hoped that Breuxias would manage to do the same.

Rising from his seat on a nearby table, Yax'Kaqix shut the Lady Frolov's journal with an audible snap. Stepping between Dor and Breuxias, the elf offered the book to his friend.

"It's all in here," Yax told him. "Take a look if you want."

Waving it aside, Breuxias asked, "You're taking his side now?!"

"What's happening here isn't Dor's fault," Yax replied, returning the book to him. "It started long before any of you were ever born."

"I'm sure the Lord's journal, the one from the lockbox, tells the rest of the story," Dor interjected, "but I haven't had time to read it yet. No way in the Nine Hells am I going to open myself up to that book. Not after seeing what Lord Frolov did to his family."

Wincing again as Rafasi probed the open wounds on his side, Sir Caayl asked, "And what did he do? What went on here?"

"What's still going on here," Rayne corrected him.

Turning to Breuxias and the others, Rafasi interjected, "If you want to argue about this, take it out into the hall. This man needs rest, not stress. The Goddess's powers can purge the infection but won't mend this corruption of the flesh. I'll have to collect a few things first. Which one of you is going to help?"

The sudden assertiveness of the priest surprised him. Caayl guessed that it surprised the others too. For a moment, no one spoke.

Yax broke the silence when he answered Rafasi. "I'll come with you. But we won't go far. We've covered the fact that splitting up is a bad idea."

"Good," Breuxias said, snatching up Dor by his collar. "While you're doing that, we can have a little talk about this journal, that chest, and whatever the Hells else you're hiding from me."

"Sounds lovely," Dor replied. "Looking forward to it."

Breuxias pushed the calamitous mage into the hallway. Yax and Rafasi followed them, keeping an eye on the volatile duo. Relief washed over Sir Caayl when Rayne shut the heavy door behind them.

Sighing, Caayl thought, *we're alone. Finally alone.*

Returning to his side, Rayne stroked his bearded cheek. As he turned to face her, Caayl gasped as the pain in his side flared anew. As the agony increased, so did the hunger. Though he hurt all over, he felt a particular ache deep in his loins; he longed for her to soothe his ache, satiate his hunger.

Smiling mischievously, Rayne kissed him. He returned the kiss, crushing her to him desperately. As they embraced, he could feel the heat of their passion burn hotter than the pain. Awash in the ecstasy of contact long denied, he kissed her over and over again.

As Rayne nibbled her way down his neck, Caayl managed to say, "I've wanted you from the first moment I laid eyes on you, from the first day your family came to stay on the estate."

Pausing, she replied, "You wanted me even as a child. Silly boy, you were barely eight winters old when we met. And me scarcely over a dozen."

Loved, he'd meant to say. But his craving for her perverted his speech as it had polluted his thoughts.

"I can't believe we've been apart for so long. I've sacrificed so much for oaths that seem meaningless now." Pulling her tighter against him, he added, "What are they worth without you?"

The hunger burned inside him again. It caused his blood to boil. Consumed with passion and desire, he found himself unable to speak coherently. Had what he said made any sense? Did he even care?

"It's not your fault," Rayne responded as he kissed his way down her neck. "We're here, together. It was meant to be. We shouldn't worry about the past now. Instead let's focus on..."

As Caayl bit into the soft, sensitive spot above her collarbone, she let out a low moan. Feeling her hot sex grind against his own, he almost climaxed instantly. Mere layers of fabric separated them from indulging their passions.

Ignoring the pain and even his most sacred vows for the all-consuming hunger, he lifted the spritely woman and sat her on the table roughly. With a grunt, he pulled her leggings free, flinging them onto the cold floor. Her taut thighs tightened around him, causing him to exhale sharply.

Rayne hesitated for a moment. She looked concerned, hesitant even. He wanted to see ecstasy.

Taking the sword he'd been born with in hand, Caayl entered her, sheathing himself to the hilt in her welcoming wetness, causing her entire body to shudder. Tightening against him, she moaned. Grabbing him by his salt-and-pepper mane, she pulled him to her, crushing her lips to his. Their tongues danced and played together.

She's hungry too, he thought, returning her kiss.

Feeling his climax building too soon, the inexperienced knight slowed down, trying to hold back, but Rayne's hunger met if not exceeded his own. She held him tightly, bucking wildly against him.

Her eyes never left his. Fixated on each other, they made furious, frenetic love on top of the table. In this foreboding place, their act itself felt like a rebellion against the evil lurking here, two points of light coming together to shine brighter against the growing darkness.

"Oh...my...Goddess!" Caayl exclaimed.

Burying himself deep inside her, he flooded her with his seed. Her iron grip on him slackened somewhat, but her velvet glove still held him firmly. She pumped him languidly, milking every drop from his erect manhood.

As his passion cooled, his hunger waned, satiated for a while. Guilt replaced his waning hunger. What else had this act caused him to rebel against? And what would it cost him in the end? Recalling his blasphemy at the point of release, Sir Caayl hoped that his Goddess would forgive his trespass against Her.

He tried to pray to Ishta'Kahl for forgiveness but discovered he could not concentrate on the nebulous, on the divine. Though his words flew up, his thoughts remained below. Rayne was too real, too immediate. She consumed his every thought, every desire. Ishta'Kahl would understand, right? She would see the depth and purity of their love and forgive him this one blasphemy, allow him this one indulgence.

Kissing him on the neck, Rayne cooed, "I love you."

"I love you too, my goddess," Caayl whispered.

***

Rafasi followed Yax'Kaqix down the hall, away from the scene of a heated argument between Breuxias and Dor. Both men promised the priest and the elf that they'd settle their dispute without bloodshed, but Rafasi didn't know whether or not to believe them. Breuxias was a mercenary, little better than a hired killer in the priest's opinion. And, if Dor's tale held water, the wizard had been responsible for sinking the *Nightsfall*, leading to the death of most of its crew.

"Are you sure it's a good idea to leave them alone?"

The elf paused for a moment, taking a look back at him.

"They'll either work it out or they won't," Yax responded. "I can't do it for them. When Breuxias gets like this, there's no reasoning with him. He'll beat his head against that Dor until it opens one way or another. I don't think forcing the wizard to talk is the correct strategy. It'll encourage him to keep lying to us. If we gain Dor's trust, we'll be able to coax him into confiding in us. I believe that he has good intentions, but he's bound to a certain level of secrecy so he speaks in riddles."

"Whatever method works," Rafasi commented. "At this point, I'd like some answers. What's with that chest for instance?"

"Do you dread what it contains as much as I do?" Yax asked.

"Have you felt it too?"

"The unclean presence? When that chest was open back in the village, my brain exploded with searing pain. My senses reeled from the corrupting energies stored within that blasted box. I felt it before, on the ship and then on the beach. But it was fainter, weaker then."

Rafasi had detected a malignant influence at both locations. However, until Dor's admission in the cave, he had assumed that it was the elf himself. The harrowing stories about Yax's people, the Elves of the South Isles, terrified him as a child. Now he accompanied one of the fierce, wild Unen'ek through the corridors of a haunted keep.

Yet Rafasi felt protected rather than threatened by Yax'Kaqix. The elf exuded quiet calm even under the direst of circumstances and possessed the reassuring presence of a natural leader. He loathed admitting that to himself much less the elf. His sacred oaths as a priest of Ishta'Kahl charged him to protect others, not rely on them for protection.

"So it's not one of us," Rafasi said. "It's the chest."

"Not the chest itself," Yax clarified, "rather what it contains…or whom it contains."

"Whom it contains?" he shuddered, "I don't like the sound of that. What do you mean?"

"Just a hunch," the elf replied, shrugging his shoulders.

"Would you care to share your hunch?"

"No, not really," Yax answered. "I dislike being an alarmist almost as much as I hate being wrong."

"You're a complicated one," Rafasi teased, trying to alleviate some of the tension.

"You don't know the half of it."

"Do tell?"

"Trying to get a confession out of me, priest?" the elf asked. With a wry grin, he added, "Because that's not likely."

Rafasi's own heartbeat filled the gulf of silence left in the awkward moments after both men's failed attempts at levity. In the interim, they located an armoire full of silk linens. With a renewed sense of purpose, the priest led them back toward the library with an armload of bedclothes.

Rafasi didn't want to be away from Sir Caayl for too long. He feared the knight might turn impure thought into sinful action. Though temptation was ripe as Rayne in this wild world, it had to be avoided by those chosen by the Goddess to serve her divine plan.

Despite her portfolio as a goddess of healing, mercy, and protection, Ishta'Kahl did not forgive her acolytes as easily as she did the rest of her flock. As paragons of her faith, the Moon Goddess expected them to be examples to the world. If they strayed from her shining path, the chosen served as examples to the rest of her worshippers, examples of why not to incur the wrath of Ishta'Kahl.

"What do you intend to do for the knight?" Yax asked, pulling Rafasi out of his quiet contemplation.

"First, I'll bless the last of the river water. Then I'll use it to cleanse the infection from the wounds. A simple healing ritual will not be enough to mend the flesh. For that, it will take nightly ministrations for at least a fortnight."

"Primitive but effective," Yax replied, much to the priest's consternation. "What do you intend on doing about restoring his youth, his vitality?"

"There's nothing easily done about it," Rafasi admitted, "at least not to my knowledge. Healing that advanced would be the provenance of a high priest, a rank that I do not see a simple pilgrim such as myself attaining anytime soon."

"There are other methods," the elf hinted.

"And what would you have me do?"

"Not you, priest," Yax replied. "If the bulk of my luggage had not gone to the bottom with Gneut's caravel, I'd handle it myself. As it stands now, I won't be able to find the proper ingredients until we make it to Myth. *If* we make it there."

"I didn't realize that the Choj'Ahaw were trained healers."

"We are trained as healers as well as killers. The nature of war is a double-sided coin. As Lords of War, we must know both sides with equal proficiency in order to manage the chaos of battle. However, this particular remedy is not a manipulation of the Aethyr but rather an alchemical application, and it's definitely not something that I learned in the service of my people. Some knowledge is forbidden, even amongst the Unen'ek, and must be stolen rather than learned."

"Alchemy? Forbidden knowledge? Surely you speak of necromancy," Rafasi spat, crossing himself with his holy symbol.

"There are gradations of necromancy," Yax retorted, "not all of them involve animating corpses, creating homunculi, or trafficking with spirits. Time itself is an aspect that can be manipulated with the right alchemical concoction. Personal time doubly so."

"Time manipulation?" Rafasi interrupted, "What does this have to do with Sir Caayl's condition?"

"There's a potion I can brew that will restore his lost youth. "It can erase the damage caused by the wraith, reverse the knight's personal time, so to speak. It's hard to explain. Humans do not see time as my people do."

"Is that why elves live so long compared to humans?"

"One of the reasons," Yax responded, "at least if you ask the monks at the High Temple of Kümatz, the sacred keepers of time itself. They understand the cycle of ages to a greater degree than most, but even they do not have all of the answers. Certain secrets are reserved for the Cosmic Dragon to reveal when we stand before Him again at the end of this cycle."

Rafasi decided not to start a religious debate with the elf, not yet anyway. Yax felt comfortable enough to expound his beliefs to him, but the priest did not know how to respond without offending him. His curiosity aroused, Rafasi relied on the favored techniques of practiced confessors, careful listening and selective yet soulful querying.

The priest asked, "And how do you know this potion will work?"

"Because I've used it to great effect in the past," Yax answered, averting his eyes from the other man's own.

"But why would you need such a thing? You're virtually ageless."

"It wasn't for me," Yax admitted. "I brewed it for my wife."

"Your wife? Did she get attacked by one of those foul things?"

"No, I did it to extend her lifespan. She was human."

The proclamation shocked Rafasi into silence. The Winaq'che elves took humans as mates on rare occasions, but the practice was almost unheard of amongst Yax's people. In fact, most humans on Faltyr shared the Unen'ek's aversion to interspecies unions, including those in Rafasi's homeland of Panglov.

The taboo had originated in the Dark Times after the Cataclysm. If the old stories could be believed, Rafasi recalled, one bad seed had been enough to sow discord between the races of men and elves. A half-breed upstart, an Ireti bastard named Ra'Tallah, had seen to that when he'd drawn the known world of Faltyr into a nightmarish conflict. The Great War had not ended until Artemis, the original mage-king of Moor'Dru, slew the devilish sorcerer. In their final apocalyptic battle, these two great magicians had sundered the Meshkenet Mountains, burying the remnants of the Ireti Empire beneath a sea of sand.

Artemis's final prophecy foretold long-dead Ra'Tallah would rise again to bring an end to this cycle of ages. After the Cataclysm, elves and men drifted apart to preserve the future of Faltyr, to avoid fulfilling the Prophesy. None that lived during those Dark Times would risk bringing the half-blood reincarnation of that Ireti devil into the world. More than a dozen centuries removed from those dark days, most of the peoples of Faltyr still observed that superstitious taboo.

Yax's answer beggared Rafasi's exhausted brain. So many questions arose at once that the priest did not get a chance to ask any of them. As they approached Dor and Breuxias outside the closed door of the library, Rafasi noticed that neither of the two men seemed the least bit hostile with the other anymore.

In fact, Breuxias and Dor conversed in a conspiratorial fashion. A listener, even an eavesdropper by nature, Rafasi disliked not knowing what they said almost as much as he hated himself for being nosy and intrusive. Hated the sinfulness of it, he reminded himself.

Spotting their approach, Breuxias intercepted Rafasi and Yax before they reached the library. Whatever the giant of a man had to say, it seemed important. Anger had disappeared from Breuxias's face, replaced by a lusty gleam that lit his black eyes. Rafasi had dealt with enough merchants and gamblers in his wilder days before joining the priesthood. He recognized a motivation as basic as greed. But it was greed tinged with something else. Wonder perhaps, Rafasi mused.

"Tell him what you told me," Breuxias said, prodding Dor.

Dor looked from Breuxias, to Yax, and then to Rafasi. However, he did not speak. Instead, Dor hesitated, allowing several silent, tense moments to pass in the hallway.

Rafasi excused himself to tend to Sir Caayl's wounds. He could take a hint. However, in the interest of self-preservation, the wily priest left the door behind him cracked slightly, and the acoustics of the stone hallway made for easy listening. Little did he know that the knowledge he'd gain from eavesdropping on their conversation would be his undoing.

Chapter 14

Kaladimus Dor hated repeating himself, but he accepted that it was in his best interest at this point. The rules of the game had changed drastically with the revelations contained within Lady Frolov's journal. If the Hallowed Vessel remained in the subterranean cove, the Council certainly didn't leave it there without protection.

In fact, Dor feared that the whole damned keep was an elaborate trap designed to kill any of those foolish enough to seek the prize. Once the blood demon had corrupted Lord Frolov, the Council had been forced to send Protectorate Magi to deal with Sierris and her brood.

When confronted by this powerful evil, the Protectorate Magi found themselves either unable or unwilling to destroy them all. The protective wards trapped the remaining undead within the grounds of Frolov Keep to serve as eternal guardians for the Hallowed Vessel.

Dor wondered if the wyvern had been summoned from the pits of the Underworld to act as another sentry. If not, how did it figure into the equation, if it fit into the equation. Either way, how in the Nine Hells would they kill it or avoid it long enough to escape?

Although powerful in his own right, Dor did not feel that he would be able to fight his way to the ship alone. His own survival and the success of his mission now rested on trusting the mercenary captains of Finders Keepers. He had dealt with the famed adventuring guild on one previous occasion. He had been satisfied with the results despite the quirky, even irksome, personalities of the particular guildsmen he'd employed in the recovery of the chest's contents. Dor hoped Yax and Breuxias would fare better than those poor bastards.

Trying the "honest" approach once again, Dor confided in Breuxias about the existence of the magical ship but did not go into details about its true nature. Not enough time remained before Rafasi and Yax returned for that tale to be told.

Dor could not bring himself to overcome his own natural prejudice against religious zealots like the holy man and the holy warrior. He believed that those with the best intentions often made the worst choices. After this disastrous mission for his master, he considered himself to be a living testament to that caveat.

Dor informed Breuxias that Spensir and several others had known of the ship's existence for some time now. He told him about Gneut's deathbed confession, including the compass, spyglass, and the maps. And reiterated the warnings on the steles in the village and summarized the pertinent information gleaned from the Lady Frolov's journal.

"So that's what the gnome was after," Breuxias exclaimed, "and he got all of us involved! If Gneut was alive, I'd kill him myself."

He had no doubt in his mind that the mercenary would follow through with such a threat given the opportunity.

Already knowing the answer, Dor asked, "What should we do?"

He relished those times when he could solve a mundane problem without risking a magical solution. Breuxias reacted as he anticipated. Dor hated manipulating his friend, especially after deceiving him earlier, but the situation demanded it.

Breuxias said, "If it still exists, we find that ship and get off this damn island."

"If we can beat Spensir to it, but he's got the maps and the items. They'll eventually lead him to it, assuming he hasn't stumbled upon it already."

"Don't worry about that spineless cunt," Breuxias spat. He gestured toward the returning elf and added, "Yax and I know how to handle backstabbers and bushwhackers. Otherwise we wouldn't be members of Finders Keepers."

After Rafasi excused himself to deal with Sir Caayl's festering wounds, Dor relayed the same information to Yax. Dor brought the elf up to speed on the magical ship, its location in a subterranean cove below Frolov Keep, and the likelihood of mortal peril between them and the Hallowed Vessel.

Yax waited until Dor had finished speaking then asked him a single question. "Do you think that Lord Frolov's journal will point the way to the cove's entrance?"

"Possibly."

With a slight smile curling his thin lips, the elf responded, "If you can't find the answer there, then we'll have to take those maps from Spensir by whatever means necessary."

"Damn right," Breuxias said. "Spensir knew the value of that ship, so he killed Donal and then ran off with the compass and the maps. I knew we should've never trusted that miserable sonuvabitch. If I have anything to say about it, he won't live long enough for me to make that mistake again."

"My thoughts exactly," Yax said.

Dor dreaded what secrets the Lord's diary might hold, but knew that he would have to examine it as soon as possible. Otherwise, he would have someone else's blood on his hands. Perhaps this book would hold the answer to the elf's question as well as the answers to his growing list of questions about Frolov Keep.

After settling back into his seat at the table, Dor extracted both journals and his own mission log from the almost bottomless pouch. Fumbling about with an inkwell and a fresh quill, he prepared to examine the Lord's journal.

Despite the urgency of their situation, Dor refused to open his mind to the violent, murderous mental impressions left behind by the late Lord Frolov. A scribing spell would have to suffice this time. So Dor guided the animated quill as it copied the contents of one text to another. *Just stay focused,* he reminded himself as the quill scratched out script in the Lord's bold hand.

Cranthus Frolov viewed the appointment to the remote island fiefdom as the chance of a lifetime. He considered it an honor to be entrusted with the stewardship of one of the few remaining Hallowed Vessels, a relic of the last war against the Elves of the South Isles. An engineer as well as a registered magus, Lord Frolov had hoped to glean many secrets from the ship of legend. Instead, he had fallen under the seductive sway of Sierris.

In all probability, Sierris had targeted Lord Frolov, insinuating herself into the life of his family as the twins' nanny. The ageless beauty had aroused jealousy in his wife and his daughters had feared her. Infatuated with the witch, he'd ignored their feelings.

Dor discovered that Cranthus had observed something wrong with the porcelain-skinned woman. Sierris avoided the chapel much to his chagrin, preferring to observe religious services in her private chambers. In addition, Lord Frolov reiterated his wife's observations regarding Sierris's lack of appetite and aversion to direct sunlight.

Cranthus lamented her unnatural influence on the men in his service, even the clergymen. He even wrote of his jealousy of these other men and its eventual repercussions. Dor read about how the Lord's unhealthy obsession with the scandalous woman had escalated to murderous consummation of their affair in a single sanguine evening.

Having caught Sierris with one of his knights, Cranthus had flown into a rage, caving in the young man's skull with an iron-shod bucket. The death of her lover had seemed to arouse Sierris to new heights of passion. Before the knight's body had grown cold, Lord Frolov had added his seed to the dead man's own inside the insatiable seductress.

From that night onward, Lord Frolov's entries became sporadic and fragmented. Dor realized that he read the words of a man going insane. According to Cranthus's own words, betraying his marital vows ate at his sanity less than slaying one of his own soldiers.

The angry ghost of the young man seemed to haunt Cranthus, accounting for his disproportionate guilt and degraded mental state. Though his head priest denied such a presence lingered in the keep, the Lord believed that the specter was no mere hallucination. Having dealt with the restless dead at Frolov Keep, Dor had to agree with him.

In his grief, Cranthus had fallen under the sway of the one person with whom he shared the truth about the young knight's death. Claiming to have been visited by a similar shade, she had promised to protect Lord Frolov from the vengeful spirit of her murdered lover.

Sierris had also promised to love Cranthus and not judge him for his crime of passion. After all, he'd loved her enough to kill; no man had ever loved her that much before. Even as she spoke those words, the Lord wrote, he had not believed them. Instead, he felt a burning, compulsive desire for her that transcended rational thought.

Their torrid affair escalated in the wake of the murder. Sierris pushed the boundaries of discretion, demanding that each night's affections be more public than the last. Word of the affair soon reached Natalya's ears. Lord Frolov had dismissed the rumor as idle gossip but later discovered that Sierris had confessed to his wife.

Lady Frolov ended up catching them together on two separate occasions. Dor noted with revulsion that the Lord had enjoyed having his weeping wife watch as he spilled his seed inside his new lover. Her grief had made their passion all the sweeter.

A thunderous clatter interrupted the tragic tale. Feeling his concentration on his scribing spell slip, Dor waited for the inevitable flash following the thunder. Not again, he thought frantically. Fighting the rising panic in his chest, the master-of-disaster watched the shuttered window for any sign of lightning.

The sound repeated itself, but no flash accompanied it. If not a storm, Dor wondered, what had produced that noise? The wyvern wailed in the courtyard, as if it were answering his question. The winged beast's high-pitched cry shattered his concentration on the spell.

The quill shot across the room toward Yax'Kaqix who appeared to be asleep. The elf reached up and caught the projectile with detached ease. Opening his wild, inhuman eyes, he stared across the library. Dor felt Yax's gaze bore into him.

"We will discuss this at a later time," the elf said, "if we live through this night."

Before Dor could offer an apology, Yax rose from his seat and headed for the battened window. Drawing his wand, he spat what sounded like a curse. With a single blast, the elf blew the heavy shutters off their rusty hinges.

As Dor joined Yax at the window, he caught sight of their winged stalker atop the crumbling domed roof of the temple. As stained glass shards rained down into the chapel, screams rose up from its dark interior. The rampaging wyvern shrieked in response, its high-pitched cry drowning out those of the terrified sailors trapped below.

***

Meanwhile, inside the besieged chapel, Spensir was happy to be alive. After the beast's ambush in the courtyard, he had ordered all lights extinguished, postponing their search for the secret entrance.

If the monster proved to be nocturnal, he knew they'd have to wait until daybreak to continue their hunt for the Hallowed Vessel. Unfortunately, the winged monster had returned before the sun. After their intrusion into Her temple, he knew Gilly was right about one thing. He doubted Damarra would hurry to the blasphemous sailors' aid.

He watched in horror as the massive creature's thunderous assault threatened to collapse the entire domed roof of the chapel. Rolling away from his impromptu bedding, he avoided being killed by masonry and rotten support beams crashing to the floor.

Spensir squinted through the dimness and the dust, relieved to see that Vorta had survived. However, countless cuts covered her exposed flesh, a condition similar to his. The falling debris had left the lovers bloody and battered but not beaten.

Someone cried out like a dying animal from amidst the pile of debris. The monster responded by shrieking again, causing another shower of glass slivers to fall from the dome. The combination of the temple's dim interior and the beast's racket prevented him from finding out which of his comrades had been trapped beneath the rubble.

Vorta tapped him on the shoulder repeatedly. Turning toward her, Spensir noticed a figure rising from the edge of the debris field. Judging by the stocky silhouette, Fergus had escaped of his own accord. That meant Gilly had to be the one howling for help.

"We've got to get out of here," Vorta shrieked in his ear.

Already shaken by the surprise attack from above, the verbal assault on Spensir's eardrum proved too much for his frayed nerves. He reached out and slapped Vorta across the face. She grew deathly quiet, staring at him with murderous intensity. He would have apologized had it been in his nature. Instead, he grabbed and shook her. Born an irascible bastard, he would likely die as one, he thought.

"Stop screaming and start running," Spensir snarled. "Go with Fergus, I'll get Gilly."

"I...I can't. Not without you," Vorta stuttered, fear choking her voice. The strongest woman he had ever known, Vorta did not admit to needing anyone or anything lightly. So when she did, he listened.

She came from a background that few women on Faltyr survived, much less escaped. She fled her broken home as a teen after ending her father's string of indecencies and abuses with a sharp kitchen knife, a torch, and a flagon of lamp oil. Evading capture from the local authorities, Vorta made her way to the ancient port city of Kingsport. Unlike the countless harlots on the streets of that vast city, she relied on guile, light fingers, and a sliver of steel to survive.

According to Vorta, she didn't put much faith in men until she'd met him. She considered him to be the exception to her rule, a man who treated her like an equal and loved her despite her vicious, violent nature. He didn't even deserve it. He felt unworthy.

Spensir looked at the pile of debris and then back at the face of his lover. Seeing the red welt rising on her face, he understood that their love was not perfect but it was genuine. He fancied them a match made in the Nine Hells, two demon lovers adrift on a sea of fire.

Spensir kissed Vorta roughly but passionately. Her lips yielded to his own as he drank in her taste one final time. Whether they lived or died this night, he resolved to do it by her side. He figured that he owed her that much.

"Alright," he relented, leaving poor Gilly to fend for himself. The old man's screams followed Spensir into the night.

Spensir clambered out of one of the rear windows of the temple. Spying no immediate threat, he turned to help her through the window frame. He flattened himself against the structure, waiting alongside her in the shadows to see if Fergus or Gilly would make it.

Fergus emerged from the ruined temple, carrying the map case clutched in one hand. Spensir scolded himself for forgetting one of the three keys to their salvation. Though the items had led them here, their prize still eluded them. The map of the island didn't indicate the location of the Hallowed Vessel beyond the vicinity of the temple. The compass needle remained fixed on the ridge spur but offered no further leads to the ship of legend.

Perhaps there was another way to divine the vessel's precise location. After all, its owner had hidden it right beneath their feet. *Of course*, Spensir thought, *the spyglass!*

Withdrawing the device from inside his shirt, he surveyed it for any signs of damage. The sighting instrument looked to be intact. In spite of the shipwreck and their ordeals on the island, not even a scratch marred its perfectly crafted lenses.

Extending the spyglass, he pointed it at the overgrown grass at his feet. What he saw took his breath away. The view shifted from grass, to soil, and then to rock before giving way to a confusing series of tunnels honeycombing the landform. His stomach churned. The nauseating feeling reminded him of bad experiences manning the crow's nest on rough seas.

As Spensir adjusted the focal length of the device, it penetrated farther into the depths of the labyrinthine complex. Its lenses brought the interior of a subterranean cove into startling focus. And, lo and behold, he spied what had to be their coveted prize. Frayed hawser ropes secured the bollards of a rotting plank pier to the starboard side of a magnificent ship, a lorcha missing its figurehead.

"The Hallowed Vessel," he mused aloud.

"You've found it?" Vorta and Fergus asked at the same time.

"I can see it. But how in the Nine do we get to it?"

"There's got to be another way," Fergus commented.

Vorta asked, "Wouldn't they have had to sail it here?"

Grabbing her again, Spensir kissed her.

"Out of the mouth of a babe," he jested, releasing her.

He devised a plan of action. It involved a dangerous, desperate assumption, but proved to be their best bet in these circumstances. Shouting to be heard over the beast's shrieking, he relayed the kernel of his idea to Fergus and Vorta.

"We sneak around yonder tower while that beastie is occupied. Make for the gate and then the village. We'll slip back to the river and then swim for it from there."

"Swim for where?" Vorta asked, looking perplexed.

"The cliff face. Below the keep. There's got to be an opening into the cove. They had to sail the ship in there somehow."

"But we would have seen it."

"Not if it was concealed by magic."

"If it's hidden, how're we going to find it?"

Tucking the spyglass back into his waistband, Spensir replied, "Leave that to me and this 'ere little wonder."

"Are you sure about this?" Fergus interjected.

"Enough to stake my life on it...and yours. Now follow me."

Spensir headed toward the tower, surprised that Fergus had dared question his orders. His subordinate's lack of confidence disturbed him but he dismissed it. What did a simple quartermaster know about leadership anyway? Spensir was the captain after all, and the captain would have his prize.

Chapter 15

Despite his aged appearance, Rayne found Caayl quite insatiable. After securing themselves inside the library's anteroom, they made love several times. Now as the knight slumbered on her exposed bosom, Rayne stroked his salt-and-pepper hair once again. Though he slept soundly, sleep eluded her. Conflict raged inside her.

She had been unable to find a convenient time to mention the Hallowed Vessel to Caayl or any of the survivors in the manor house. After serving with Spensir and the others on multiple expeditions, she wanted to give him the benefit of the doubt. Why would they have murdered Donal and taken off with the maps? Even now the whole situation made no sense to her, unless Vorta had something to do with it. *That had to be it*, she concluded.

Rayne considered the troublemaking bitch nothing but bad news. Ever since Spensir had fallen under her sway in Kingsport, he'd gone from selfish and irascible to violent, moody, and ruthless. Insanely jealous, Vorta had even driven a wedge in Rayne and Spensir's longtime friendship, turning him against her shortly after his "promotion" to first mate.

The *Nightsfall*'s original first mate, Obadiah, had disappeared under similar circumstances as Donal Cadogan. Gneut conducted no investigation, unwilling to believe the worst about Spensir. The captain had promoted him to first mate following Obadiah's funeral.

However, rumors persisted amongst the crew that Spensir, prompted by Vorta, had pushed Obie overboard during a raging tempest off the coast of Panglov. Until the disappearance of the Cadogan twin, Rayne had never paid any heed to the idle gossip whispered amongst the *Nightsfall*'s crew. Her loyalties remained with her friend, long after he ceased treating her as such.

Now, she didn't know what to believe. Had she allowed her feelings for Caayl to betray her allegiance to Spensir and the other crewmembers? For better or worse, she had cast her die with those in the manor. At least she'd done it for love.

Thanks to her superb hearing, Rayne didn't mistake the wyvern's attack on the chapel for thunder. In fact, the sound of broken glass intermixed with human screams brought her off the table so fast that she almost rolled the sleeping knight onto the floor. Fortunately, the knight caught himself, staggering to his feet.

Alarm evident in his voice, he inquired, "What's going on? Are we under attack?"

Pulling on her leather basque, she responded, "Not us. But I think those poor bastards in the chapel may be."

Dressing in haste, the lovers spared little time for affection. Even so, Rayne liked that Caayl helped tighten the last few straps on her leather breastplate. Leaning into him, she enjoyed his warmth, settling for the diligent squire rather than the animalistic lover.

Returning the favor, she girded his weapon belt about his waist. Smiling coquettishly, she snuck in a hug amidst aiding her knightly love. Looking up, Rayne could tell by the wolfish grin on his face that her brief embrace had not gone unnoticed.

Caayl kissed her and said, "I wish we had more time—"

Placing a finger to his lips, she interjected, "We have the rest of our lives."

"Agreed," he replied, his familiar, boyish smile returning.

Entering the main library, Rayne let him lead her. She rarely followed any man, save Gneut and her father, but she would follow her love through the gates of any of the Nine Hells.

Approaching the others at the open window of the library, Caayl commented, "I'd hoped we might actually get some sleep."

"No chance of that with you," she teased.

Turning from his place at the window, Breuxias jested, "You can sleep when you're dead. Right now, we have much work to do."

Though she feared the tall man's answer, she asked, "Work?"

Breuxias gestured across the courtyard at the besieged temple. From the window, she could see the winged beast perched on the ruined stained glass dome of the chapel, using its tail in an attempt to spear the sailors trapped below. The creature displayed a rudimentary level of intelligence by shifting support beams and smashing away panes of glass that impeded its hunt. Intellect made beasts even deadlier in her experience but it did not make them invincible.

Mercifully, when the wyvern withdrew its stinger from inside the chapel, no victim dangled from its menacing tip. The monster opened its triple-hinged mandibles, revealing a wide, toothy maw. Its frustrated shriek caused Rayne's sensitive ears to ring.

Though Yax cringed under the audible assault too, she thought he looked unimpressed by the wyvern's display. If anything, the Wand Bearer appeared bored by it.

Breuxias did not share his companion's impassivity toward the situation. Frustration and quiet rage colored his face as he watched the monster's attack on the temple.

"I'm done," Breuxias spat. "I'm sick of running. Let's fry this damn chicken."

"Agreed," Yax said. "The hunt begins."

"Hunt?" Rayne asked. "Are you serious?"

"I believe that the Goddess steered us to this accursed place to cleanse it," Sir Caayl replied. "So let's do it."

Rafasi said, "I agree. Let us pray Ishta'Kahl protects us all."

Rayne could not believe that Caayl had consented to this madness. What did they hope to do against a foe so powerful? A veteran of many campaigns in her own right, her expertise involved small-unit actions and missions that utilized her roguish skills. Taking on something the size of a juvenile dragon required a level of might and magic far beyond the ken of what she could muster.

Trying to inject some rationale into the conversation, she asked, "And how do you intend on slaying this beast?"

"I agree with Rayne," Dor said, joining the others at the window. "I can't think of a single way to do it that won't likely kill all of you in the process."

"I'm having the same dilemma," Yax said.

"Don't worry," Breuxias boasted, "I've got that covered."

"You've got it covered?" Yax asked. "Now I am worried."

Breuxias smiled broadly. Turning to the wizard, he asked, "Can you make something bigger without killing us all in the process?"

"Bigger?" Dor replied, sounding baffled but intrigued.

"Yeah, bigger."

The scarred, tattooed brute came off as someone whose plans often involved wrestling something to the ground and then ripping off its appendages. Rayne did not like Breuxias's insinuation. The first image that sprang to her mind involved a giant version of him leaping onto the temple and tackling the wyvern.

But Breuxias had a simple, elegant idea that might actually work if implemented correctly. If it didn't get Yax killed first, she fretted. The plan called for the elf to draw the beast away from the temple and then distract it long enough for Breuxias and Dor to slay it. Yax would not be alone though. Someone would be there to run interference if things went sideways.

"I'll--" Caayl began, only to be cut off by Rayne.

"I'll do it," she volunteered, surprising everyone. "So let's do this before that thing out there eats more of my friends."

As they exited the bronze double doors, Rayne pointed the handful of arrows toward the ground. If they had to flee, she didn't want to have their razor sharp tips anywhere near her. Running with scissors could be dangerous, but running with arrows could be downright deadly.

Rayne and Yax crept across the courtyard, allowing their eyes to adjust to the darkness. As her vision shifted to the new spectrum, she scanned the area between them and the temple for Glynn's bow. Although Breuxias had pointed out its general location from the upper window, finding the abandoned weapon amongst the undergrowth could be tricky.

Crossing the overgrown bailey, she tried to keep her focus on the weeds and off of the raging wyvern. Though knowing the creature by name brought some level of comfort, her primordial fears of all dragon kith and kin erased her earlier bravado. As she advanced, Rayne forced herself to fight the panic rising in her chest.

Strolling beside her, Yax'Kaqix hummed to himself in the tongue of the Unen'ek, a dialect all but a mystery to her. Blasé about the whole affair, he moved in an almost lackadaisical fashion across the bailey of the haunted keep. To her, the preening elven Wand Bearer embodied coolness under fire, a relic of a bygone age.

Sudden movement beyond the broken tower drew their attention. Before Rayne could discern the identity of the figures moving past the shattered structure, Rafasi's voice bellowed from the window of the library.

"Spensir's getting away! He's heading for the gate!"

Blind by natural design but certainly not deaf, the wyvern snapped its eyeless head around in the direction of the sudden sound.

"Thanks," Yax yelled. "Now we all know, fool!"

Rayne watched as the wyvern leapt from the temple dome, swooping toward her and Yax. Unable to tear her eyes from the menace, she cried, "What do we do now?"

"Back to the keep," he barked. "We're aborting."

Spotting Spensir heading toward the gatehouse, she knew that she had to stop him. They needed those maps and she needed answers.

"To the Nine with that," she replied, dropping the handful of arrows. "I'm not letting them escape with the maps."

Leaving Yax to distract the wyvern, Rayne sprinted toward the open gate. Hazarding a look behind her, she watched in awe as the elf spun, twisting out of the way of the monster's tail as it whizzed past his head. Striking the ground hard, he rolled into the undergrowth.

Realizing the immediacy of her peril, Rayne dove to the ground, sliding on the hard gravel of the carriage road. She grunted as the force of the impact knocked the wind out of her. The wyvern overshot her small form lying in the gravel roadbed, its claws missing her vulnerable flesh.

Bruised and bloody from her power slide on the rough stone path, Rayne staggered to her feet. Regaining her balance, she hurried to intercept Spensir and his cohorts. Sprinting past the Lord's stables, she realized that their circuitous route around the sundered tower would allow her to intercept them. But what would she do then?

Alone against three armed individuals, one of them her dubious friend, Rayne prepared for hostile negotiations. Lifting her long-bladed fighting knife, she assumed a defensive stance between Spensir and the gate.

As he ran for the gate, Spensir cried, "Get outta my way!"

"Never!" She cried over the shrieking sound of the wyvern. Out of the corner of her eye, she could see Yax blazing away with the jade wand, trying to buy her time. "You're not going anywhere with those maps."

Spensir set his jaw and drew his sword.

"I'm not dying here," he shouted. "We're gettin' to that ship if'n I go around you or through you. Now move or you're dead!"

Despite his harsh words, Rayne remained unconvinced. Though his voice dripped with venom, fear filled Spensir's eyes. To her, he looked more like a panicked steed than a cornered lion.

The crunching sound of gravel drew her attention, ending their brief standoff. Caayl approached at a rapid pace, making a mad dash across the courtyard toward the gate. Pain stitched his face, but he accelerated rather than slowed as the blinding sensation increased.

Spensir slipped around her as the knight's approach distracted her. By the time she spun back around, her former friend had gotten a good lead toward the gate. Even as Spensir fled, Caayl maneuvered to cut him off before he reached it. Both men ran as if possessed.

Fergus attempted to flank her and Rayne reacted, sending her dagger deep into his exposed belly. He grunted as the blade skewered his liver, coating her hands in his sticky, warm fluids. Fergus was no longer a threat. But where was Vorta?

The stabbing pain in Rayne's vulnerable bosom provided the answer to that question. Looking down, hot blood already dribbling from her lips, she saw a stiletto embedded in her chest. Turning slowly, she faced her attacker. Vorta held Rayne in her arms as if the duo were locked in a macabre dance step. Smiling wickedly, her killer twisted the vicious blade, causing Rayne to cry out despite her best efforts.

Sir Caayl glanced back at her, his eyes full of horror and fury. As Spensir tried to rush past him, the knight screamed like an infernal beast. Swinging downward, he sliced the first mate from collarbone to buttocks.

Bathed in the blood of his enemy, Caayl turned toward the women. Wiping the back of his hand across his face, he only managed to create more of a mess. The knight looked unhinged.

Jerking the stiletto from Rayne's bosom, Vorta tossed it away into the night. Choking on her own blood, Rayne struggled to breathe as Spensir's wench lowered her to the ground. She watched as Caayl advanced on Vorta. The grin on his face seemed inhuman, even demonic.

Stepping away from her victim, Vorta smiled at Caayl. Looking left, looking right, she had nowhere to go. Yax and the wyvern fought near the manor, and Caayl positioned himself between her and the gate.

"You can't kill an unarmed woman, can you, knight?" Vorta taunted. The shaky singsong quality to her voice failed to mask her terror. "You took an oath. You can't do anything to me. I'm a defenseless damsel now."

When Vorta relied on her natural charm to save her, Rayne realized she'd not only doomed herself but damned Caayl as well. Screaming again, he swung across Vorta's midsection, slicing her open and spilling her guts onto the gravel. As bitter tears ran from the corner of her eyes, the mortally wounded wench sunk to her knees. She clutched at her innards as desperately as she clung to life.

Summoning the last of her strength, Rayne beseeched Caayl to stop, to show mercy, but he stood unmoved. Looming over Vorta, he raised high his broad sword and stabbed downward. The blade penetrated her throat, not stopping until it was sheathed hilt-deep in her torso.

Placing his boot on Vorta's chest, he kicked the dead woman backward to retrieve his gore-covered blade. Her savaged corpse fell over onto its back, landing beside Rayne on the unforgiving stone, leaving both women's lifeless eyes to stare up at the starry night.

***

Yax'Kaqix stood at the open window of the Lord's library. His glowing eyes narrowed to mere slits as he watched the wyvern ransack the temple across the bailey. The cries of those trapped inside the chapel mixed with the shrieking sound of the frustrated, hungry creature.

Yax admired the display of ferocity and fury. The wyvern proved an impressive beast but not an invincible one. In his considerable combat experience, nothing was invincible. Means existed to thwart, subdue, or slay anything on the face of Faltyr or inside its rotten core for that matter.

For him, the real question became collateral damage. Any invocation capable of damaging the wyvern would set the aging temple ablaze or raze it to the ground with Spensir and the maps inside. Collapsing the structure could prevent them from making it to the ship at all. At least without rappelling gear and a perilous swim.

However, one solution offered a higher chance of success: to lure the wyvern across the courtyard toward the manor house. He doubted any of the others, save Breuxias or Rayne, would be fast enough or strong enough to survive in the open bailey alone with the rampaging creature. For the plan to work, Breuxias had to be on the roof with Dor which left Rayne to run interference if required.

Even if he risked the fallout from his more fiery spells, Yax knew that it would be almost impossible for him to cast a devastating spell on the run. Channeling the energy required to stop the wyvern in its tracks would take enough time to leave one vulnerable to attack. This quarry was no goblin horde or ogre tribe. This monster was what Breuxias referred to as a "one-hitter quitter."

So how would they slay it without getting themselves slain? Breuxias had provided the answer; for once, his idea might succeed without radical improvisation or a near-death experience on his part. Apparently, his friend labored under the delusion that he was either invincible or insane. Last time Yax checked, he was neither. As he reflected on their past association, he regretted telling the human his favorite Unen'ek proverb: An elf's life upon Faltyr is warfare.

But he would not be alone in this endeavor. Rayne surprised him by volunteering to accompany him. Sir Caayl protested her involvement, but she made him see reason. Rafasi and he spoke bravely enough, but Yax considered the holy warriors of little use in a wyvern hunt. He'd rather have the half-elf guarding his back with Glynn's bow than suffer through the pious pair of humans watching out for his soul.

Parting ways with Breuxias on the stairs, Yax teased, "Keep an eye on that one. Dor's liable to be as dangerous as the wyvern."

"Thanks," Dor replied, grinning despite the elf's jest.

"Don't do anything stupid down there," Breuxias chided.

"I wouldn't think of intruding upon your area of expertise," Yax gibed, saluting his comrade.

"Come on, mage," the brute began, turning for the stairs. "We'll die of old age before the Old Man here gets tired of his own jokes."

As he and Rayne descended the stone steps to the ground floor, Yax prepared himself for the trials ahead. Chanting in his native tongue, he summoned the energies necessary for the weaves that would be required to ensure his survival in the upcoming encounter. Although he would be unable to use the most devastating spells in his arsenal, he knew stacking several defensive layers would boost his survivability.

Emerging from the double doors of the Lord's manor, Yax strode out onto the porch. Looking up at the veiled moon, he watched as clouds swam across its pale face. Even without the aid of starlight, he saw everything within the walls of Frolov Keep with startling clarity. Even for an elf, Yax possessed superb dark vision; he'd honed the ability during centuries of fighting minions of the Underworld.

They covered less than half the distance to Glynn's bow when they spied motion between the temple and the sundered tower. Spensir, Vorta, and Fergus raced across Yax's field of vision. But he didn't see any sign of Gilly, the *Nightsfall*'s carpenter.

Before Yax could decide how to incorporate this new variable into the plan, the pot went to pieces.

Rafasi's voice bellowed from the window of the library, "Spensir's getting away! He's heading for the gate!"

The warning alerted the wyvern as well as the fleeing sailors to their presence. And Yax let the foolish priest know the import of his mistake. The monster leapt from the temple dome, swooping toward them.

Her eyes riveted on the menace, Rayne cried, "What do we do now?"

"Back to the keep," Yax barked. "We're aborting."

"To the Nine with that," Rayne replied, dropping the handful of arrows. She pointed to the sailors rushing toward the gatehouse. "I'm not letting them escape with those maps."

The pot crumbled all around Yax. She rushed to intercept Spensir and his coconspirators, leaving him to face the wyvern alone. The winged demon dove at him, tucking its wings to speed its descent.

Twisting out of the way of the monster's lethal tail, Yax felt the stinger whiz past his head. Striking the ground hard, he rolled away into the bushes, happy to have something soft to cushion his fall.

As the wyvern maneuvered for another pass at him, he sprang to his feet, drawing Starkiller from his belt. The end of the wand flared to life, firing one blast after another at the beast. The wyvern howled as the searing-hot beams sought and then found their target.

On his periphery, he caught sight of Rayne sprinting past the Lord's stables. Raising her elven blade, she assumed a defensive stance between Spensir and the gate. Sighing with relief, Yax hoped that her luck would hold out against Spensir and his cohorts. For the moment, he had bigger prey in mind.

As the wyvern dove toward him again, he raised the hand bearing the cursed spider ring. Though the nasty thing took a physical toll on anyone not native to the Underworld, elves could wear it for some time without incurring any significant side effects. However, calling upon the powers of the ring was painful, even draining. Still, the item came in handy during tight spots like these.

The ring responded to his mental command instantly. Yax ground his teeth together as his blue blood flowed into the ring, providing the fuel for its dark magic. Calling upon one of its abilities, he anchored strands of webbing to the gatehouse and the broken tower. Then he utilized the same simple rope trick he'd used on the deck of the doomed *Nightsfall* and later on the burned bridge. Through the Aethyr, Yax tied the sticky silk into a series of complex knots, effectively creating a net.

Unable to halt its forward momentum, the wyvern slammed into the webbing. Plummeting to the ground, it struggled to free itself from the improvised trap. As the wyvern clawed and snapped at its tethers, Starkiller fired blast after blast into the thrashing beast. The white-hot energy burned holes through its wings and left the scales protecting its back and flanks glowing red as the eyes of the elf.

Yax hazarded a glance toward the manor house, spotting Dor and Breuxias amidst the ruined siege equipment on the roof. However, the sight of Sir Caayl and Rafasi sprinting out of the manor alarmed him. Yax's concern turned to annoyance once it became clear that the humans had different destinations in mind. While the knight closed on Rayne, Rafasi headed toward the Temple of Damarra.

Yax needed additional factors to manage on this battlefield like he needed another hole in his ears. Though he had commanded untold thousands of men, elves, and even dwarves in his lifetime, the majority had been trained combatants following a cohesive plan of action. Sir Caayl was blinded by his concern for Rayne, and Rafasi was no soldier at all. In Yax's mind, despite their good intentions, they might as well be meat for the beast.

Still, some hope existed for the do-gooders. If Yax could get the wyvern into position, Breuxias and Dor would get their shot at dispatching it once and for all. Firing the wand as he ran, he took a circuitous route toward the manor, keeping the wyvern well away from either Rafasi or Sir Caayl. However, Yax underestimated the beast's strength and agility. It almost cost him his life.

Spreading its web-covered wings, the wyvern leapt into the air like a springing cat. Yax rolled out of the way at the last instant, avoiding the crushing weight of the beast as it crashed to the ground.

The eyeless monstrosity's jaws snapped after him, but he moved faster. Drawing Demon Queller with his free hand, he cut upward in the same motion, severing one of the wyvern's sensor cones protruding from the corners of its tri-hinged mandibles.

Emitting an ear-piercing shriek, the wyvern backed away from him, swinging its tail defensively. Leaping backward, Yax evaded the razor-sharp stinger of the berserk beast. Using his momentum, he executed a series of back handsprings designed to put as much distance as possible between him and the wyvern before it could relocate him.

Risking a quick glance toward Rayne's last position, Yax saw the disaster about to unfold. Caayl sprinted toward her and the others at a rapid pace, making a mad dash across the courtyard toward the gate. Spensir fled in the direction of the gate, but the knight maneuvered to intercept him. His lead on Caayl waned with each passing second.

The elf wished his allies success as he turned to face his own opponent. As the wyvern maneuvered into the final trap, he signaled Breuxias and Dor by firing a single blast from the wand into the sky.

Yax watched as Breuxias hurled a ballista bullet from the roof of the manor. As the stone projectile reached the apex of its arc, Dor emitted a ray of magical energy from his open palms. The hurled stone swelled to the size of a boulder before crashing down on the exposed backbone of the wyvern. Crushed like a bug, albeit a gigantic one, the beast lay twitching in the courtyard, viscous green fluids oozing from every orifice.

With the wyvern dispatched, Yax shifted his attention back to the situation at the gate but far too late to alter its tragic resolution. Sir Caayl stood alone amongst a field of corpses. Fresh tears streaked his gore-covered face. Yax reminded himself that all victories came at a price. Judging by his vacant stare, the knight had paid too much this night. He'd likely never be whole again.

Chapter 16

A single source of illumination lit the courtyard. Sir Caayl stared at Rayne's burning form amidst the conflagration. The dancing flames sheathed the fallen woman, obfuscating her form as the raging pyre consumed her.

Tears stung his tired eyes but neither the smoke nor even the gruesome sight of his beloved's body upon a pyre caused him to weep in such a fashion. By the gods, it was the smell. Despite the pungent odor of the dead beast, the sweet stench of Rayne's charred flesh invaded his nostrils, a particular smell all too familiar to a veteran of the Blood Wars.

Caayl found it difficult to take a breath. The knight had stood by unfazed as Orson's troops put entire elven tree cities to the torch, rounded up the survivors like livestock, and then shipped them south, never to be seen or heard from again. Now, the death of a single half-elven woman had reduced him to tears.

He'd loved Rayne from the first instance he'd laid eyes on her. And his love for a single half-breed had been enough to shield him from the mass hysteria and hate that had swept through the populace of Oparre in the wake of King Orson's Purity Laws.

The torch he'd carried for Rayne had been the reason why he had risked everything to save her people's greatest hope. His treasonous act had led him south to Kingsport and into her welcoming arms. He had taken their chance meeting in a tavern as providence rather than coincidence.

How could he have been so wrong? Hadn't the Goddess put his unrequited love in his path as a reward for standing up against genocide and tyranny? Or had Rayne remained forbidden fruit despite his sacrifices?

Sir Caayl had violated his vow of chastity. He had risked what honor he had left for a taste of Rayne on his lips. Now she was dead, her body stacked on a bonfire like so many of her elven relatives. The horrible irony weighed upon his soul.

Had Rayne been slain to punish him for his indiscretions, his sins? Had she paid the price to remind him of his sacred duty to a higher power, one that looked as harshly upon blasphemers as oath breakers? After all, he had become both in the span of the last year.

Love blinded me, he lamented. His fateful decision to pursue Rayne had caused him to breach his sacred vows to Ishta'Kahl. His affection for his childhood love had distracted him from his sacred duty, from his promises to the Goddess and the fellow knights of his Order. While others risked their lives to stand against the king, he squandered their sacrifices on the fruits of temptation, sin, and lust.

But his love for Rayne had also led him. If he had not loved her, he would not have taken the actions that had caused him to flee his homeland. As a result, his love for her had not only saved lives but had restored hope to an entire people. His love for her had guided his every action from childhood until this fateful night. In fact, Caayl had sworn to love her until his dying breath long before swearing any oaths to Ishta'Kahl.

His moral quandary arose from this paradox. He could not reconcile his faith in his Goddess with his love for Rayne. In the end, he knew that he could not choose. His loyalties would have remained divided for the remainder of his days. So Ishta'Kahl had chosen for him.

He wept fresh tears. The duty-bound knight wiped them away from the corner of one eye. Holding that forefinger aloft, Caayl noticed that the light from the pyre seemed to coexist within the teardrop. Something about the duality of the firelight comforted him. Even as Rayne's body burned, he knew that her soul had flown free.

Now her soul existed elsewhere. Where had she gone? Would she be accepted into the Gates of Heaven, or would she be tortured in one of the Nine Hells? Or could her father's people be right? Would she transition from one mortal shell to another?

As his fragmented mind turned to elves, Sir Caayl became aware of Yax'Kaqix's presence at his side. The elf stared at him with intensity that rivaled his preoccupation with the pyre. Could Yax read his mind? Or see the stains upon his soul? Either way, the ancient being might have answers to the nagging questions that had set his brain ablaze. At this point, any answer would be reassuring as his own crisis of faith prevented him from finding solace in his own beliefs.

Eyes riveted on the flames, Caayl inquired, "What do you think happens when we die? Do we move on or just fade away?"

Instead of answering immediately, Yax gestured to the night sky. Caayl cast his eyes skyward. The Silver Lady and the brightest stars shined through the lingering cloud cover. Even now, Ishta'Kahl kept watch over him, judging him from afar.

Finally speaking, Yax asked, "And what would you say if I asked you to define the nature of stars?"

Caayl replied, "I suppose, if I were to believe my nursemaid, they're pinpricks in the curtain of night through which Kahl the Creator's light shines. But, if I were to believe those who initiated me into the inner mysteries of the Church, they are the wives of Kahl.

"At the dawn of time, the All-Father wept lonesome tears as he roamed the sea of eternal night. His countless tears drifted like seeds upon the wind, carrying forth his greatest hope, a desire for a mate. The fires of creation erupted inside these tears, transforming them into the burning brides of Kahl. Our sun, Damarra, the womb of all life on Faltyr, is but one of them."

"Poetic but inaccurate," Yax responded. "These flaming balls of gas are the true engines of creation for life in this universe. And the balls of rock and water that surround many of them are home to all manner of life. Even in a finite universe, variety is nigh on infinite. But Faltyr is not one of them. Not originally.

"This blighted sphere you call Faltyr is an alien construct, an incubator for a race older than all of us. In my language, we do not call this place by this name. We call it Ono, the Egg. And we wage the Eternal War against the faceless masters of the Underworld and their minions who will stop at nothing to see the Egg's contents nourished, incubated, and hatched, ending life as we know it.

"My people are called the Unen'ek because we are the Children of the Stars. The Cosmic Dragon sent us to cleanse this hollow world of the unholy seed that grows within it. And we cannot fail."

Sir Caayl did not find this unexpected response reassuring. His worldview of Faltyr as a planet seeded by matter from a star brought to life by the will of the Creator comforted him, making him feel a part of something greater, grander, and even universal. Yet, he considered the entire concept of the world as a giant egg incubating some faceless evil maddening, especially if the elves sought to destroy it.

"So what is the point if that is true?" Caayl asked.

"The point is that the same battle being fought here is happening all over the universe in one form or fashion. On alien shores, vastly different species wage unceasing wars against the forces of tyranny and oppression working to return us to the hell of an eternal night devoid of hope for another morrow. Every civilization is a direct by-product of this fundamental conflict between light and dark. We must all choose our side and play our parts. However, most beings live and die ignorant of the conflict itself much less the roles they play in it."

Bewildered by the implications of the elf's revelations, the knight asked, "What does that have to do with where we go when we die?"

Yax responded, "If one was to believe the Old Ones, it has everything to do with it. Those who dedicate themselves to the dark will descend into the Nine Hells to serve their new masters. The faceless masters consume the victims' souls in order to nurture the seed at the heart of the world. Those who fight for the light earn the joys of the heavens to nourish their spirits, purify their souls, and prepare them to wage glorious battle against the dark in their next incarnation."

The knight's brain reeled at the implications. Instead of the multitude raised by Yax's revelation, Caayl asked a single question.

"Where do you think Rayne will go then?"

"From what I observed, she liked to play both sides against the middle," Yax adjudged. "If that is true, I feel sorry for her and pray for her salvation."

"Why so?" Caayl inquired, dreading the elf's response.

"The Old Ones say that the hottest hell of the Underworld is for those who remain neutral in the eternal conflict."

He failed to find comfort in Yax's answer. Instead of a blissful image of Rayne soaring aloft to a new life on a distant world, his mind's eye fixed on the image of his beloved burning for eternity. For his sins, would he burn alongside her? If not heaven, would they at least have hell?

Sighing, the knight confided, "Initially, I joined the King's army to do my duty for king and country. When I swore my allegiance to the Order of Ishta'Kahl, however, I assumed I was dedicating myself to the powers of light. I was wrong. So horribly wrong.

"My kingdom has been twisted by the darkness that corrupts the countryside, the churches, and even the crown. Its people have been led astray, fighting a war that won't end until it drowns the world in blood. Sadly, I was one of them for a time yet my love for a good friend reminded me of my true loyalty to my heart."

"She was more than a friend, I'll wager," Yax commented.

"Aye, in truth she was," Caayl admitted. "We loved each other very much."

"Wouldn't King Orson be furious if he learned that one of his knights loved a woman tainted with elf blood?"

Sir Caayl grunted in agreement. Eyes returning to the pyre, he began, "He had his own son executed for the same treason. My king is mad or possessed. Sir Ausic was right. The Blood War grows in size and scope with each passing day as countries are dragged into the fight."

Yax lamented, "And with the Queen of Silent Brook doomed to die in a dungeon, there are none left on the mainland that can stand against Oparre's might."

"Hope is not lost, my new friend," he replied. "Of my crimes of inaction, I did not add the life of Queen Shy'elle or that of her unborn child. Ausic and I failed to save our Prince, but his forbidden love and their child were saved by these very hands."

"What are you trying to say?"

"On the night Orson ordered his son executed, Ausic and I were supposed to take care of the elven Queen. We couldn't do it. So we fled. He took Shy'elle in one direction, and I rode south with a decoy. I broke my oath. Threw my life away. Fled king and country to end up in the arms of my love. And now she's..."

Caayl's statement remained unfinished as his grief overcame him. Yax closed the distance between them, placing one sympathetic hand on the knight's shoulder. As he stared into the elf's emotion-filled eyes, he realized Yax had suffered losses greater than any human could experience in a single lifetime.

In a conciliatory tone, the elf admitted, "I have thrown away a dozen lives. Walked away from fate. Turned my back on fortune and lost loved ones that no fortune could ever replace. It never gets easier. Not in all of the centuries between my birth and this awful night. I've mourned a wife and my son. You can't save everyone. It's when you stop trying, however, that you start dying."

"I'm trying," Caayl began, wiping his eyes. "But it's harder by the day. And this...this is too much. I want to throw myself on that fire and join her yet I can't break another promise. I have to live, if only for that reason."

"Look at the bright side. Why worry? At this rate, none of you are going to make it off this island alive anyway."

"At least there's a bright side." Sighing, the knight added, "In case I don't survive, I want you to make me a promise."

"A promise?" Yax asked, sounding skeptical. "Elves don't take oaths lightly. Unlike humans, we tend to honor them."

"It's important! The fate of your people is at stake."

"The elves of Silent Brook are not my people," the proud Unen'ek reminded him. "The Winaq'che chose to beat their swords into plowshares and live amongst your people. Where has it gotten them?"

"Will you doom an entire people because of ancient strife and prejudice? Will you be no better than my bloody king?"

After a long moment, Yax responded, "Fine. Confess your sins. Unburden your soul and secure my oath."

The elf traced an arcane symbol in the air between them, leaving fire in the night that slowly faded to nothing. When Yax had finished, Caayl began speaking his mind, his heart, and his soul. Before he had finished the whole sorry tale, the knight's veracity had recruited a powerful ally to his cause. He bound the elf to him with something stronger than magic, something that would ensure the success of his mission should he perish from the face of Faltyr. A promise.

***

Entering through the main entrance of the crumbling cathedral, Rafasi held the lantern before him, allowing it to light his way into the structure's pitch-black interior. Polychromatic glass shards from the ruined window crunched under the soles of his shoes.

Someone or something groaned from outside the reach of the lantern's light. Instead of eliciting fear, the sound filled the Rafasi with resolve. Undeterred, he advanced into Damarra's temple.

Addressing the injured party, Rafasi asked, "Are you hurt? Do you require assistance?"

Another echoing groan issued from the room beyond the vestibule. He prayed that it belonged to Gilly and not some vengeful specter haunting the temple. The exhausted Priest of Ishta'Kahl had performed enough exorcisms for one evening.

As he entered the expansive apse of the church, Rafasi spied a pile of debris that filled the center of the room. Maneuvering around the ambulatory, he searched for the source of the sound until he located the injured carpenter. Steeling himself, the priest focused on the task at hand rather than on the horrifying desecrations that had been perpetrated inside this once holy place.

Gilly lay trapped below a section of timber, one of the rotting beams that had been supporting the now-defunct dome. Though conscious, he did not sound coherent. *Likely a concussion*, Rafasi thought.

Seizing an altar pole once used to light and snuff candles, he tested the length of ash. It proved flexible but strong, having survived the brutal humidity of the island courtesy of a thick layer of varnish. Inserting it between the fallen beam and a sizeable chunk of mortar, Rafasi levered the section of timber off of Gilly's leg.

Winded from his exertions, he took a seat on the temple floor beside the freed carpenter. He positioned the lantern so that he could examine the patient, relieved to see that Gilly remained stable despite his ordeals, although now unconscious. The old man was either hardy or lucky, perhaps even blessed.

Removing the battered haversack from his shoulder, Rafasi delved into its contents. His healing kit had been the single piece of his luggage that the priest had been able to recover from the wrack of the *Nightsfall*. Truly a blessing from the Goddess.

Rafasi extracted a small glass jar from the bag. Uncorking it, he wafted its vapors beneath Gilly's hawkish nose. The older man gasped for air as he returned to consciousness. Tears streamed from his eyes as he swatted at the noxious jar, nearly knocking it from the healer's hand. Laughing despite their dire straits, he replaced the cork and returned the jar to the contents of his healing kit.

"Are you tryin' to gag a maggot with that, Father?"

"Nah, just wanted to wake you from your nap, grandpa," the priest responded. "Wouldn't want you missing out on the fun."

Gilly winced as Rafasi straightened his shattered leg.

"Great," the old man spat through clenched teeth. "A healer with a sense of humor is about as useful as a doxy with a sense of smell."

"Language," he reminded the surly old sailor.

"Sorry, Father. Force o' habit. Am I gonna make it?"

"With proper treatment, you'll live," Rafasi said, flashing a tired but genuine smile. Already exhausted, he knew that his greatest exertions yet lay ahead.

Digging into his kit again, the healer extracted a short, wide ceramic jar. Smearing some of the jar's contents on his hands, he applied the minty poultice to either side of Gilly's arrow wound. After wiping his hands on his robes, Rafasi exchanged the poultice jar for a metal cylinder. Uncapping the container, he poured its silvery contents onto the broken leg. The priest tossed the cylinder back into his bag, satisfied with his preparations.

Their location remained Rafasi's primary concern. The evil forces dedicated to Darconius had desecrated the temple in a thorough fashion. He hoped the light of Damarra and the strength of her daughter, Ishta'Kahl, would penetrate the shadow looming over Frolov Keep. In fact, he went a step beyond hope; he prayed for it.

"In the names of the Daughter, Ishta'Kahl; the Mother, Damarra; and the All-Father, Kahl the Creator, I pray for your healing light, your cleansing fire, to flow forth from you to me, your humble servant. I ask this not for myself but for this poor man. He is not perfect but he is one of your creations. I ask that you fill me with your light, with your fire, so that in your names I may heal this man, restore his flesh and nurture the spark of creation that lies within the soul of all humankind. I ask this not for myself but for Gilly. I ask this in your names."

Channeling the powers of his Goddess, his hands started to glow, building in intensity as he placed them over Gilly's wounds. Face contorted in pain, the old carpenter tried to jerk away. However, Rafasi latched onto him, forcing his patient to the floor.

The priest closed his eyes as the brilliant light radiating from his hands became too much to bear. Gilly thrashed as it flowed from the healer through him yet Rafasi held him tight.

Having exhausted himself as well as the power of prayer, Rafasi released Gilly. The priest sank to the floor beside the carpenter. As he did so, the Goddess's healing light vanished, plunging the interior of the apse back into near darkness.

The weary priest lay there in the small circle of light cast by the lantern. The after-image of the Goddess's fiery light remained before his eyes. As Rafasi blinked, the two balls of fire partially eclipsed each other on the back of his eyelids. He saw in them the Goddess and her Holy Mother, the moon and the sun. Their light had indeed penetrated this dark place.

Rising to his feet, Rafasi felt like a lamb born anew, albeit a sleepy one. Yawning, he retrieved the lantern from the floor. Leaving Gilly to rest, he went in search of water. After his latest exertion, the priest felt as if he'd crossed a desert with a mouthful of sand.

Though further dangers might lurk within the walls of this haunted keep, Rafasi rejoiced that the Goddess still watched over him. He had been a fool to place his faith in men, especially Sir Caayl. What did he need from a fallen knight who would abandon oaths to king and country, one who would violate his sacred vows to Ishta'Kahl? When a priest needed help, he prayed to the gods and goddesses of Faltyr. With their divine aid, why would Rafasi need to rely on mere mortals?

Chapter 17

Breuxias strode across the courtyard toward the bodies of the slain sailors. Behind him, Dor continued to blather about the technicalities of his purported invisibility spell. If the troublesome wizard was a master of anything other than disasters and intrigues, Breuxias concluded that it had to be excuses.

"Whatever," he responded to Dor's remarks. "I don't want to hear about how concealing us from something without eyes is different than being invisible to people. That's obvious."

"We're still alive, aren't we? So the spell worked."

"We're still alive because that thing is dead," he corrected Dor. "And that's no guarantee either of us will live through this night, especially if I can't trust you."

"But—"

"No buts, you're worse than my children about making excuses. At least I can trust them not to put a lightning bolt up my arse when my back is turned."

"You have children?"

"You sound surprised," Breuxias commented.

"Not really," Dor replied. "But it helps me understand why you treat me like a child. You're as bad as Proleus in that regard."

"Proleus?"

"One of the Council of Three," Dor said. "Proleus was the sole member to oppose my selection for this mission. He'd have trusted it to the grasping hands of his apprentice."

Breuxias marked the mage's evident distaste for both individuals. He hoped Dor held him in higher regard than either of them. After all, he had made a genuine attempt at friendship with Dor before the wreck of the *Nightsfall*. He'd even gone so far as to vouch for Dor when Spensir had tried to lynch him.

Squatting beside the first mate's body, Breuxias could feel the mage's eyes on him. Searching Spensir's body for the maps, he ignored Dor for a moment. Breuxias located the compass and spyglass but the maps eluded him. He decided to take Spensir's sword as well, securing the sailor's weapon belt below his magic girdle.

Looking back at Dor, he could tell the mention of the Council of Three had sent the mage's mind back into his shadowy past.

"Check the woman," Breuxias ordered but Dor didn't respond. He barked, "Mage! Did you hear me?"

"Wha…"

"I said, check the woman."

Fixing his eyes on Vorta's brutalized body, Dor sighed. Spurred to action, he knelt beside her and searched her for the map case.

Breuxias checked Fergus's corpse but realized that the quartermaster did not possess the maps. He did, however, take the leaf-bladed sword as it might come in handy.

As Dor rolled Vorta's body onto its side, Breuxias examined the compass and spyglass. The compass needle pointed at the temple rather than magnetic north. He checked the position of the stars to be sure he wasn't mistaken. Curious, he thought. As he peered through the spyglass, Breuxias noticed it enabled him to see through the night with the clarity of an elf, or even a dwarf for that matter.

The brute considered neither of these revelations as important as the discovery of the Iron Circle of Moor'Dru emblazoned on both items. His anger rose as he stared at the sinister symbols. He returned his attention to Dor in time to see the mage extract the map case from beneath Vorta's body.

Blood covering his hands, Dor checked its contents. Holding the maps aloft, he waved them at the brute. Eliciting a frown rather than approval, the troublesome magician returned the documents to the map case. Dor placed the strap of the map case over his shoulders. As he did so, the leather tube came to rest on top of his magic pouch, the Iron Circle prominently emblazoned on both of them.

"They're all here," Dor cheered. "Nice to have my map back too."

Breuxias rushed at the mage, fighting the urge to kill him on the spot. Tired of games, tired of intrigues, and most of all tired of excuses, he vowed that Dor would tell him the truth this time, one way or the other.

Dor started at the suddenness of Breuxias's advance, but the larger man gave the dangerous wizard no time to react. Instead, he seized the mage by his throat, lifting him several feet into the air.

Interrogating Dor even as the mage struggled to breathe, Breuxias growled, "What do you mean, back in your possession? Explain yourself. I'm sick of your lies! What're you hiding?"

"I . . .can . . .explain," Dor gasped, struggling to draw a breath.

"I'm listening," he responded, tightening rather than loosening his grip. "Time's wasting!"

"I . . .needed . . . transport. Mission . . . required . . .it."

The brute eased up on his grip, albeit slightly. His other hand drifted toward the gem set in his magic belt. No novice when it came to interrogation, he had been on both sides of it on several occasions.

"This is your final chance to confess," Breuxias said. "Make it good or I'll twist off your head."

Holding Dor mere inches from his face, he stared into the mage's panic-filled eyes. He wanted Dor to plumb the depths of his dark orbs for any sign of a bluff; he didn't bluff about matters of life and death. He wanted Dor to realize it, even if it killed him. In the brute's mind, this lesson would prove valuable, even if the mage's first chance to apply it came in his next life.

Drawing in what could be his final breath, Dor started to speak. Breuxias listened as the mage told him about his frantic search for a way out of Oparre as the authorities closed in around him. After overhearing Gneut's story about the ship in a port tavern, he had exchanged the map case, containing a detailed map of Moor'Dru and its outlying islands, for passage home to Myth. Fighting to take a breath, Dor assured Breuxias that Gneut had possessed the other maps before their chance encounter in Kingsport.

"So you risked all of our lives to complete some damn mission for the Council?"

"I had no idea Gneut would want to come here straightaway," Dor pleaded. "You have to believe me."

Disgusted, Breuxias tossed him as easily as the ballista bullet. The mage stumbled over the scorched chest, landing on his backside. Rubbing his bruised throat, Dor glared at the brute.

"And why should I do that? All you've done is lie."

Breuxias towered over him, his massive arms folded defensively. He considered the mage's confession to be a good start, but he knew that they were still a long way from full disclosure.

"I didn't realize the extent of the dangers here until I saw the markers," Dor explained. "I wanted to tell you everything but I've been sworn to secrecy by my oath to the Council of Three. I can tell you that the original Protectorate Mages that were sent here trapped the horrors haunting this keep. They deemed it necessary to protect the ship."

"Now we're getting somewhere." Interrogating Dor further, he asked, "Protect the ship from whom?"

"From anyone trying to steal it. Please understand. I'm sorry to have gotten you and the others involved. That wasn't my intention. I never wanted anyone to get hurt, much less killed. I just wanted to go home!"

Breuxias could tell from the miserable, almost pathetic, expression on Dor's face that he had told the truth this time. He even empathized with the young wizard. Breuxias extended a hand, but the mage stared warily at the hulking shadow looming over him.

Breuxias admitted, "Believe me, I understand the oaths of wizards and the extent of their intrigues."

As a young man, he had gotten caught up in the affairs of Metron Illbringer and his charismatic, conniving apprentice, Nistra. While performing an errand for Illbringer, he had suffered extensive burns that forced him into an extended convalescence in the wizard's tower. Once there, Nistra had drawn him into her bed and, by extension, her web of lies. For a while, he had even been manipulated into believing that Nistra carried his baby. In the end, he had slain his rival, Sir Andor, over an unborn child sired by the honorable knight.

Changing the subject, Breuxias inquired, "The glyphs on the map case and these other items are similar to the one on that chest of yours. Care to elaborate on that, or is it a state secret too?"

"They're all variations on the Iron Circle, meaning they're all tied to Moor'Dru," Dor confessed. "The compass and spyglass belong to the ship concealed below this keep. As for the chest, its contents are a state secret and one you want no part of. Trust me. If it wasn't my burden to bear, I wouldn't have a damn thing to do with it."

"Whatever," Breuxias spat. "You've gotten your last warning. Endanger my life with your lies and I'll kill you. Understand me?"

Breuxias realized Dor would only reveal so much. Too bad he couldn't open up the mage with Spensir's rusty blade and read his innards like a diviner. *So be it*, he thought; *we all have our secrets.*

Dor accepted the extended hand. As the other man helped him to his feet, he replied, "Got it."

Breuxias tried to release Dor's hand but found that he could not. Dor had him locked into a grip that defied explanation much less brute strength. He had either managed to cast a weave without words as he sat on the ground or relied on some conjurer's trick to mimic magic.

"And, if you ever put your hands on me again without my permission, I'll kill you. Got it?"

Judging by the intense look in Dor's eyes, Breuxias believed him. The young mage seemed as deadly serious as the mercenary himself had been moments ago. Perhaps Dor might make a good friend after all. Sniveling cowards who hid behind oaths to shirk responsibilities to those around them deserved no respect in his opinion. But Breuxias respected anyone willing to defend those same oaths with their lives.

Smiling with newfound respect for the beleaguered young man, the brute said, "Agreed. I expect nothing less than your best efforts because it'll take that to slay me."

Releasing his new friend's hand, Dor responded, "Understood."

"Good," Breuxias said. "Let's get back to the others."

***

Rafasi returned to the apse of the cathedral, carrying a bucket. Gilly sat on one of the few pews that had survived the dome's disintegration in the wake of the wyvern's assault. Rotating his restored shoulder, the old carpenter marveled at the restored flesh.

"I see you're feeling better already," Rafasi said, setting the bucket down on the pew. He dipped a tarnished goblet in the container.

"Truly a miracle, Father," Gilly said, bending his leg without any visible sign of pain or lack of mobility.

"Thank the Goddess," the priest responded, offering the goblet to the other man. "I am merely her vessel. Now drink this. Your body will be in sore need of it following your ordeals."

Eyeing the cup, the carpenter asked, "What is it?"

"Water," Rafasi explained, "Wasn't sure about the cistern out back, so I purified it and then blessed it."

"Bah! Water?" Gilly spat, recoiling. "Holy at that. Are ya tryin' to poison me?"

Smiling at the old man's jest, he urged, "Drink it. You need to rest while the others decide how to proceed."

"I reckon they'll go after Spensir and the others with that flyin' devil dead."

Rafasi realized the *Nightfall*'s carpenter didn't know he was the sole survivor of Gneut's ill-fated crew.

"I'm afraid that won't be necessary. They're gone."

"High-tailing it is what Spensir is good at," Gilly said then laughed. "That yellow-bellied bastard left me for dead."

"Then perhaps you can find some measure of peace. Spensir, Vorta, and Fergus have not fled. They're dead."

"Dead? Aye, serves 'em right for leaving me behind. Became meat for the beastie, did they?" the carpenter chuckled.

"Nay. Fate had a different plan for them, a tragic one. Rayne tried to take the maps from Spensir and he wouldn't let them go without a fight. In the ensuing melee, Vorta slew Rayne. Sir Caayl flew into a murderous rage, killing the rest of your crewmates. At least that's how it appeared from this side of the courtyard. I could be mistaken. My ears serve me better than my eyes on a moonlit night."

Rafasi regretted that his faith in Caayl had proven to be such a disappointment. He had believed the Goddess had led the two men to each other for a special purpose. However, so far, the priest had seen the knight violate first one and then another tenet of his sacred vows to the Order of Ishta'Kahl.

Rafasi wondered if his purpose was to offer the knight-errant forgiveness for his actions, but that required the other man to seek absolution. Contrary to the Goddess's mercy, Sir Caayl seemed to be interested in invoking the jealous deity's wrath. Instead of falling to his knees before Ishta'Kahl to beg Her forgiveness, the knight prepared a heathen's pyre for the half-elven woman in the courtyard.

Looking away from Rafasi, Gilly said, "The maps, huh?"

"Aye," he confirmed. He added, "As soon as the others find them, they'll be after the ship, I'll wager."

"The ship." Gilly gasped, turning back toward the priest. "How'd you know about that? Did Rayne tell you about it?"

"I overheard the mercenaries discussing it with that mage." Rafasi grinned. "Stone walls and high ceilings make for nice echoes."

"A healer and an eavesdropper," the carpenter chuckled. "A man of many talents, aren't we, Father?"

"Those are the least of them," the priest boasted. "What do you know about the ship?"

"Supposed to be on this blasted island. We were gonna port here and let them acquire it."

"Them? The mercenaries?"

"Extra muscle. But they didn't know what we was after. The captain kept it all pretty hush-hush."

Rafasi picked up the lantern again. Turning the wheel on its side, he extended the wick to its maximum length. The circle of light doubled in size around them, allowing him to get a clearer look at his surroundings.

As he wandered around the ambulatory, the priest inquired, "But why did Spensir bring you here? To ransack this temple? To inflame the hot-tempered Sun Goddess to smite you all? For your trespasses, may Ishta'Kahl protect you and Damarra forgive you."

He cast the light from the lantern over the desecrated and rededicated altar. The altarpiece now portrayed blasphemous scenes of the Underworld and its faceless master, Darconius.

"Let's hope Darconius doesn't take offense to your intrusion either," Rafasi added. "Looks like whoever usurped control of Frolov Keep worshipped the Faceless One."

He prayed for their protection, using the last of the holy water to cleanse the altar stone. As he did so, a putrid smell wafted across his nostrils, causing him to gag. He fought the urge to be ill.

"The taint of evil here is almost enough to make me retch."

"Tis not the evil spirits you smell, Father, but the foul stench o' that dead beastie. Even growing up in a fishing village, it's near enough to turn my stomach."

"Perhaps," Rafasi inquired, "But why here? Why would you look for a ship inside a temple?"

"Not in the church," Gilly corrected him. "Under it. According to the maps, the entrance is located here."

"Under it," he mused, twirling his beard with his free hand. "It makes sense. All of these temples are built on similar principles. Passageways and rooms hidden throughout." Rafasi ran the lantern along the seams of the walls, the edges of the buttresses, and even the joints cut in the floor.

Wringing his hands, Gilly asked, "Whatcha doin' there, Father?"

"Most crypts have hidden entrances to prevent grave robbing and other ghoulish pursuits. Given the geography, I wouldn't be surprised if they are part of an extensive system of caverns."

The lantern flickered as Rafasi passed it along the seam of a wall adjacent to the apse of the temple. He ran the lantern back along the seam. They watched as it flickered once again.

The priest approached the pedestal abutting the closest wall. Examining its exterior, he located a switch underneath the lip of the abutment. Without hesitation or deliberation, he triggered the mechanism, confident it would reveal the entrance to a hidden crypt.

The pedestal recessed into the wall, revealing a cut-stone slab set into the floor. Gears and other machine work became more visible to him through the seams around the slab. A recess in the corner of the false floor panel contained a short lever. Rafasi assumed the mechanism triggered the slab covering the concealed entryway.

Wiping away the dust with his sleeve, he noticed a sigil burnt into the stone slab itself. This symbol bore a close resemblance to the one on the stone markers in the village and the one on Dor's chest. Rafasi recognized it as a variation on the traditional Iron Circle of Moor'Dru. Either way, it was a warning.

"What is it?" Gilly asked.

"Wizard's work," the priest spat. "It appears these magi were thorough in their examination but not in their exorcism of this foul place. Let us hope they have done a better job here."

"Don't have much choice, do we, Father? Can't swim home."

"Prayer can only do so much. Sometimes you have to take a chance and have faith in the wisdom of your actions."

Reaching out with his free hand, Rafasi grabbed the lever.

As soon as he pulled it, the priest realized his mistake. The Aethyr-powered mechanism set into motion, nearly leveling the temple around them. The walls shimmied and shook as a shock wave passed through the entire structure. Pieces of mortar and stone rained down around both men. The Goddess protected them still, Rafasi trusted. After all, the falling debris did not kill or injure either of them.

The stone section in the floor retracted into the wall. In its place, a set of narrow stairs led to a stygian abyss below. Rafasi noticed that the waning light of the lantern failed to penetrate to the bottom of the stairs. Unable to determine how much fuel remained in the lantern, he knew that they would have to hurry; otherwise, they would need to rely on the disastrous magician and the mercenaries to show them the way to the ship. Rafasi never had faith in them and he lost what little he had in Sir Caayl when he stumbled upon him and Rayne together after the exorcism of the wraith.

Gilly grabbed Rafasi as he started down the stairs. Fear filled the carpenter's wide eyes. The whole ordeal had spooked him badly.

"Don't you wanna wait on the others, Father?"

"I'll take the Goddess's protection over the company of their kind any day, my friend; paid killers, murderous magicians, and fallen knights," Rafasi replied, shaking off Gilly's grip. Continuing down the stairs, the priest muttered, "I'm done putting my faith in the fallible."

"Having been shot by one of them buggers already, I'm inclined to agree witcha, Father," Gilly whimpered, following the priest into the crypts below.

The lantern's faint light illuminated the rows of vaults lining the walls of the catacombs. Rafasi saw skeletal remains in every one of them. Random bones littered the stone passageway beyond the stairs.

"On second thought, I weren't never too damn bright," the old man reconsidered, turning back toward the staircase.

"There's nothing to fear here," Rafasi said, grabbing Gilly this time. "What did you expect to find in a crypt? It's dust and bones."

"We prefer to bury our dead at sea for a reason; we don't like looking at 'em."

"At least they don't look back."

"Thank the heavens for small favors."

"Thank Ishta'Kahl," Rafasi chuckled.

After traveling a short distance, they discovered an archway on the left hand side of the corridor. It opened into a new chamber. Open vaults similar to those in the passageway lined three of the four walls. But the skeletons within this section of the crypt wore finery and vestments befitting nobles or senior clergy. Their garments and jewelry identified them as either acolytes or adherents of Damarra. Judging by the dust and decay, all of them died long ago.

Four granite sarcophagi dominated this chamber located on a raised platform in the center of the room. One lid remained intact. Another sat slightly askew while the other two lay broken on the floor.

The lantern did not reach the fourth wall of the expansive room. Rafasi advanced toward the central platform. He planned to use the higher ground to discern whether or not this room was a dead end. If this crypt didn't lead to the ship, one of the others contained within the labyrinthine catacombs should take them to it.

Approaching the first of the open sarcophagi, he lifted the lantern, illuminating its ghoulish contents. The soft light revealed a bone and flesh corpse wearing the tattered vestments of a High Priest of Damarra. The corpse existed in a different state of preservation than the others in the crypt. To Rafasi, it bore a closer resemblance to an Ireti mummy than a mere skeleton.

Beneath the dead priest's tattered regalia, a gold amulet glinted in the lantern light. Clearly not the rosy sun-shaped disc of Damarra, the sigil on the amulet represented dread Darconius, the same unholy symbol used to profane the desecrated temple above the catacombs.

Here lay one of its corrupters, Rafasi surmised. Cursing and crossing himself, he spat on the platform beside the sarcophagus. Moving on, he shined the lantern over the stone coffin with the shifted lid, revealing something far more horrifying than the symbol of an evil, primal god. Its light revealed ruffles, lace, and a tiny mummified hand with painted nails.

He recognized the sunken face of one of the twins pictured in the Frolov family portrait. Her golden locks remained as perfect now as the day her mother painted them. Feeling faint from the stale air, the priest staggered backward before steadying himself against the adjacent sarcophagus.

A bloodcurdling scream cut short Rafasi's prayer for the poor girl's soul. He turned in time to see a desiccated corpse seize Gilly by the head. The crypt thing dug its bony fingertips into his vulnerable eye sockets.

Blood and vitreous humor spurted forth from his ruined eyes as they ruptured, causing the doomed carpenter to howl madly. His legs kicked in little death spasms as the creature drew the dying man to its fleshless lips. Rafasi watched in mute horror as its pronounced canines pierced the old man's flesh.

As the creature fed on Gilly's lifegiving fluids, the priest realized the true scope of the danger. He faced a pack of hungry vampires, alone. The warning above, he thought. It marked their nest.

A scratching behind him drew his attention. Turning toward the cluster of sarcophagi, Rafasi raised the symbol of the Moon Goddess but it was too late to protect him from the servant of the Darconius. The undead priest lifted him aloft with ease, its red eyes boring into him.

"Ishta'Kahl—"

"Will not save you here," the Priest of Darconius interjected.

The vampiric priest sank its fangs into the other man's exposed throat, silencing the Priest of Ishta'Kahl's prayers permanently. As the blood demon drank from him, Rafasi's hand slipped from his holy symbol as his life slipped from this world.

Chapter 18

Dor slowed as he entered the rubble-strewn interior of the temple. He moved through the building cautiously. With the hazards posed by its deteriorating state, the crumbling temple might prove as dangerous as whatever lurked below.

Pausing beside Yax and Breuxias at the top of the staircase that led to the crypt, he asked, "What are we going to do?"

"Too late to do anything about it now," Yax observed. "The ward's broken."

"If that priest isn't dead already," Breuxias remarked, "remind me to strangle him."

Sir Caayl walked past Dor without comment, his eyes fixated on the stairs as he entered the vault. He held aloft a torch in one hand and his sword in the other. Dor assumed that Caayl had taken the torch from Rayne's pyre. He did not fail to note the poetry of the knight literally carrying a torch for his dearly departed.

Sinking the *Nightsfall* had cost a number of lives, but he considered Rayne's death the hardest of all to bear. The realization that he'd cost Caayl his one true love almost overwhelmed him. Dor forced himself to focus despite the emotions welling up inside him.

Their experiences on the island had transformed the knight and, by all appearances, not for the better. Covered in blood, sweat, and grime, he looked like a merciless butcher rather than the pious cavalier Dor had met on the *Nightsfall* a few months ago. The young wizard recognized the haunted look in Caayl's eyes. He'd seen it often enough in his own.

In the short time he'd known the knight, Dor noted many parallels in their lives. Having been responsible for so much death and loss, he felt as flawed as Sir Caayl, as tortured by his past. Something about that realization comforted as well as disturbed the magician. Judging by the condition of his robe, he wagered that he looked as rough as the knight, if not worse.

Dor stopped at the top of the stairs as the inscription over the entrance to the catacombs caught his attention. He read the glyphs burned into the stone, learning that Rafasi's trespass had doomed him and the carpenter, perhaps them all.

Sir Caayl descended the unlit staircase followed by Yax and Breuxias. They advanced along the passageway, ignoring the catacombs' ghoulish contents. Sword and wand at the ready, Yax walked just ahead of Breuxias. Both sellswords trailed the knight by several paces.

As Dor hustled down the stairs, he activated the blackened staff clutched in his left hand. The end of his staff burst into flames, adding a potent new source of illumination to combat the darkness. The light drew his eyes to the vaults lining the walls of the passage. Skeletal remains filled each and every one of them.

Catching up to Breuxias, the mage tapped him on the shoulder. Dor whispered, "We have to get out of here."

"That's what we're doing," the brute retorted. "The ship lies below. You said so yourself. C'mon."

Raising his voice slightly, Dor said, "You don't understand. This is bad. Even worse than I thought."

"Everyone's dead but us," Breuxias barked. "Of course, it's bad! It's downright horrific. But how could it get any worse?"

Down the corridor, a familiar female voice began to recite a singsong incantation. But it couldn't be Sierris, could it? Bones shivered and shook in the vaults around them, sending up a thick cloud of bone meal and dust. Dor coughed and sputtered as he stumbled along the sloping passage.

Wiping the dusty remains of countless dead from his face, the mage snorted, "Thanks. You had to say it."

Sir Caayl cried, "By the gods! What have we done?"

The knight stood in the entryway to an expansive crypt adjacent to the main passage. As Yax and Breuxias rushed in that direction, Dor trailed after them. Reaching Caayl's position, the terrible trio witnessed the same gruesome sight that had so fixated the knight. Dor felt his jaw slacken and his blood run cold.

Rafasi and Gilly were unrecognizable. The ravenous blood demons had torn them to pieces, strewing their body parts and innards about the raised platform and the antechamber of the crypt. The drained bits and pieces of the meddlesome priest and the grizzled carpenter served to rejuvenate the starving cabal of demons.

The vampires had yet to drink their fill, so their orgy of blood continued. Lord Frolov feasted on one of Rafasi's tanned limbs. And his longtime companion, the dread Priest of Darconius, gnawed on a section of intestine as if it tasted like fresh blood sausage straight from the Brackwald.

Sierris stood in an open sarcophagus behind the undead lord. Dor found the necromancer as beautiful as she was terrifying. Bathed in the blood of the priest of Ishta'Kahl, the half-dressed witch gestured as if conducting a symphony of terror. Though her minions concentrated on feeding, she watched Dor and the others, her black eyes boring into his own from across the crypt, yet she did not let their presence interrupt her ritual. In fact, her chanting rose toward crescendo.

Not all of the undead inside the crypt treated Dor and the remaining survivors with such casual disregard. As the vampiric knight suckled on the bloody stump of Gilly's neck, it cast its glowing red eyes in their direction. The blood demon discarded its current repast in favor of fresher prey. Snarling, it stalked across the crypt.

The carpenter's limbless torso landed in the puddle of viscera covering the stone floor. The remaining Frolov twin sat amongst the gore, enjoying her own meal. Holding a liver in her bloody hands, little Sanya tilted her curly head back. She squeezed the ruined organ, forcing its sticky contents to rain down upon her eager lips. She lapped at the bile and blood, relishing every drop. The remaining fluids streamed down her fae face and splattered onto her frilly dress.

Sierris finished her spell before Dor could disrupt her weave. Instead, he watched as disassociated bones pulled together before his eyes, reassembling all but the most deteriorated bodies in the chamber. Animated skeletons moved in the vaults lining the walls of the crypt.

As the skeletal reinforcements surrounded them, Dor returned his attention to the cabal of vampires. Sir Caayl moved to block the vampiric knight's advance, spurring the child vampire to sudden, violent action. Sanya leapt to her feet, charging the tarnished Knight of Ishta'Kahl. He raised his sword in a defensive posture, but Dor realized too late he had no intention of attacking the undead child. Caayl's bloody, bold resolution wavered this once. And it cost him.

Sanya cleared the distance between them with a single powerful leap. Tearing at his throat, she bore the knight to the floor. Blood spurted from his savaged neck, coating Sanya in a fountain of crimson.

Without hesitation, Breuxias rushed forward. As Sanya bared her tiny fangs, he took one mighty swing. The heavy blade of the first mate's sword ripped rather than cut her head from her slender neck. Her curly blonde pate bounced across the chamber into the shadows.

Lord Frolov screamed, "No!!! I'll kill you, bastard!"

Sierris reined in the Lord with a single mesmerizing look.

"We shall flee," she declared. Turning toward the other egress from the crypt, she added, "The servants will handle this lot."

Turning to his few remaining subjects, Lord Frolov mechanically repeated his mistress's orders. Though his eyes never left Breuxias, the Lord followed Sierris toward the rear exit of the chamber, a viable egress now that the protective ward had been disabled. The animated skeletons and lesser vampires moved to cover their retreat.

Dor huddled closer to Breuxias and Yax as the mindless skeletons surrounded them. As the two mercenaries cut down skeleton after skeleton, Dor raised the blackened staff.

He shouted, "Cover me! I'll need a few moments."

The Protectorate Mage wove a particularly dangerous incantation, one available to him thanks to the wondrous staff, a parting gift from old Salaac. Far more than a torch or tool for banishing angry spirits, the black staff allowed him to channel the fires of the Nine Hells.

Though they exchanged concerned glances, Yax and Breuxias swept into action without protest. Dor wagered that the battle-hardened mercenaries had relied on solutions just as dire, just as desperate. He hoped they didn't end up two more people dead because of him.

Yax fired a rapid series of blasts from Starkiller, halting the advance of the armor-clad vampire. The undead knight howled in pain, struggling to shed its red-hot armor. Free of its sizzling hauberk, the vampire drew its rusty broadsword and charged the elf.

Yax whirled his leaf-bladed sword about him in a blur of motion. Two headless skeletons fell to the floor. Even as other skeletons around him clawed at his vulnerable limbs, Yax focused on the threat of the charging vampire knight.

Sparks flew as Yax's vicious blade intercepted the broadsword. The vampire's attack battered the elf backward until its corroded blade snapped against the keen edge of the magic one. The vampiric knight swung the basket hilt of its broken sword, smashing the weaker elf to the floor.

Swarming skeletons clawed at Yax as he lay on the ground. Dor fought to keep the others from ripping his ally apart, but there was no way he'd be able to make his way to the downed elf. Fortunately, as Yax stirred, Dor realized that he wasn't unconscious only stunned. Though the elf didn't appear seriously injured, blue blood flowed from a dozen or more shallow wounds on his exposed appendages.

Using sword and staff, Breuxias fought with an agility and speed uncommon for men his size. Spinning the simple wooden staff about him in a dazzling display, he shattered one skeletal assailant after another with precision blows. However, countless skeletons moved into the room in their herky-jerky fashion, steadily replacing the fallen. Breuxias swept the curved blade back and forth across the undead horde, cleaving limbs and crushing skulls, in an attempt to reach Yax'Kaqix.

"If you're going to do something," Breuxias shouted to Dor, striking down another skeleton, "now would be a good time!"

Disastrous Dor responded by positioning the flaming staff parallel to the floor. As he held it at hip level, rivulets of lava snaked down the burnt black exterior of the staff. The lines of liquid fire swam the length of it, rushing toward the tip. And then nothing happened as the staff's flame sputtered and died.

The awesome heat, sound, and pressure of a controlled volcanic eruption buffeted the narrow confines of the crypt. As a cone of pure hellfire spewed forth from the end of the staff, blinding light flooded the crypt. The spell bathed everything between Dor and the priest of Darconius in liquid flame. The fiery spell reduced any skeleton in its trajectory to ash. It consumed the evil priest too, sending his infernal soul screaming into the Nine Hells.

The surviving vampires howled and hissed, baring their fangs. They backed away from the source of the awful light. Their snapping teeth and inhuman cries rose in intensity until the spell fizzled, plunging the crypt back into darkness.

The flaming jet disappeared as quickly as it manifested, leaving the tip of the staff with the luminosity and potency of an ordinary torch. The amount of devastation wrought by the dangerous spell shocked everyone in the room, even Dor. In fact, it genuinely surprised him that the Hellfire spell hadn't killed them all.

Sierris recovered faster than the other vampires. Plucking a sword from one of the skeletal warriors, she raced for the door recessed into the back wall of the crypt. Lord Frolov and the vampiric knight took longer to recover and it cost them.

Yax swept his blade around in a circle, severing the legs of every skeleton within reach. Seizing the initiative, the elf arched his back and sprang to his feet. Bleeding from countless wounds on his exposed extremities, he raised the jade wand clutched in his left hand.

Before the vampiric knight could recover, he fired two rapid bursts of energy into its exposed torso. Screaming and smoking, the wounded vampire clawed at the evasive elf. Yax dodged away, using his momentum to launch himself into an impressive back flip. Landing in a crouch on the wall, the elf adhered to the vertical surface thanks to the sticky properties of the spider ring.

Filed teeth clenched with grim determination, Yax launched himself from the wall with an incredible leap. Clearing the throng of undead, he rolled with the impact of his landing. Springing to his feet again, he brought his sword around in a flash and cleaved the vampiric knight's head from its neck.

As skeletons closed in around them, Breuxias uttered the command word for his belt. The gem in the magic girdle flared to life as the skeletal dead clawed at his arms and bare torso. He cleared a path around him with a swing powerful enough to turn skeletons to bone meal.

Spinning on the ball of his foot, Breuxias hefted the staff like a spear. Lord Frolov turned to run but reacted too slowly. The brute hurled the staff with all of his enchanted might.

The blunt staff impacted Lord Frolov in the back with enough force to explode from his chest. The improvised projectile exited the wound accompanied by a fountain of blood and bone. Striking the far wall of the crypt, the staff splintered into a thousand gory slivers.

As Lord Frolov's ruined body crumbled to ash, Sierris shrieked loudly enough to cause Dor physical pain. Dropping both chest and staff, Dor clapped his hands over his ears. Her face transformed, revealing the demonic nature that lurked beneath her heavenly visage.

"You'll pay!" Sierris vowed. "You'll all pay for trespassing here. This is my island now!"

Sierris's hands contorted in a series of arcane gestures. The witch flung one gesticulating hand out toward Breuxias and Dor. Black tendrils of corrupted Aethyr energy streaked across the crypt. The lethal weave spared nothing in its path, disintegrating the skeletons caught between the warring spell casters.

Dor grabbed his staff but didn't have time to retrieve the chest. Raising the imbued item like a shield, he shouted in the old tongue of Moor'Dru. As the Protectorate Mage finished the incantation, a shimmering hemisphere of blue energy encircled him and Breuxias.

The tendrils engulfed the Aethyr shield, writhing along its surface like an octopus probing its prey. The struggle proved violent but short-lived as his shield resisted the necromancer's attack. As the tendrils turned to black smoke, Sierris screeched in frustration.

If looks could actually kill, Dor would have fallen dead under the witch's withering gaze. She retreated into the doorway at the back of the crypt. Even as she raced away from the battle, fresh ranks of the undead emerged from the outer corridor of the extensive catacombs.

The sheer amount of bodies buried beneath the Temple of Damarra alarmed the Protectorate Mage to no end. How many generations of noble families and clergymen had been interred in this foreboding place? Had her spell been powerful enough to animate them all? What else had it animated in the process? Would they have to fight Spensir and company all over again or face off against an undead wyvern?

As alarming as Dor found these worrisome thoughts, they did not terrify him as much as the idea of Sierris beating them to the Hallowed Vessel. Even without the compass and spyglass, the ship of legend remained an artifact of tremendous power. Dor couldn't allow the ship to fall into Sierris's possession. His sworn duties as a Protectorate Mage required him to stop her at all costs.

On the other side of the chamber, Yax appeared reluctant to leave his remaining allies in a crypt full of the walking dead. Dor didn't blame him. The undead horde outnumbered them, even after the damage wrought by his fiery spell.

Smashing the skull of another skeleton, Breuxias shouted, "What in the Nine are you waiting for? Don't let that bitch get away!"

With a slight nod to his allies, Yax pursued Sierris into the catacombs below the crypt. Dor and Breuxias stood against a legion of biting, clawing skeletons bent on their destruction. Leveling the staff in the direction of the mindless dead, he prepared to show them why his mentor, Braigen, had dubbed him the "Master-of-Disaster."

***

Yax'Kaqix tracked Sierris through a sloping series of twisting, turning passages beneath the catacombs, yet she left a visible trail through the thick dust and cobwebs. The patches of luminescent mold growing along the walls and floor of the corridors aided his keen dark sight in tracking the elusive necromancer.

The cultures of mold formed a series of large, unfamiliar glyphs. Yax recognized the glowing mold to be a species similar to those used in Free Dwarf colonies. Multiplying rapidly in this environment, the colonies required constant manicuring or a hermetically sealed vessel that restricted their growth cycle. He postulated that they provided directions to the underground cove. Judging by the abrupt change in her route, Sierris labored under the same delusion.

Yax supposed the witch could be leading him into a trap. He had a motto for these types of situations: when in doubt, bet on a trap. That particular caveat rarely led him astray, although it contributed to his reputation as being paranoid.

His constant vigilance did not fail him on this occasion.

The passageway widened up ahead, exposing a grotto illuminated by another patch of the glowing mold. As he rounded the fat stalagmite protruding from the floor of the cavern, a shadow played across the opposite wall. Bringing the blade about in a flash, Yax glimpsed nothing in the dimness, yet he felt someone, or something, watching him. He spun back around, thwarting the vampire's stealthy approach.

Sierris wore a gore-covered diaphanous dress that clung to her substantial curves. Her pale-as-death skin served as a sharp contrast to her long black hair. The dried blood caked at the corner of her toothy grin added to the necromancer's predatory aspect.

Sierris manipulated one slender hand into a series of gestures, invoking the arcane powers at her command. Tentacles of inky blackness erupted from the floor of the cavern to ensnare him. The tendrils writhed about his body, forcing both hands up and away from his wand. Sierris stalked toward him, confident her spell would hold him.

"You've slain my mate and disrupted my plans." Baring her fangs, she added, "But you did free me. So, now, I'll repay the favor."

"That so?"

Bound but not beaten, Yax ceased his token resistance against the painful confines of the necromancer's spell. By biding his time, he'd drawn her close enough to employ the spider ring. Opening his left hand, he fired a ribbon of webbing into her smirking face.

Sierris staggered backward, clawing at the sticky material. While she struggled with the webbing, Yax called to Demon Queller in his native tongue. The searing blade leapt from his hand, whirling about his body in a blur of motion. The smoking tentacles writhed and squirmed before dissipating into the floor of the grotto. When called by its master, the sword returned to his outstretched hand.

He charged Sierris as she cleared her eyes of the webbing. His overhand swing almost became a killing blow, but she blocked it. The collision of the two swords created a shower of sparks. Demon Queller bit deep into the witch's sword, chipping the inferior blade.

Their next exchange proved fast and brutal with quarter neither asked nor given. They fought from one end of the cavern to the other. Both combatants moved with celerity, but the vampire moved with supernatural quickness. However, Yax's masterful skill with a blade kept him fighting on even ground with the blood demon.

Lashing out with a tiny fist, she hammered Yax in the chest, flinging him backward. Landing on his heels, he staggered to a stop several feet away. As Yax recovered his balance, Sierris prepared another weave with one spasmodic hand.

Practically leaping into its master's free hand, Starkiller blasted Sierris before she could finish casting her spell. She started a new weave, but Yax interrupted her with another glowing missile. Though the damage appeared minimal, the multiple impacts from the wand kept disrupting her concentration. The irritating series of blasts drove her from focus to frenzy.

Howling in frustration, Sierris flung her nicked-up weapon at him. Turning sideways to narrow his profile, the experienced duelist pulled Demon Queller to his chest and uttered a quick enchantment. He lashed out with the speed and precision of a cobra, the elven blade striking the flying sword at its tip. Demon Queller sliced through the weaker weapon from blade to pommel. Its two smoking halves clattered to the grotto floor.

Yax rolled Demon Queller over the back of his hand. In this close proximity to the undead thing, its blade radiated enough heat to sear his flesh. His display produced the desired effect, making the pain worth the gamble. Shock and awe crossed the pale face of the female vampire. Fear crept onto her countenance in their wake.

"There are older and scarier things roaming the night than you, fiend," Yax warned as he took a threatening step forward.

Sierris turned and fled into the inky depths of the catacombs beyond the phosphorescent chamber. He pursued the panicked female vampire through a twisting maze of passages. Spying Sierris at the end of a corridor, Yax fired a salvo from his wand at her.

The projectiles missed the evasive blood demon, illuminating a sheer drop into the black below. Sierris slid to a stop, almost plunging over the precarious edge. He halted a few paces beyond him.

"You won't get away that easily," Yax cautioned her.

She wheeled around, facing her pursuer. He had cornered enough wounded beasts in his day to know that they're liable to fight fiercer than ever. He circled toward the side passage to the right of the precipice. She had yet to notice it. For better or worse, Yax had her full attention now.

"It'll be a leisurely stroll to the ship once I've drained you dry, elf," Sierris spat through her prominent fangs. Her human mask contorted, revealing the bloodthirsty beast lurking beneath her perfect porcelain skin.

"Promises, promises," he replied, putting his wand in his belt.

Raising his open palm, Yax started chanting. A ball of spiraling flame materialized out of the Aethyr, called forth from the elemental plane of fire. As he released the sphere, it flared with the terrible intensity of a small star.

Sierris conjured a shield of inky-black energy, but her last minute defense came with explosive consequences for both spell casters. The fireball collided with her shield. The ensuing blast of concussive energy sent them flying in opposite directions.

Groaning, Yax rose from the cold floor of the chamber. Already on her feet, Sierris charged toward him. Calling Demon Queller to him, he caught the sword on the run. Rushing toward her, he roared like a dwarven berserker.

Avoiding a head-on clash with the frenzied vampire, Yax'Kaqix pirouetted on the ball of his foot. Spinning away from her claws, he swung Demon Queller at shoulder level. The elven blade found its mark, slicing through her exposed neck.

The vampire's hissing head sailed past him, landing with an audible plop. Her body stumbled and fell forward, coming to a rest several paces from its severed head. Battered and bleeding, he slumped to the damp floor.

Yax blinked for a long moment. As his eyes fluttered open, he wondered if he'd fallen asleep. Sierris's body had not finished the process of rapid decomposition, so he hadn't been slumbering. Thank the fates, he thought. Breuxias and some of the other guildsmen called him "Old Man" already. Had the brute stumbled upon him asleep by the remains of an adversary, Yax would have never heard the end of it.

A single point of light drew his attention as shadowy figures approached from the direction of the grotto. Summoning his own inner fire, the worn warrior drew strength from its warmth for a final push to reach the ship. He dragged himself to his feet, ready to welcome friend or foe at the point of his sword.

As Breuxias and Dor entered the chamber at the end of the corridor, Yax hunched over the smoking remains of Sierris. One of them made a jest about him looking the part of the vulture, but he was too tired to care. The weary elf felt the weight of his many centuries, but he tried to hide it from his associates.

Relieved to see his companions alive, Yax'Kaqix sheathed his sword, careful not to let his demeanor waver. Vain and proud, he held himself to impossibly high standards. He viewed life as a forge, and he was being tempered by its trials and tribulations. Demon Queller remained unmarred after untold centuries of conflict, so its master felt like he should be as unfazed by his experiences. As he reflected upon his earlier concerns, Yax realized he had contributed to Breuxias's delusions about his aura of invulnerability.

Yax asked them, "Can you get us to the ship? I think I'm ready to leave now."

Poking at the ashy remains, Dor responded, "I believe so. But I'll need the compass. It's one of the pieces missing from the Hallowed Vessel."

"You didn't mention that it was missing anything."

"We've got two of them, the compass and the spyglass," Dor replied. "There are others, but we've got the maps to find 'em. Don't worry. It'll function without every piece but not a hundred percent."

Yax and Breuxias exchanged doubtful glances. Finally, the brute handed the compass to Dor.

"Hurry up," Breuxias urged. "There's no telling how many of those skeletons are back there. I doubt we got them all."

Dor opened the compass's ornate lid, holding the instrument out before him. Its arrow spun on its axis, pointing toward the passage exiting the chamber to the right. Satisfied with the compass bearing, Yax trusted the others to lead the way.

He followed the others down a steep, winding set of stairs cut into the natural stone. The steps wound down until they emerged from the ceiling of the subterranean cove. Torches ensconced along the wall of the expansive cavern flared to life as they descended the staircase. They illuminated the cove as well as their prize.

Moored to a narrow, dilapidated pier, the Hallowed Vessel shone like a precious gem, despite a layer of dust and grime. Rundown storage buildings huddled alongside the dock, their plank roofs rotted away. Untouched by either age or the elements, the ship of legend stood in stark contrast to the moldering decay around it.

Yax regarded the Hallowed Vessel as a work of art, even by elven standards. If he had to classify it, the ship resembled a lorcha, a fusion of eastern and western sailing technologies. Its sails appeared identical to those utilized on Chi'Zhan junks and Unen'ek warships. His people had revolutionized Chi'Zhan shipbuilding millennia ago, and their styles had maintained close similarities, even in the wake of the Cataclysm. The hull of this vessel had a sleeker design, like the shallow draft longboats favored by barbarian raiders.

He realized that Dor's hypothesis had been correct. The ship was incomplete. As they reached the dock, Yax could see that the bow ended abruptly where its figurehead once rested. And neither the anchors nor the sails radiated the same magic as the rest of the ship. Less powerful spell casters than those who'd crafted the Hallowed Vessel had cast the protective spells woven into them.

Impressed by this ship of legend, Breuxias whistled his appreciation as they walked out onto the decaying dock.

"Pretty elaborate for the ass end of nowhere," he commented. "But how are we three going to be able to crew it and sail our ragged hides back to civilization?"

As Yax tested the durability of the gangplank, Dor said, "We have to use the true name of the ship in the old tongue. The captain can then command the Hallowed Vessel to sail with little or no crew. The magic bound into it is very powerful indeed. Not the kind of magic to tamper with without enough expertise in the art of spell craft."

Breuxias replied, "Aren't we lucky to have you along then?"

Dor explained, "These weaves are almost beyond me. If I happen to misinterpret anything or botch the spell, it would be catastrophic."

Following the elf up the gangplank, the brute responded, "Don't let us down then."

Ignoring the middeck cabin for the time being, Yax led them up to the aft castle of the ship of legend. Familiar with similar styles of ships, he deduced the location of its wheel. However, he did not expect the heavy-duty pedestal standing next to the ship's wheel.

Apparently, the ancient magi of Moor'Dru had copied more than the basic design of Unen'ek ships. Yax gazed upon a primitive version of an elven control console, a management device for the enchantments woven into their ships of the line. The panel facilitated control of the ship, but it also acted as a sophisticated antitheft device, tying the captain to his command via a telepathic link.

If the console worked like its elven cousins, the Hallowed Vessel would obey a single master. Its captain either had to be slain or stripped of command utilizing a special sanguine ritual. Amongst the Unen'ek, the sole way to abdicate the responsibility of this honored position required taking one's own life. Yax wondered how closely the shipwrights of Moor'Dru had copied that final detail.

Yax hungered for the power that this vessel would afford him. With the Hallowed Vessel at his command, no enemy would dare stand against him or his companions. With all of its parts at their disposal, they would unlock a relic so powerful that they'd be able to take on a fleet of warships or a flight of dragons.

He realized that the commander of the Hallowed Vessel would also be its slave. He had no more desire to be chained to a permanent duty station, even a mobile one, than he aspired to be Lord of the Jade Throne. The elf valued his personal freedom too much for that kind of commitment.

As a result, a lifetime dedicated to the Hallowed Vessel sounded like a prison sentence to Yax'Kaqix. However, a human from Moor'Dru might be convinced that taking command of the ship of legend was not a burden but an honor, a birthright. If Yax could find someone gullible enough, he might even be able to convince the fool that fate had chosen him.

Turning to Dor, the elf grinned toothily. If the mage didn't end up killing them all, Yax's idea just might work. Only time and the mutable hand of fate would tell.

Chapter 19

Kaladimus Dor stood before the glyph-covered control console of the Hallowed Vessel. Finishing the first part of the activation spell, he fitted the compass into an indentation on the top of the panel. He then read aloud the second part of the spell. As he fell silent again, the mage slid the spyglass into place beside the compass. After full insertion into the pedestal, the device's rear lens glowed green.

A noticeable hum pierced the relative stillness of the cove as a powerful wave of magical energy rippled through the ship. Three rows of crystals grew out of the console. Awestruck, Dor glanced at Yax, but he seemed unfazed by the dramatic revival of the long-dormant ship.

"Is that it?" Dor asked the world-weary elf.

"One final passage. But we need the true name of the ship to complete the enchantment."

"Not a problem. I spotted it under the painting of the ship in the manor." Withdrawing his mission log from the depths of his pouch, he added, "I copied it down in here. But it didn't make any sense to me." Dor flipped through the book until he located the right page.

Yax chuckled when Dor showed him the entry. "Didn't make any sense, huh?" the elf commented, removing a signal mirror from one of his belt pouches.

Holding it against the page at an angle, Yax tilted the mirror until it caught the light from the console properly.

Dor blushed in embarrassment. The damn word was backward. "Oh! *Seadragon.*"

Dor repeated the ship's true name in his native tongue. He waved his hand over the three rows of crystals, causing them to glow in response. Though the outer rows were iridescent, the central row maintained a steady white shimmer. The array of lights on the console left Dor staring in confusion.

Yax inquired, "Is there a problem?"

Not knowing what to do next, Dor asked, "How do we command the *Seadragon* to take us where we want to go?"

Breuxias quipped, "Sail it? It is a ship after all."

Ignoring his comrade's smartass response, Dor eyed the display with a heady mix of hesitation and anticipation. Its glimmering, winking lights reminded him of the fantastic tales of the Aethyr ships that had roamed the wide world of Faltyr during the Golden Age before the Cataclysm.

Judging by its appearance, the Hallowed Vessel—the *Seadragon*—was a relic crafted by magicians obsessed by the legends of the Golden Age. His ancestors had created not only a symbol of bygone days but also one of unfathomable power. Dor felt unworthy of standing on its ageless deck, much less taking command of the *Seadragon*.

Yax had intimated as much, hadn't he? But why would the elf want Dor to be its new captain? After the sinking of the *Nightsfall* and the sanguine events on the island, why would Yax want him to take command of the Hallowed Vessel? Was it his destiny? Or did Yax have some ulterior motive in mind?

"Are you sure?" Dor asked, his voice trembling.

"For the last time," the elf scolded, "take the wheel, imagine a destination, and hold on tight."

"But why me? Surely, you can do it."

"Oh, I can do it. In fact, I want to do it," Yax admitted. "But you're going to do it. It's time you learned some control and responsibility, especially if you're going to be traveling with us."

"Yeah," Breuxias prodded. "And don't sink this one, at least not with me aboard."

"I'll try," Dor muttered, stepping up to the ship's wheel.

"Don't try," Yax admonished, "just shut up and do it."

Sighing, Dor relented, seizing two of the handles on the ship's wheel. He spoke the word for "seadragon" in the secret language of his Order so loudly that it boomed like thunder inside the subterranean cove. As the distorted name of the Hallowed Vessel echoed back to him, a thousand hot pinpricks set his palms ablaze with pain.

Recoiling, Dor released the wheel. Its wooden handles and his palms were covered in blood, his blood. He examined his bloody hands, but he did not find any open wounds. The ship's magic had healed the damage it had inflicted upon him without leaving a single scar. He watched the wheel as the wooden handles absorbed his sacrifice.

After wiping his hands on his ruined robe, he took hold of the sticky handles. *No gain without pain*, he reminded himself. Grasping the handles, Dor jerked reflexively but the pain he'd anticipated did not come. Much to his relief, the ship required no further bloodshed to seal their magical bond.

As the *Seadragon* responded to its new captain's mental commands, the mooring lines untied themselves. Dor gasped as the ties withdrew up the side of the ship and then coiled around their housings. As the ropes settled into place, the lines securing the rigging went into action, manipulating the sails into the ready position. A flutter ran through the sails despite the pronounced lack of a breeze anywhere within the confines of the cove.

As the rudder creaked, the wheel turned in his hands. Though he commanded the ship, the *Seadragon* performed every task on its own. Slowly but surely, the ship tacked and turned until its bow faced the channel that would hopefully lead them out to sea.

The empty deck of the *Seadragon* stood in stark contrast to that of the *Nightsfall*. As unseen hands manipulated the Hallowed Vessel's rigging, Dor recalled the bustling deck of Gneut's caravel when he'd first boarded it in Kingsport. The ship's complement had grown as they'd sailed east, toward Myth.

Every one of them dead now, lost thanks to Gneut's damn fool obsession with the ship of legend. *Too many of them killed by my hand*, Dor lamented. He wanted to weep for the dead but discovered that the tears would not come. Had he grown too haggard for tears, perhaps too bitter? He had neither the energy nor the inclination to probe too deeply into his frayed mental state.

Dor did not speak for a long time. None of them did. The three survivors of the wreck of the *Nightsfall* watched in silence as the Hallowed Vessel passed through the false wall that had concealed the location of the subterranean cove from the outside world. The mage looked over his shoulder as the *Seadragon* emerged from within. He saw a sheer cliff face. Even now, the illusory wall remained seamless.

The *Seadragon* entered the river channel, giving him a clear view of a new dawn blooming on the horizon. His harrowing time in Frolov Keep turned out to be longest night of his young life, even worse than recovering the contents of the chest from the sunken temple on the western edge of the Sands of Sorrow.

Dor knew he should be elated but found no joy in their escape. After their ordeals on the island, he was happy just to be alive. He looked away from the island and the foreboding keep perched high upon the precipice overlooking the sea. If he never laid eyes on either again, it would be too soon.

No one spoke until after the *Seadragon* cleared the bay and made its way out to sea. Damarra crested the horizon as the ship turned toward the destination on Dor's mind: Myth, his home. Though he bathed in the light of the new day, the sun's rays failed to warm him.

Shivering inside his robes, Dor broke the silence.

"I can't believe one person's obsession with this ship led so many people to their doom. It's tragic. What do we do with it now?"

With a chuckle, Breuxias answered, "Do? Captain Gneut, my most recent employer, is dead. As is his crew. The ship is ours, all of ours. Finders keepers."

"Indeed." Yax added, "Finders keepers."

Dor echoed, "Finders keepers."

A smile slowly spread across his face. Acceptance by this bloody brotherhood of adventurers warmed him better than the rays of the morning sun. As he eyed the scorched lid of the chest where it sat by his foot, he wondered if he would have to go it alone after all.

Perhaps Breuxias and Yax would help him safeguard the nefarious contents of the chest until he could get it safely into the Council's hands. In doing so, his newfound brothers and their ship of legend might tip the balance and ensure the success of Dor's mission to save not only Moor'Dru but all of Faltyr.

But that would be another story.

THE END

The Glossary

Term	Definition	Type
Aethyr	The invisible energy of creation-and-destruction that is believed to permeate the universe. This is the energy that all beings that utilize magic draw upon to alter the fabric of reality.	Philosophy
Agranak	Ruinous city where Yax'Kaqix was once turned to stone by a beholder. Breuxias witnessed the event.	City
Ak Islands	Small chain of volcanic islands considered the nexus of the Jade, Nubari, and K'akla Seas. These islands are home to colonies of Unen'ek, Nubari, and even Lizardmen.	Place
Animated Dead	Wandering, controlled, and intelligent versions exist; this classification includes the following: zombies, skeletons, mummies, and flesh golems	Undead
Apsu	God of the Oceans, Currents, Waves, and Sea Life; viewed as an angry sea creature of chaotic and stormy disposition. Sailors, fisherman,	Deity

coastal dwellers, and anyone who must travel by way of the expansive, dangerous seas of Faltyr make sacrifices and offerings to Apsu. Called Dagon by the Nubari.

Aray	God of War, Glory, Battle, and Patron of Soldiers and Mercenaries; called Guan Di by the Chi'Zhan, Säj, and Tzuk	Deity
Aremythias	City-state on the island of Corr Deyraire. This port is where the Nightsfall picked up the members of Finders Keepers.	City
Arpithia	This ancient port city is the capital of the Empire of Arpithius and is its most populous city.	City
Arpithius (Empire of)	This nation used to be known as the Western Baax Empire. It is located on the western tip of Ny, south of the Empire of Chi'kakal. Baax rulers split their empire long ago, after securing a prime spot for trading, fishing, and mining along the Jade Coast. This tumultuous empire has long been a thorn in the side of its neighbors.	Nation

Artemis	Powerful sorceress in antiquity (pre-Cataclysm). She fought against the dark aims of Ra'Tallah and forced his armies from Moor'Dru. Artemis pursued the Ireti wizard to the Mesh'Kenet mountains and fought an apocalyptic battle there. She sacrificed herself to destroy Ra'Tallah. In the process, the mountains were sundered, the Sands of Sorrow were created, the Nubari home islands were sunk, and the Cataclysm ended Faltyr's last golden age. Prophesy holds that she will return when Faltyr needs her most.	Person
Asta	Captain Gneut's older sister. Crewmember on the Nightsfall. A middle-aged gnomish female.	Person
Asterion	A small island kingdom north of Panglov, located in the Pelican Gulf. The city-state of Minotas used to hold dominion over this nation until Yax'Kaqix, Breuxias, and the surviving members of several other mercenary companies deposed its ruler.	Nation
Atoss (Kahl)	Atoss is the creator of Ogres and the world around them. He is depicted carrying a large club. He created the world so he would have someplace to hunt and harvest. He is a skilled mason and constructed Mok'Drular for his first people so they might have safety from the humans. Ogre equivalent of the deity Kahl.	Deity

Ausic (Sir)	Knight of Ishta'Kahl; traitor to the crown of Oparre; helped Queen Shy'elle escape from the dungeon at Grymsburg.	Person
Baax	The Baax people originated on the eastern coast of the main continent on the peninsula of the same name. These olive-skinned traders, sailors, and shepherds arose out of barbarism to become a major empire before splitting into Eastern and Western empires. The eastern empire is long gone, conquered by the Gre peoples that formed the Crimson Phoenix. However, the Western Baax Empire still survives as the Empire of Arpithius.	Peoples
Baax Sea	Sea bordering Panglov to the east and the Crimson Phoenix to the south.	Ocean/Sea
Baraviel Sea	This deep, cold body of water is located northwest of Faltyr.	Ocean/Sea
Bardo	Old Baax city located to the north of Siobhan across the lake. This used to be the hub of trade in this region but has long fallen into decay. It is now little more than a fishing village and religious community.	City

Basklor	The Ogre god of war and revolution. He brings death to those who oppose his people and protects them from their enemies. He is depicted as riding a giant six-legged horned beast into battle wielding a giant spear. He has a son, Choss, by Shanoit who was after his power so that she might control the Underworld. Choss was considered impure by Karin and was cursed by her so that he would grow into a hideous being. This angered Basklor and Shanoit. The two attempted to kill Karin but were unable. They did manage to strip her of all her power and memory and cast her soul into another dimension with the aid of Cheshyll. Atoss became angry at this and sent his angels to bring Basklor to him. Basklor was banished to the Underworld by Atoss. Atoss sent his creation Maax'Ytalia to bring his wife home.	Deity
Bhaga	Lillith's sister and her opposite; Bhaga is the Goddess of Good Fortune, Gambling, Fate, Accidents, and Divorce; she stayed to serve Kahl even after her sister's banishment from the Celestial Court; called Fu Shen by the Chi'Zhan, Säj, Tzuk	Deity

Brack	A race of tall, light-haired, and pale-skinned humans that originated as barbarian tribes in the Brackwald. Learning from the empire-builders around them, the people of the Brackwald later unified under the banner of the Brack Empire, now the tripartite Brack Union.	Peoples
Braigen	Kaladimus Dor's mentor. Protectorate Mage from Moor'Dru. Fled Moor'Dru during the coup led by Proleus. Whereabouts unknown.	Person
Breuxias	Mercenary captain of Finders Keepers guild. He is tall and muscular but not overly broad. His body is heavily scarred and tattooed. He wears a mystical item called the Belt of the Titans. Breuxias fought alongside Yax'Kaqix and Kan'Balam on the island of Asterion. He set sail on the Nightsfall with fellow guildsmen, Yax'Kaqix and the Cadogan Brothers.	Person
Broken Lands	Rocky, shattered region of Faltyr located east of Silent Brook and north of Crimson Phoenix. Barbarians, demihumans, and ogres call it home.	Place
Caayl (Sir)	Knight-errant of Oparre. Adherent of Ishta'Kahl. House of Regula. Rayne's childhood love.	Person

Cadogan, Donal	Member of Finders Keepers mercenary guild. Fraternal twin brother of Glynn Cadogan. From the Crimson Phoenix.	Person
Cadogan, Glynn	Member of Finders Keepers mercenary guild. Fraternal twin brother of Donal Cadogan. From the Crimson Phoenix.	Person
Cascandra	Goddess of Rivers, Springs, Waterfalls, and Dryads; called Xi-Bo by the Chi'Zhan, Saj, and Tzuk; called Sarasvati amongst the Ugra.	Deity
Caswyn	God of trade and negotiation.	Deity
Ch'ab	Translation "Penance". This island is located south-southwest of O'nal.	Place
Chahuk	Translation "Place of Thunder". This is the smallest of the South Isles. Located west of Sibal. This is a stronghold of Lizardmen who reside in the jungles here. They rarely venture outside their island, so the Unen'ek leaves them to their own devices for the most part.	Place
Cheshyll	He is the Ogre god of jealousy, greed and thievery. He steals from all and hordes his treasures into caves throughout Faltyr. Atoss encased him in scales, ripped a small hole in his sack of plunder and split his tongue for betraying him. Depicted as a large, scaly ogre carrying a sack with a small hole in the bottom to	Deity

show that greed and theft do not pay.

Chichu'äm	Goblin & Elven Deity of the Underworld; represented as the Queen Spider embracing the Inner Sun of the Underworld. Elves view Human god, Darconius, to be the agent or offspring of this elder being.	Deity
Chi'kakal (Empire of)	Empire situated on the western edge of Faltyr's main continent (Ny). It is ruled by the Chi'Zhan peoples whose dynasties stretch back to a time before the Cataclysm. Today, this empire is a multicultural mix, having conquered areas settled by Ugra, Säj, Baax, and Unen'ek peoples. The Long Road passes from the Tumbletruk Mountains in the east through the southern part of the country, paralleling rivers until it reaches the Gulf of Shang'tze.	Nation
Chi'kal	This is the ancient capital of the Empire of Chi'kakal and the ancestral home of the Chi'Zhan people. It rests high in the mountains at the source of a mighty river that flows west to the Gulf of Shang'tze. The city is rumored to be guarded by dragons loyal to the emperor of Chi'kakal.	City
Chi'Zhan	One of the most ancient cultures of humans to have survived to Faltyr's present day. These people are defined by their golden skin tones, almond-shaped eyes, and dark hair.	Peoples

Though they are related to many of the Mongoloid tribes located on the western half of the main continent, the Chi'Zhan are by far the most advanced culturally, technologically, and magically. Every Emperor or Empress of Chi'kakal has come from the enduring Chi'Zhan dynasty.

Choj'Ahaw	Literally translates as "Lord of Battle". These elven Wand Bearers are the equivalent rank of a General in most armies. They are highly trained in alchemical, magical, and martial arts and are often regarded as a one-elf army.	Position
Choss	This ogre deity is the offspring of Basklor and Shanoit. He was born out of wedlock and was considered impure by Karin. He was cast into the wastes of Faltyr and manifested into a hideous beast resembling a man-sized Ogre. He is the patron saint of half-Ogres and other bastard children of the Ogres of Faltyr.	Deity
Corr Deyraire	This small island is home to a Baax legacy kingdom that was instituted to rule its native Nubari inhabitants. This island is long-time stopover on the route to Moor'Dru so it has become a melting pot of cultures.	Nation
Council of Three	The Council of Three is the highest level governing body of the island of Moor'Dru. This body politic is responsible for passing all laws,	Political

regulates taxes, directs military offense/defense measures, and dictates trade relations with other nations. The Council is comprised of three ruling mages: a High Mage, a Mediator Mage, and a Protectorate Mage.

Crescent Bay	Wide, shallow bay on the east coast of the Crimson Phoenix.	Bay
Crimson Phoenix	This centuries-old human kingdom dominates the Baax peninsula and is home to both Gre and Baax peoples. This is one of the more tolerant kingdoms in respects to the rights of elves, gnomes, fae, and other demihumans. Opposes the genocide and naked aggression of Oparre.	Nation
Damarra	The Sun Goddess of Faltyr. She is the wife of Kahl and the mother of Ishta'Kahl (and all peoples of Faltyr). Also known as Shamash (amongst the Ireti and Baax).	Deity
Darconius	The Bringer of Darkness, Awakener of the Dead, and chief god of the Underworld. Born of Kahl and Damarra but always portrayed in opposition to his father and mother. Some sages record that the roots of this religion are more ancient than the Trinity of Worship (Kahl, Damarra, and Ishta'Kahl). Elves consider him and his worshippers to be agents of Chichu'äm.	Deity

Decadus	A period of ten years on Faltyr.	Calendrics
Demon Queller	The powerful elven blade carried by Yax'Kaqix.	Object
Dor, Kaladimus	Protectorate Mage of Moor'Dru. Also called The Master-of-Disaster, Disastrous Dor, and Maelanfaidh (son of the servant of the storm). Dor boards the Nightsfall in Kingsport on his way home to Moor'Dru.	Person
Dragon	Term for a magical race of nearly immortal beings that are reptilian in origin. They go through several changes throughout their lifetime, molting and growing in size until they become an Adult, then a Wyrm, then a Titan, and finally a Celestial (or Cosmic Dragon). They all possess at least one breath weapon, utilize Aethyr magic, can fly, shape shift, and even shrink in size to fit their environment when necessary.	Peoples
Dwarf	Free and Deep Varieties of these short, stout, and hardy humanoids exist in the Underworld. They have an ashen complexion and are allergic to sunlight, unlike their Gnomish cousins. Male dwarves are hairy and tend to be bearded. Despite common misconceptions, female dwarves do not typically have facial hair. Excellent dark vision. Resistant to most poisons, toxins, gases, and radiation. Able to navigate the	Peoples

Underworld with uncanny accuracy. Unparalleled craftsmen and artificers who make steel rivaling elven steel. Technology more advanced than their gnomish cousins. Free Dwarves live in fortified siege states under mountains all over Faltyr. Deep Dwarves live in the bowels of the Underworld, still toiling away for their Faceless Masters.

Eastgate	This fortified city is the easternmost jewel in the crown of Oparre. It is located on the border of Panglov, on the edge of the Sands of Sorrow. The new route of the Long Road passes through here now instead of Imputnim to the south.	City
Enech	Former Baax capital city that is situated on the southeast coast of the Crimson Phoenix.	City
Eresh	Goddess of Death and the Dead	Deity
Eternal War, The	The term for the sacred war fought for countless millennia between the elves of Faltyr and their allies against the forces of the Underworld and the minions of Chichu'äm.	Philosophy
Fae	Collective term for a number of different species that are all considered to be creatures of magic. They have wildly varying shapes, sizes, levels of intellect, and magical abilities. Some are little more than glowing butterflies while others are	Fae

haughty nearly immortal lords of their own magical realms.

Faltyr	The planet on which the Cycle of Ages Saga takes place. The majority of its surface is water with a few large continents. Features countless islands and races. Has one lunar satellite in orbit around it.	Planet
Fergus	Bullish quartermaster on the Nightsfall. Spensir's ally.	Person
Finders Keepers	Famous guild of mercenaries and adventurers based in the Crimson Phoenix. Yax'Kaqix, Breuxias, and the Cadogan Brothers are all members of Finders Keepers.	Business
Five Elements	Ja'-----divine representation of water, spring, east Lum-----divine representation of earth, autumn, west Kaj-----divine representation of air, winter, north, cold, ice K'ak-----divine representation of fire, summer, south Nawalik-----divine representation of spirit, void, the inner sun	Philosophy
Fraustmauth	Also spelled Frostmouth or Fraustmouth. This ancient city is the capital of the Crimson Phoenix. A few hundred years ago, this was the northernmost Baax border city before being conquered by Gre invaders. The city gets its name from the notorious winters created	City

	by the cold currents of the Pelican Gulf.	
Frolov Keep	Remote island fiefdom located off of the coast of the main island of Moor'Dru. The secret destination of the Nightsfall.	Place
Frolov, Cranthus (Lord)	Mage lord of Moor'Dru. His fiefdom was the island setting for the events of COAS: Finders Keepers. Charged with protecting the Hallowed Vessel.	Person
Frolov, Natalya (Lady)	Lord Frolov's wife. Mother of the Frolov twins.	Person
Frolov, Natasha	Sanya Frolov's identical twin.	Person
Frolov, Sanya	Natasha Frolov's identical twin.	Person
Ghost	Disembodied spirit of the dead, usually with unsolved business.	Undead
Gilly	The aging carpenter on the Nightsfall. Spensir's ally.	Person
Gneut	Gnomish captain of the Nightsfall. His obsession with obtaining the Hallowed Vessel led to the events of COAS: Finders Keepers.	Person
Gnome	The terrestrial cousin of Faltyr's dwarves. These creatures are almost identical to dwarves, except for having tanned or ruddy complexions and no allergy to sunlight. Gnomes tend to live in isolated mountain cities but many wander the world of	Peoples

Faltyr due to their natural curiosity. They are skilled craftsmen, inventors, jewelers, engineers, miners, alchemists, and illusionists.

Goblin	Blanket term for a number of subterranean species that live within Faltyr's Underworld and that often emerge at night to plague humanity and other surface races. The Unen'ek elves and some Winaq'che fight the Eternal War against these creatures; Free Dwarves fight against them as well. Goblins are referred to as Mas (Masu) in both Unen'ek and Winaq'che dialects.	Peoples
Goblin (Hobgoblin)	Larger and stronger than True Goblins but not as smart or cunning; used as beasts of burden, gladiators, & myrmidons by their smaller cousins. Most accept their role in the caste system due to the religious dogma taught to them from childhood; however, some do chaff under its constraints.	Goblin
Goblin (Kappa)	An aquatic species of goblin that typically lives deep in the lightless abyssal seas or roams the subterranean waters of the Underworld. Saltwater and freshwater species exist. Feature webbed hands and feet and are excellent swimmers; breathe air or water with equal proficiency. Most live in tribal chiefdoms but there are many wild schools of these beings	Goblin

roaming the depths.

Goblin (Kobold)	A small, vicious, & cunning species of goblin that serves as a slave race of myrmidons and scouts for their larger, smarter cousins. Kobolds are notorious troublemakers that make good skirmishers but poor soldiers. Kobold females give birth to litters several times per year.	Goblin
Goblin (True)	True goblins are intelligent, vicious, wily, and allergic to sunlight. They possess bulbous black eyes, big noses, sharp teeth, and long clawed limbs. Goblins are good craftsmen & tool makers; and make perfect miners as they can burrow with claws & tools. They have superb dark vision in addition to excellent hearing and a powerful sense of smell. Goblins are omnivorous but prefer meat (live or dead). They tend to live in stratified chiefdoms (have a caste system that spans across multiple species of goblin). These True Goblins consider themselves the masters of all Goblinkind and use the others to serve the sinister purposes of Chichu'äm and the other faceless masters of the Underworld.	Goblin
Golden Wedge, The	The proper term for the pyramid-shaped copper-gold tip of an elven wand.	Object

Gre	Fair-featured race of humans descended from barbarian tribes of the Broken Lands. Organized into powerful kingdoms in antiquity and moved south to raid the lush Baax countryside. Participated in the destruction of the Ireti and Baax Empires. Modern kingdoms of Ny ruled by descendants of the Gre are Oparre, Ror, and the Crimson Phoenix.	Peoples
Grymsburg	This is the capital city of the Kingdom of Oparre. Situated on the shores of Lake Haven, Grymsburg is considered to be an impregnable fortress.	City
Gulf of Oparre	Shallow body of water located south of the Sands of Sorrow. Kingsport is situated on the western side of this gulf.	Gulf
Gulf of Shang'tze	Body of water located on the western edge of Ny. The Long Road ends at the port of Xine on the shores of this body of water. The roots of Chi'Zhan culture developed here tens of thousands of years ago.	Gulf
Half-elf	Anyone with enough elven blood to be noticeable is considered a half-elf. Generally considered a bad omen, these interspecies couplings are frowned upon in many religions and regions of Faltyr. The Winaq'che elves do not hold this belief, so their domain (Silent Brook) has long been	Hybrid

home to mixed blood outcasts looking for a place of refuge. The ears of half-elves are almost always pointed, and their dark vision and hearing is akin to an elf.

Hallowed Vessel, The	The prize sought by Captain Gneut. This ship of legend is rumored to harbor great power and bestow upon unnaturally long life upon its chosen captain.	Vessel
Harbin (Father)	Priest of Darconius who masqueraded as a Priest of Damarra. During his lifetime, Father Harbin was a close friend and ally of Lord Frolov.	Person
Hermopolis	This is the oldest city-state in the Western Baax Empire (now known as Arpithius). This fortified port city is the hub of all trade as well as all conflict with the Chi'Zhan peoples to the North and Unen'ek peoples to the South.	City
High Mage	The senior member of the Council of Three that governs the island of Moor'Dru. Salaac was the last High Mage of Moor'Dru before being deposed by Proleus. The High Mage helps to govern the island of Moor'Dru; manage its trade relations; appoints its ambassadors and judges; levies taxes and tariffs; and has the final say in passing new laws.	Position

Hippocampus	Messenger of the Gods, Traveler between Worlds, the Gate Keeper.	Deity
Human	Endless variations on a common hominid theme; mostly harmless.	Peoples
Imputnim	Port city on the border of Panglov and Oparre. It used to be a stopover on the Long Road. The Dead Road stretches west of here into the Sands of Sorrow towards sunken Laeg.	City
Inanna	Goddess of Beauty, Love, and Passion; antithesis of Serene; called Kama by the Chi'Zhan, Säj, and Tzuk.	Deity
Ireti	An ancient race of long-limbed, lean, and olive-skinned humans that ruled the longest-surviving human empire on the main continent. Their peoples built some of the human wonders of the world and had advanced knowledge of alchemy, magic, architecture, astronomy, and more. Ireti dominion did not end until after the Cataclysm reduced their empire to a shadow of its former self. Ra'Tallah was the last emperor of the Ireti Golden Age and triggered its ruination.	Peoples
Ireti Ocean	Deep, wide sea located south of Faltyr.	Ocean/Sea
Ishta'Kahl (Naracleyes)	The Moon Goddess and favored daughter of Kahl and Damarra. She is the goddess of healing, protection, planting, nature, fertility, and birth.	Deity

The Ogre people revere this goddess as Naracleyes and often leave a candle burning in their window seals at night to pay homage to this goddess.

Jade Sea	Area of heavy trade west of Arpithius and Chi'kakal.	Ocean/Sea
Jerishiya	Town in the nation of Panglov.	City
Kahl	The Creator, The All-Father, the Chief Deity of Faltyr's predominant pantheon of deities. Kahl represents nature, creation, and time. Known as Chi'Zhan-Di amongst the peoples of Chi'kakal. Damarra (the Sun) is one of his brides. Kahl's favorite daughter is Ishta'Kahl.	Deity
K'akla Sea	Deep sea located west of the South Isles, the home of the Unen'ek elves.	Ocean/Sea
Kan'Balam	Translation "Snake Jaguar". This half-elven warrior was the only begotten son of Yax'Kaqix. Kan died while fighting to stop the goblin invasion of Asterion. Breuxias became his best friend.	Person
Kappa(s)	A nasty species of aquatic goblins that can survive in fresh or saltwater.	Goblin
Karin	Wife to Atoss. She is depicted as a pregnant ogre woman with twins about her feet. She was cast into another dimension by Basklor and Shanoit. She is the goddess of life and grants power to her followers to	Deity

	create it. Her followers are often very devout in their beliefs and are honorable as they are pure in nature.	
Kautar	God of Artifice, Craft, Construction, Engineering, Smithwork, and Mathematics; called Kotar amongst the Gre, Knorra, and Brack; called Qatar amongst the Ireti and Baax.	Deity
Kell	God of insight, knowledge, and language. He was Kahl's first creation. Guards the Rock of Kell for his Father.	Deity
Kelpie (Dire Seahorse)	Demonic half-horse, half-sealion creatures of the Abyss. Reek havoc on shipping, coastal settlements, fishermen, and island nations.	Hybrid
K'in	Elven word for the Sun (Damarra).	Star
Kingdom of Oparre	Though called a kingdom, it is really the largest empire on the face of Faltyr. Its xenophobic ruler, King Orson II, now wages a genocidal war that threatens to drown the main continent in blood.	Nation
Kingsport	Originally an Ireti city, this sprawling maze of streets and slums was renamed by the early rulers of Oparre. This city is the largest port in the Kingdom of Oparre. It is situated at the terminus of the Asimii River, the longest river on the main continent.	City
Knights of Ishta'Kahl	Holy order of noble warriors devoted to the Moon Goddess. They	Religious Order

routinely take vows of chastity as they are all grooms of Ishta'Kahl and the sworn protectors of all who sleep under her watchful eye.

Knorr(a)	Collective term for the fierce, wild barbarian tribes of the Broken Lands. Singular term is Knorr; plural is Knorra.	Peoples
Kolomal	Translation "Salvation". This island is located west of Cha'b. It is home to many temples and religious communities.	Place
Kümatz	The King of Dragons is revered by Dragons as well as the Unen'ek and Winaq'che elves as an immortal being, a god living in the Cosmic Sea.	Deity
Lake Haven	Ancient impoundment located in the heart of the Kingdom of Oparre. The Asimirii River flows through this impoundment on its way south to Kingsport. Grymsburg located on the shores of this great lake.	Lake
Lillith	Goddess of Misfortune, Fate, Accidents, Divorce; Kahl's first wife; cast out by Kahl for the light of Damarra; becomes the concubine of Darconius and the mother of his dark spawn.	Deity
Logous	The easternmost point on the Long Road. This is the capital city of Panglov and a major port.	City

Long Road, The	The term for the series of roads, trails, rivers, and passes that leads from Panglov to Chi'kakal. This "road" was established in antiquity, long before the Cataclysm, but has changed routes throughout the ages.	Road/Trail
Lucha	Elven word for Faltyr's lone moon.	Satellite
Lunare	plural (Lunares); lunar months used in the calendrics of the New Calendar; 28 days long; 13 Lunares constitute a solar Cycle/Year (Annum); 1 Dreneri Winter 2 Imbolok Spring 3 Originus Spring 4 Raynmilla Spring 5 Lucalla Summer 6 Clanauysh Summer 7 Tryum Summer 8 Aderhast Summer 9 Pashalanot Autumn 10 Alphoresis Autumn 11 Supinis Autumn 12 Wintaris Winter 13 Eriskartis Winter	Calendrics
Maasetilia (Maax'Ytalia)	Goddess of wandering, journeys, and adventure; she is the Wild One, the Whirlwind. She was created by Kahl to keep a balance in nature. This deity is the patron saint of forests, druids, hunters, and even foresters who seek to placate the spirits of nature. Her symbol is the spiral or	Deity

directional. The Ogres call this deity Maax'Ytalia and depict him as a tattooed Ogre wielding a double-bladed battle axe.

Maelanfaidh	According to Yax'Kaqix, this is a type of sorcerer (purported to be mythical) who blurs the lines between elven and human ways of channeling the Aethyr. This method of using magic sometimes results in catastrophic side-effects as those experienced by Kaladimus Dor, a living example of a Maelanfaidh.	Position
Marduk	Proleus's apprentice. Protectorate Mage of Moor'Dru. Pursued Dor through the Sands of Sorrow on at least one occasion.	Person
Maru	The northernmost kingdom of the Ugra people.	Nation
Mediator Mage	One of the three classifications of registered Magi on Moor'Dru. The highest ranking Mediator Mage serves on the Council of Three that governs Moor'Dru; he/she serves as caretaker of schools and universities; oversees the historical and religious duties of the Council; and votes on all new laws proposed by the High Mage. The Mediator Mage who sits on the Council is charged with safeguarding certain forbidden Magickal Arts, such as contact with the Golden Ones of Solodonus.	Position

Meshkenet Mountains	The shattered remains of this mountain chain are clustered on the coast of the Pelican Gulf, forming a natural barrier between Oparre and Panglov. The rest of this mountain chain was sundered during the Cataclysm resorting in the creation of the Sands of Sorrow.	Natural Formation
Metron Illbringer	Insidious sage who made a bargain with Breuxias to decipher a letter from Breuxias's father in exchange for procuring a dangerous item. The Illbringer allowed Breuxias to recuperate in his tower after the disastrous mission to recover said item.	Person
Minotas	This city-state used to hold dominion over the island kingdom of Asterion. Its corrupt ruler, Aeogius Rex, was deposed by Yax'Kaqix, Breuxias, and others following the events that led to the death of Yax's half-elven son, Kan'Balam.	City
Mok'Drular	Megalithic ruins of an Ogre city located in the Meshkenet Mountains on the edge of the Sands of Sorrow.	City
Mollinar (Dominion of)	Formerly a sovereign nation. Now part of the Kingdom of Oparre. Located on the Nubari coast.	Nation
Moor'Dru	This island nation is home to a culture of magic-users, mystics, and naturalists. As a result of the heavy	Nation

predominance of magic, Moor'Dru's form of government is a mageocracy, meaning that none may rule unless they possess the ability to wield magic. Though this nation would seem a natural enemy of Oparre, Proleus led a coup here, seized control of the island, and signed a non-aggression pact with Oparre.

Mount Belgulla	Highest peak in the Tyrus Mountains on Moor'Dru. Can be seen prominently from the port of Myth.	Natural Formation
Myth	A major port city on the main island of Moor'Dru. It is not only the former capital of Myth but also the home of Kaladimus Dor and his master, Braigen.	City
Nargawald	Until a generation ago, the Nargawald was a sovereign nation located between Oparre and Silent Brook. This nation was absorbed by Oparre following the marriage of its ruler to the former crown of Oparre. In antiquity, Nargawald referred to the sprawling forest; it was logged into oblivion by a series of kingdoms ruled by Brack and Gre invaders.	Nation
Nas'r	God of Lies, Intrigue, Deception, and Illusion; a trickster god referred to by many different names by humans, gnomes, and ogres; seen as an agent of Chichu'äm by the elves of Faltyr	Deity

Nergal	God of Disease, Pestilence, Poison, and Rot. Placated more than worshipped.	Deity
New Calendar	This is Faltyr's post-Cataclysmic calendar. The current year as of the events of COAS: FINDERS KEEPERS is 1575. Year Zero on the New Calendar equates to Year 34,063 on the Sacred Calendar used by Faltyr's elves and sages.	Calendrics
Nightsfall	Caravel owned and operated by Gneut the Gnome. Kaladimus Dor sinks this ship near a remote island on the coast of Moor'Dru.	Vessel
Nistra	Metron Illbringer's conniving apprentice who tricked Breuxias into believing that she was pregnant with his child. It turned out the child belonged to Sir Andor, the man Breuxias killed in a duel to preserve Nistra's honor.	Person
Northgate	An impenetrable fortress that guards the passes leading north from Oparre into Brack and west into the Tumbletruk Mountains. The Long Road passes through this city.	City
Nubari	A swarthy race of people who have existed on the main continent of Faltyr for as long as the Ugra. Their golden age has long past and these people live in a state of barbarism	Peoples

once again, subservient or belligerent to the interests of larger empires that hold hegemony in the region. Uthenea, Mollinar, Oparre, Corr Deyraire, Moor'Dru, and the Ak Islands count Nubari descendants amongst their peoples.

Nubari Sea	Shallow sea located southwest of Faltyr.	Ocean/Sea
Ny	Faltyr's main continent. Pronounced Nī.	Continent
Oameni	Culture of dark-haired, dark-eyed, pale-skinned peoples inhabiting the region west of the Brackwald. Though united by a common language and culture, these warring tribes never unified before modern times. Their lone previous attempt at unification led to disaster as it provoked a murderous response from the Brack Empire. These tribes now exist as a conquered people who are either subservient or belligerent to the interests of the Brack Union. Many have chosen the harsh life of nomads, braving the area dominated by the Tzuk horsemen.	Peoples
Oculus Malus	The one-eyed son of Kahl and Damarra. He is revered as the Father of Demihumans. Oculus Malus disobeyed his father and mated with his sister, Serene. Brother, sister, and the twisted offspring of their union were banished to the most	Deity

desolate reaches of Faltyr. Later, this rebellious son of Kahl tried to lead his demihuman hordes against Kahl and his favored children, humanity. In the final battle, Oculus Malus cast an evil glance upon his father and was smote down by a ball of light. This dead, twisted god was consigned to the Underworld and referred to as Oculus Malus thereafter. Many demihuman tribes across Faltyr have taken up worship of Oculus Malus under many corrupted tribal names. His symbol depicts as an eye within a circle, often weeping blood.

Ogre — *Peoples* — Race of giant humanoids who prefer to live in mountainous regions of Faltyr's main continent. Though Ogres used to be an advanced race with highly sophisticated building techniques and adept control of magic, alchemy, and astronomy, civilized Ogres are rare in post-Cataclysmic times. Many tribes have been reduced to barbarism or nomadic/pastoral lifestyles to survive in a world dominated by human kingdoms.

Ohno — *Planet* — The elven word for Faltyr; this word translates as "egg". Reflects their belief that the planet harbors something sinister within its core.

O'nal — *Place* — Translation "Stomach". This organ-shaped island is located southeast of

	Xoc'ne.		
Ophanim		Also called Thrones. Intelligent, malevolent, and dangerous psychokinetic beings covered in eyes. Several variations on these floating orbs of death are recorded across Faltyr, including Abyssal (aquatic) & undead versions.	Creature
Orson (King)	I	Former king of Oparre. Current ruler's late father. Supposedly poisoned by renegade sorcerer in 1526. Known as "The Evil One" for his bloody, imperialist policies.	Person
Orson (King)	II	Current king of Oparre. Persecutes Blood War on main continent of Faltyr. Hates elves, fae, magic-users, and all other creatures of magic.	Person
Paneasta (Shalentis)		The god of celebrations and frolic. This god is the patron of the arts, music, and poetry. He is often depicted as a young man with a bottle of wine in one hand and set of pan pipes in the other. He is similar to Dionysus. Ogres call this god Shalentis. He is often depicted as an obese ogre pouring wine into goblets as he dances to an ogre drummer beats. He is also the god of gluttony and laziness.	Deity
Panglov		This arid nation is a mix of sandy deserts and rocky mountains	Nation

crisscrossed by countless caravan routes that lead west across the continent of Ny. The start of the Long Road, the ancient land route to Chi'kakal, is found in eastern Panglov. In the current conflict, this nation is neutral, having a non-aggression pact with both Moor'Dru and Oparre.

Pelican Gulf	Horseshoe-shaped body of water between Ror and the Crimson Phoenix.	Gulf
Porobal	Translation "The Burning Place". This island is located west of Sibal and is dominated by a series of active volcanoes.	Place
Proleus	Dictator currently ruling Moor'Dru after overthrowing the rest of the Council of Three. Usurped and killed Salaac.	Person
Protectorate Mage	One of three classifications of registered Magus on the Island of Moor'Dru; these magicians are specialized in applying the arts of magic to martial situations. The highest ranking Protectorate Mage on the island is one of the Council of Three.	Position
Quq	Translation "Fertile". This island is located on the southern tip of Sibal. It is considered the breadbasket of the Unen'ek islands.	Place

Rafasi	Bearded pilgrim from Panglov. He is a priest of Ishta'Kahl, a healer, and an eavesdropper.	Person
Ra'Tallah	Ireti mage-king who conquered Moor'Dru in antiquity. Sought the source of eternal life that he believed mages of Moor'Dru had stolen from him. After his armies were defeated by Artemis, Ra'Tallah fled to the area now known as the Sands of Sorrow. The final battle between these powerful wizards led to the sundering of the Mesh'Kenet Mountains, the creation of the Sands of Sorrow, the sinking of the Nubari home islands, and ushered in the Cataclysm that ended Faltyr's last golden age. Prophesized to be lying in wait for the stars to become right so that he might rise to seek his prize once again.	Person
Rayne	Half-elven female mercenary employed by Captain Gneut. Sir Caayl's childhood love.	Person
Rey'bet	Intelligent, bipedal humanoid frogmen who live in tribal societies and chiefdoms. True amphibians, they can breathe air or water. Vicious if provoked, they make war against humans, elves, merfolk, and lizardmen over trophies and territory. A typical Rey'bet possesses darkvision; can leap incredible distances; and can communicate with a complex system of croaks, clicks,	Peoples

chirps, and songs.

Rey'bet Islands	Small chain of volcanic islands dominated by thick jungles. Populated by wild tribes of Lizardmen, Rey'bet (Frogmen), and Nubari.	Place
Ror	This small mountain nation was a refuge for humans, elves, fae, and other creatures of magic until it was invaded by Oparre. Ror is an ally of the Crimson Phoenix, a kingdom that will rally to its neighbor's defense against the forces of Oparre.	Nation
Säj	This race of short, stocky Mongoloid horsemen roams the Ka'tun Plateau and the Northern Wastes. Though organized into a loose knit confederacy, these nomadic tribes try to maintain as much freedom and mobility as possible as part of their lifestyle. They are famed for their equestrians, archers, wrestlers, and musicians.	Peoples
Säj Confederacy	This confederation of clans arose in response to the dangers posed by the Tzuk empire. The riders of the Säj were forced to band together into an organized system of defense against this new threat posed by a clan of horsemen turned empire-builders. The Säj Confederacy currently controls most of the Ka'tun Plateau and vast areas of the Northern Wastes.	Nation

Salaac	High Mage of the Council of Three. Prophesized many things about the end of this current Cycle of Ages. Deposed and killed by Proleus faction. Braigen's ally. Charged Dor with recovering contents of the chest from the Sands of Sorrow.	Person
Sands of Sorrow	This unnatural desert is the result of the apocalyptic battle between Artemis and Ra'Tallah that ushered in the Cataclysm ending the last golden age of Faltyr. The sky is dominated by a swirling aurora here that makes navigation by night almost impossible. This cursed place also warps magic and drains those using it.	Place
Scydonia	A wild island nation to the south of Arpithius. These three allied islands were absorbed into the empire long ago but have yet to be fully pacified due to the wild tribes of men and beasts that roam the thick jungles that cover the islands.	Nation
Sea of Fallen Dragons	Expanse of sea bordering the northeast coast of Faltyr.	Ocean/Sea
Sea of Moor'Dru	Treacherous sea located south of Moor'Dru.	Ocean/Sea
Serene (Shanoit)	Goddess of seduction, temptation, and adultery. She tempted Kell to	Deity

gain the Rock of Kell for Oculus Malus but failed in her task as Kell was immune to her charms. In many cultures, she is the patron saint of demihumans and mixed blood elves. Ogres call her Shanoit.

Shelek	The god of magic, spells, alchemy, and the arcane. He is most widely followed by the citizens on the Island of Moor'Dru. He can communicate with all manner of things and bestow his powers upon them. Amongst the Brack and Ugra, he is known as Arcanus, while the Ireti and Nubari refer to him as Mah'jeek. Amongst the Chi'Zhan, Saj, and Tzuk, he is referred to as Lao-Tsi. His symbol is typically an open palm surrounded by stars or flames.	Deity
Shy'Elle (Queen)	Crown of Silent Brook; Queen of the Winaq'che elves; deposed and captured by King Orson's troops; Sirs Ausic and Caayl helped her escape from Grymsburg; pregnant with the Crown Prince of Oparre's child.	Person
Sibal	Translation "Rising Mist". This is the second largest island of the south island and the most populous. It is located south of Ch'ab.	Place
Sierris	Female nanny who insinuated herself into the life of the Frolov family. Eventually usurped Lord Frolov's	Person

rule through her mastery of necromancy.

Silent Brook (Tor'Binel)	This is the homeland of the Winaq'che elves. Oparre has invaded this country and occupies it as far north as the Winaq'che capital. Many of its tree cities, settlements, and peoples have been burned by the marauding armies of Oparre and its allies. Also spelled Silentbrook.	Nation
Siobhan	Modern metropolis constructed during the reign of the Crimson Phoenix over this region. It stands on the side of a lake situated on a high plateau in the middle of the country. It facilitates trade, transportation, and security throughout the interior of the Crimson Phoenix.	City
South Isles	This is the human name for the jungle-covered home islands of the Unen'ek elves. Located off the southwest coast of Ny.	Nation
Spensir	First mate on the Nightsfall. Command fell to him after the death of Captain Gneut. He also inherits Gneut's obsession with the Hallowed Vessel.	Person
Starkiller	The name of the infamous jade wand bestowed upon Yax'Kaqix by the Unen'ek elves.	Object

Taranis	God of Storms, Destruction, Rebellion, Earthquakes, and Vortices; called Shang-Di by the Chi'Zhan, Säj, and Tzuk.	Deity
Thonesh (Duchy of)	This area is a buffer state that is technically part of the Kingdom of Oparre. This duchy is ruled by Orson's bastard brother who controls the powerful city of Northgate, a fortress that guards the passes leading north into Brack and west into the Tumbletruk Mountains. The Long Road passes through here in the shadow of the walls of Northgate.	Place
Thrash	The ship's cook on the Nightsfall.	Person
Tosk'Kiante	Ogre shaman who raised Breuxias as his own son from the time that the human was a small child until his early teens.	Person
Trinitas, The	The Holy Trinity (Trinitas) consists of three religious works: Evangelium Pater Omnium (Gospel of the All-Father); Evangelium Solis (Gospel of the Sun); and Evangelium Lunae (Gospel of the Moon).	Philosophy
Troll	Tall, long-limbed, semi-intelligent monsters that heal incredibly fast unless damaged by fire, magic, acid, or sunlight. Vicious, sneaky, and persistent; wholly nocturnal. Cave, swamp, arctic, desert, and aquatic varieties known to exist.	Peoples

Tumbletruk Dwarves	This colony of Free Dwarves lives deep beneath the Tumbletruk Mountains. They supposedly helped carve the Shadowvale Pass through these same mountains, making the Long Road possible.	Peoples
Tumbletruk Mountains	This crescent-shaped mountain range is one of the highest, most extensive natural wonders remaining on the face of Faltyr. These mountains are home to communities of humans, dwarves, ogres, and gnomes.	Natural Formation
Tyrus Mountains	Mountain range on the eastern side of Moor'Dru. Mount Belgulla is the tallest peak in this range. Myth sits at the base of this range.	Natural Formation
Tzuk	A fierce clan of horsemen that arose from the ranks of the riders of the Säj. They organized along the lines of the powerful Brack and Chi'kakal empires encroaching upon their traditional homeland. In less than a century, the Tzuk swept across the Ka'tun Plateau with enough horsemen to threaten the Brack to the east and the Chi'Zhan to the south. Albeit diminished in modern times, they remain a powerful force in northwest Ny.	Peoples
Uayeb (Quintus)	5-day period following the end of the 13th Lunare; the last 5 days of the Solar Year.	Calendrics

Ugra (nation)	The oldest remaining mountain kingdom of the Ugra people.	Nation
Ugra (people)	One of the oldest surviving cultures of humans on the face of Faltyr. They are a stalwart, learned people whose own golden age ended before Faltyr's last golden age ever began. They now live on the brink in fortified communities in the mountains. Natural enemies of the Chi'Zhan, they tend to trade with the Tumbletruk Dwarves and the colonies of gnomes that reside within the borders of their siege states.	Peoples
Underworld, The	Collective term for the subterranean zones of the Hollow World, believed to consist of nine rings. Originally, it referred to the Afterlife but became synonymous with the subterranean world beneath the surface of Faltyr countless millennia ago.	Place
Unen'ek	Translation: "Children of the Stars". These are the elves of the South Isles, the original tribe of elves to inhabit Faltyr.	Peoples
Uthenia (Republic of)	Formerly a sovereign nation. Now part of the Kingdom of Oparre. Located on the Nubari coast.	Nation
Utna	Goddess of murder, strife, tyranny, and hatred.	Deity

Uxlabal	Elven concept of the soul; multi-faceted components of an immortal spiritual being.	Philosophy
Vampire	Intelligent undead also known as Lamia, Blood Demons, Vampyrs, and Jiang Shi. They are immortal unless destroyed by fire, sunlight, or decapitation. Silver and acid slow their supernatural healing abilities. Possess superior dark vision and other senses; lightning reflexes; and supernatural strength. But cannot fly or change shape without using some other sort of magical ability to do so. Must drink blood to survive (an apex predator).	Undead
Vorta	Female crewmember on the Nightsfall. Spensir's lover.	Person
Wall of Heaven, The	This megalithic series of fortifications built into the mountains themselves forms a manmade barrier between Arpithius and Chi'kakal. Powerful Chi'Zhan magic constructed this wall more than a thousand years ago as a response to the threat posed by the Western Baax Empire.	Place
Winaq'che	Translation: "Children of the Trees". These are the elves of Silent Brook, the tribe of elves that split from the Unen'ek and stayed on the mainland.	Peoples

Wraith	An energy-draining undead creature created from the tortured soul of a murder victim.	Undead
Wyvern	These winged creatures reach 40-50 feet in length and feature a barbed stinger on the end of their tails. Their mandibles feature a triple hinge to allow the creature to bite and swallow large prey in proportion to its size. At least one species of wyvern can track prey utilizing remote-sensing organs despite having no discernible eyes.	Dragon
Xine	This port city is located at the terminus of the Long Road on the west coast of the Empire of Chi'kakal. The Chi'Zhan Fleet is headquartered in this city's deep-water harbor for protection from the seasonal storms that plague the Jade coast.	City
Xoc'ne	Translation "Shark's Tail". This is the largest island of the South Isles.	Place
Yax'Kaqix	Traditional name translates as "Blue Macaw." A centuries old full-blood Unen'ek war mage, a Choj'ahaw (Wand Bearer or Lord-of-Battles). Yax is currently a captain of the Finders Keepers guild in Fraustmauth. His primary element is fire.	Person
Year Zero	Beginning of the New Calendar; Equates to Year 34,063 on the	Calendrics

Sacred Calendar of the elves of Faltyr; refers to the date that Artemis and Ra'Tallah battled and sundered the Meshkenet Mountains triggering the Cataclysm, ending the Ireti Golden Age.

Yu	This riverside city is situated in the heart of the Empire of Chi'kakal. Yu is a major stopover on the Long Road as it is famous for both its silks and its ceramics.	City
Zailya	The southernmost kingdom of the Ugra. The notorious Bandit King of Zailya not only orders raids on those who travel the High Road of the Shadowvale Pass but also manages an extensive trade network with the gnomes and dwarves of the Tumbletruk Mountains.	Nation
Zugura	Nubari city-state located on the western coast of Oparre. Fiercely independent population that lives off the sea, either as fishermen and traders or by raiding neighbors as well as passing ships. Constant thorn in the side of the Kingdom of Oparre as they oppose its rule.	City

About the Authors

Jeremy Hicks spent several years as an archaeologist before teaming up with **Barry Hayes**, his long-time friend and co-author, to realize a creative dream to turn their nightmares into fiction. The writing team of Hicks & Hayes created a dark, edgy fantasy environment known as **Faltyr**; wrote a screenplay (*The Cycle of Ages Saga: Finders Keepers*) to introduce it; and then adapted it into this novelization, which was first published by **Dark Oak Press** in 2013.

As co-owners of **Broke Guys Productions**, they have written three other screenplays, including the sequel to *Finders Keepers*. Jeremy has several short stories in **Dark Oak Press** anthologies; he has published a few more through **Amazon KDP**.

Cycle of Ages Saga: Finders Keepers was their first novel. They have also published *Cycle of Ages: Sands of Sorrow. Cycle of Ages Saga: Delve Deep* will be published in 2017.

The Master-of-Disaster is back in the exciting sequel to Finders Keepers!

www.ingramcontent.com/pod-product-compliance
Lightning Source LLC
Chambersburg PA
CBHW031322170626
46807CB00002B/524